# Tobacco Rose

A Novel

Florence Love Karsner

SeaDog Press

Ponte Vedra, Florida 32081



Cover Design: Dar Albert, Wicked Smart Designs
Ship Logo: © Dn Br | Shutterstock
Editor: Elizabeth A. White

*For*
*SeaDog, Georgie and Weezie*

*This journey started with you three long ago.*

Other Books by Florence Love Karsner

***The Highland Healer Series***

*Highland Healer (Book 1)*
*Highland Circle of Stones (Book 2)*
*Highland Bloodline (Book 3)*
*The Wolf, The Wizard, and The Woad (Book 4)*

***The Dr. Molly McCormick Series***

*We All Have Secrets*

*Famous Gullah Proverb . . .*

*If oonuh ent kno weh oonuh dah gwine, oonuh should kno weh oonuh come f'um.*

*Translation: If you don't know where you're going, you should know where you come from.*

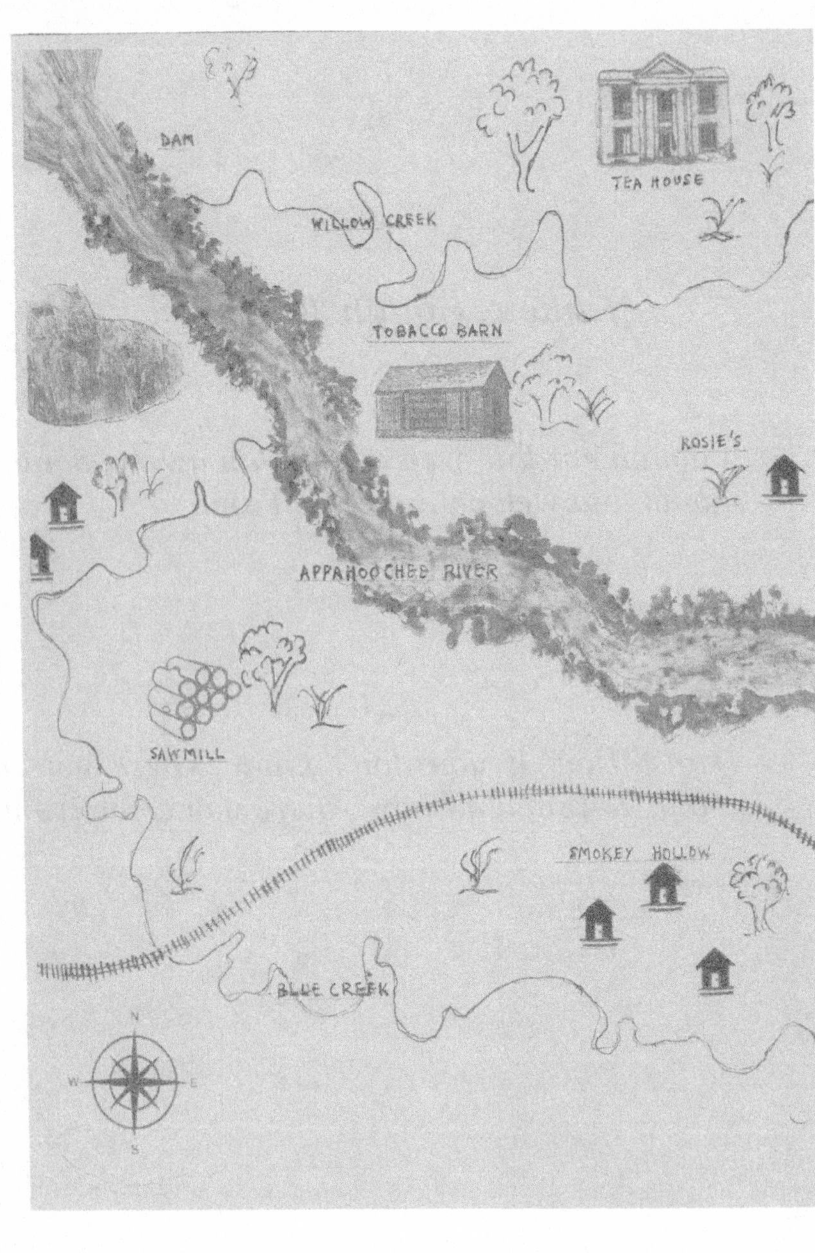
DAM
WILLOW CREEK
TEA HOUSE
TOBACCO BARN
ROSIE'S
APPAHOOCHEE RIVER
SAWMILL
SMOKEY HOLLOW
BLUE CREEK
N
W
E
S

# 1

# *Hot as Hades*

Even this early in the morning, with dew still clinging to the wisteria vine draping over the barn door, the sweltering August-hot heat had the old woman's thin, cotton dress clinging to her body. She reached her small hand into her bosom and removed a clean hanky, mopped her face and neck, then tucked the hanky back in its accustomed place.

In addition to the God-awful heat, once again the month of August presented her with unwelcome memories of another scorching summer. A summer that had brought her to her knees.

Along with these unsolicited memories, painful images flitted across her brain like dragonflies on a lily pond—a blazing sun beating down on the workers in the tobacco fields—unbearable heat—loud voices echoing in the wind—a young woman running across the yard calling to her, "Rosie! Rosie! You gotta come now!"—Mr. Sutherland hurrying to the barn telephone, yelling into the instrument at someone on the other end, "Did you hear me? I said now!"—then what seemed like hours later, the heart-stopping scream of a siren announcing the arrival of the rescue vehicle.

And the final image—climbing into the ambulance, hearing the moans and the gasping struggle for breath. Desperate sounds that had her ears closing themselves off in self-defense. And this particular image even conjured up smells that appeared to have been permanently embedded in her nostrils . . . the odors of sweat and fear.

By now, she knew the memories and images would fade away if she just kept busy and prayed. Her prayer was always the same, that one day she would not be tormented each time August rolled around and the sun ruled the universe.

She placed her small basket in the corner and murmured to herself, "I know the Good Lawd created heaven and earth, and all that is in them. But I do wish He'd given a bit more thought as to how hot He was gonna let it be in August. It's hot as Hades!"

A lone, black crow perched in the loblolly pine tree next to the tobacco barn cawed loudly as if in agreement, then lifted his majestic wings and soared upward.

The old woman's face was dark. Rich. And her skin resembled the delicate, gossamer covering of a dragonfly's wings and was stretched tightly over her thin prominent cheekbones. The crinkles at the corners of her eyes said she was either constantly squinting or laughed a lot. Or both.

She walked behind her desk and began to mentally sort through the various tasks she had to complete this day. Well, she called it her desk, but it was actually a sturdy table made from heavy oak and was as old as she was. She had toiled on it so many years its edges were rubbed smooth as a rose petal, and the surface was scratched, nicked, and stained from tobacco and spilled coffee.

Each spill, stain, and scratch was accompanied by a memory, and she would frequently trail her fingers over these in an effort to return to that particular time and place. Even unhappy memories were precious at her age, and lately, even those memories had begun to escape her.

Rosie, the elderly, black woman behind the desk, was the barn supervisor at Sutherland Tobacco Inc., and her job was to assess the newly-hired workers as they came through her employment line. She would be the one to determine what job they were most suited for.

Every summer Sutherland's Tobacco Inc. employed local young people from the surrounding area to work in the tobacco barn. Mostly teenage boys, both black and white, who were trying to make some spending money while they were out of school for the summer.

Occasionally, there might be a few females, but these girls needed to be rather hefty ones who didn't mind putting a bit of backbone into their work.

The bus with the workers from Harper's Mill had just arrived as Rosie picked up the last few tobacco leaves laying on her desk and began to string them. A couple of minutes later she heard a small cough and turned to see where the sound had come from.

Today she was definitely squinting as she peered over her rimless spectacles at the sight before her. A young girl stood at her desk looking up at her. The child couldn't be more than eight years old, and even more importantly, this girl was white!

Rosie squinted even harder now, then leaned her head to one side and bit her bottom lip as she often did when confronted with an unexpected situation. She looked directly into the young girl's face and studied it as if there might be something there that would explain the child being here in the tobacco barn. She stopped stringing the last tobacco leaf and gave her full attention to the child.

The girl remained silent, so Rosie decided she'd make an effort to sort through this unusual situation. She bit her lip once again and finally asked what she considered a most important question, "Good Lawd, chile! What you doin' in this barn? Ain't no place for a white girl, 'specially not one as lil' as you!"

The young girl gave no response, but simply stared at Rosie with cornflower blue eyes that were as large as a blood moon.

"Who yo' daddy, chile?" Rosie asked, standing up to get a better look at the girl.

"Does he know you heah in this t'backy barn?"

## 2

# *First Impressions*

The girl didn't answer Rosie's question, only stood there looking around, chewing on the tip of one of her long braids. Mesmerized. In any other setting, she'd be chattering away at anyone close by.

Her first impression—one that would leave a permanent memory—came through her small, upturned nose. The air was teeming with a sweet, crisp, pungent smell, the roots of which originated with the tobacco itself, and that was mixed with the odor of kerosene that fueled the burners and flues. Interlaced with those overwhelming scents, she inhaled the ripe, earthy fragrance of the plowed fields that ran alongside the barn. Finally, the odor of animal and human sweat told its own story.

The workers in the field were already cropping the tobacco, even though the sun had only a tenuous footing in the sky. As much as the myriad scents, the resonating voices of the workers in the field gained her attention as quickly as an undertow grabs an unsuspecting swimmer enjoying a relaxing dip in the ocean.

As the girl stood there in the early morning light, the workers began to sing. Most of the voices were male, echoing from one end of the field to the other. She couldn't understand all the words. But she instinctively knew the song was a lament of suffering and the singing a way to relieve it.

As the masculine overture ended, a sweet soprano voice rang out. Soft. Feminine. Caressing the words as she delivered her response. Yin and yang. A dance as old as time itself.

This solo was answered by a trio of harmonizing voices, deep tones that reverberated in the girl's bones. She would like nothing more than to join in this myriad chorus of sound, as it called to every fiber of her being. In her young mind, music and song was the way to express what one felt in their soul.

Rosie stood patiently, waiting for the child to answer her question. But the girl continued to stand quietly, still chewing her braid.

"Chile, come heah to Rosie," said the old woman, motioning the girl to come stand by her. The child came around the desk and went closer. Rosie gently placed her arm around her shoulder. "What's yo' name then?"

"I'm Clementine."

Rosie nodded, "Clementine. All right. Now tell Rosie what you be doin' heah."

Lifting her eyes up to the old woman, Clementine took note of the many fine wrinkles in her face, her very small nose, and full lips that needed none of the lipstick Clemmie's own mother always wore. This woman's lips were such a soft shade of pink they needed no enhancement. She had an abundance of silver hair, carefully braided and affixed in a bun at the back of her head.

Something about this older black woman, this Rosie, was like Clemmie's Nana. Warmth oozed from her. And Rosie's scent was of jasmine, as she had tucked a sprig of it within her bun.

Most of all, Clemmie relished the gentle arm cradled around her shoulder, calming her in a way she hadn't been aware she needed. She swallowed hard and spoke in a quiet voice.

"I came to work in the barn, like the others. They said they made a lot of money last year and that if I wanted, I could ride the bus up here and work in the tobacco barn, too."

Rosie tilted her head to one side, "Yo' daddy and mama know you come up on that bus?"

"Uh-huh. Daddy said 'Learning to make a dollar is a good thing. Our family has survived for generations because of a strong work ethic. It's something to be proud of.' So that's what I'm going to do." The child recited the phrase as if she had memorized it for safekeeping.

"But how old are you?"

"I'll be twelve on my birthday. That's in January."

"You eleven years old now? But you the size of a seven or eight-year-old. My, my. Didn't yo' mama feed you enough?"

Clemmie smiled at Rosie. "Yes, ma'am. Mama's a good cook, and I eat a lot. But according to her, I haven't hit my growth spurt yet. But I will. I know I will."

"Hmm. Well, I don't think there's a place for you in this t'backy barn. You're just too small to handle anything on the line."

"But I could help you, couldn't I? String the leaves like you're doing now?"

"Maybe. But you have to be fast, and you gotta be able to lift the pole and pass it to the hangers. Don't think you can do that."

She stood slowly and patted her stool, indicating the girl was to sit in her place. "Heah. You sit on Rosie's stool. I'll talk with Mr. Sutherland and see what he says I'm to do with you. Sit there now. And don't move.

"Yes ma'am. I won't."

# 3

# Geechee Rose

Sierra Rose Aiken was as much a fixture of the tobacco barn as the tobacco itself. She had started working there as soon as she was big enough to walk behind her mama and break tobacco leaves. Since then, she had worked every station and had been the barn supervisor for more years than she cared to remember. Most folks had no idea what her real name was but just called her Rosie.

When she'd been born, her mother wrapped her in a blanket and lifted her tiny body to the child's father, smiling at him as if she were presenting him with a delightful gift.

"*Keke*, I believe we should call her Rose. She's as beautiful as the flowers in my garden," she said. *Keke* was the word for father that came from their Gullah/Geechee heritage and the family still used it.

*Keke* placed the small bundle in the crook of his arm and smiled. "Rose, yes. But I think we should name her *Sierra* Rose. In honor of our ancestors who came from Sierra Leone.

He called her his little Geechee Rose, as when she was born he was still working in the coastal rice plantations around Savannah, Georgia. *Keke's* ancestors were part of a group of roughly one thousand slaves who were brought into the rice and cotton plantations of South Carolina, Virginia, and the Sea Islands which stretch from the southeastern point of North Carolina down to the northern part of Florida. Over time, these peoples were referred to as Gullah/Geechee depending on which state they lived in.

Rosie wasn't an only child. She had a sister, Tonja, some two years younger. At fifteen, Tonja was not much more than a child herself, but had an independent streak as broad as a tobacco field. At that tender age, she ran off and married a young man named Alie, and followed him to the rice fields of South Carolina.

Tonja had often complained to *Keke*, "Working in tobacco is too hard, *Keke*. Breaking the leaves, then stringing them and lifting those heavy poles. And at the end of the day, you hear the moans of the tired workers as they trudge home."

Tonja reasoned that working in the rice fields would surely be easier. She further reasoned that at least she'd be with her handsome young man . . . and being pregnant was even more reason to go with him to South Carolina.

*Keke* made a single comment. "The only good thing to come from this union is that the two of them, both Gullah/Geechee descendants, have strengthened the bloodline of our ancestors. So perhaps it will be something to hope for now. Another tie to bind our people together."

Rosie was well-acquainted with the Gullah ways, their religious beliefs, and the hope for keeping their cultural characteristics alive. *Keke* had taught her and Tonja the language of their people as soon as they could talk, and Vanna, her mother, passed on the cultural qualities: how they dressed, how they treated their children, their kin, how to cook the food.

Rosie, a widow for many years now, and her grandson were the only ones left in her family, and the only descendants of the Gullah she was aware of in this area. Tonja was still alive, or so Rosie thought. She'd not seen her for so long now she could hardly recall her face. But she could remember her voice. A soft, breathy sound Rosie could still hear in the middle of the night when the wind outside her open window whispered to her. Most probably a dream, but sometimes it seemed so real.

# 4

# Learn to Make a Dollar

Taking one last look at Clementine, Rosie stood. Her tall, thin body moving quickly—belying her years—she made her way to the boss's office at the far end of the barn. She took long strides, her thin skirt clinging to her legs. And all the while her mind whirred as she mumbled under her breath.

*I declare, I never woulda believed a lil' white girl would show up in this t'backy barn and her daddy says it's alright. What is this world coming to?*

The office door was always open, so Rosie knocked lightly on the door facing. The facing had recently been replaced with new boards made of pine from the local area and were sticky as rivulets of sap ran freely in the heat this time of year. Rosie touched the sap with her fingers then lifted them to her nose. She associated the pleasant scent with the word "home."

It was only a second before a loud voice called out. "Hey, Rosie. Come on in. Be right with you. Take a seat."

As usual, the boss was on the phone, the phone being a true luxury in this rural area. The only other one was in the Tea House, where Mr. Sutherland lived. Rosie had the greatest respect for Mr. Lawrence Sutherland. If it hadn't been for him and his daddy before him, her family might not have survived some of the years when she was a young girl herself. That had been some hard times. And then the Great Depression. Mighty hard times.

But, as her *Keke* always said, "What tries the body usually finds a way of bringing comfort to the soul." Rosie wasn't real sure what that meant, but if *Keke* had said it, then she knew it was true.

*Keke* had been a saint in Rosie's eyes. Only now, some years after his passing, did she understand how wise he was. He'd been the only one in his family who could read, and he passed on his love of reading and books to her and Tonja.

Turning her thoughts to the present problem, Rosie wasn't sure what she was going to say to Mr. Sutherland. He was a fair man to be sure, but he needed workers who could work a full day and be ready to come back for more the next. And this girl didn't fit into that category.

Mr. Sutherland placed the receiver down on the phone and came to the door. "Hey, Rosie. What's cooking?"

"Mr. Sutherland, I hate to bother you, but it's a situation I don't quite know how to handle."

"What's the problem, Rosie? Never known you to have many situations you weren't able to get a grip on." He smiled at her. Rosie was as important to him as the tobacco and was much more than his barn supervisor. His parents were long gone, and now with the most recent death, she was as close as any family he had ever had. Even when his mother was alive, he'd often found himself seeking out Rosie when he was in need of consoling or, as was often the case, when in trouble.

"Yessuh. Well, this problem has got me stumped, and I believe you may have to figure it out. You see, there's this lil' girl. She showed up this morning, coming in on the bus with the teenagers from down in Harper's Mill. There are eight or nine of them boys and a couple of girls that are working with us for the summer. You know most of 'em."

Larry nodded, "Yeah, that group seems to be working out all right as far as I know. Haven't heard any complaints. What's the problem?"

"Well, it's not them, sir. It's just that this morning a new worker came in on that bus that brings them. This lil' chile I'm tellin' you 'bout. She's only eleven. A tiny thing. And she wants to work heah in this t'backy barn. And, Mr. Sutherland . . . she's a lil' white girl!

"I asked if her daddy knows she's heah and she told me 'Yes'm, he said learning to make a dollar is a good thing.' Mr. Sutherland, she's awful small."

"Little white girl you say? Well, take me to her. Let's see what she needs. You're right, though. Sounds strange."

He grabbed his hat from the coat rack and began striding back down the length of the barn. He led the way with Rosie hurrying to keep in step with him.

As they approached the child, Rosie nodded towards her, "Heah she is, Mr. Sutherland."

At thirty-eight years old, Lawrence Sutherland was a rather handsome fellow with sandy colored hair and hazel eyes. He stood well over six feet, was broad-shouldered and muscled. He'd worked in the barns his entire life, and that alone kept him in shape.

He approached Rosie's table and could hardly help staring at the scene his eyes presented. A young girl was attempting to string tobacco leaves onto the poles, as she had seen Rosie doing. And to her credit, she was fast. Her small hands moved quickly, and her excellent eye-hand coordination served her well.

Seeing how small she was, Lawrence squatted down in order to be at eye level with the girl. Rosie had told the truth. The child was rather small, with hair as white as a magnolia blossom. Larry sensed she was shy, but apparently brave enough to ride that bus and get herself here.

"Good morning. I'm Lawrence Sutherland. Larry. And who might you be?"

The girl peered up at him with saucer-sized blue eyes that might have been ready to shed a tear. He wasn't sure.

"I'm Clementine MacKinnon. And I would like to work in the tobacco barn, please."

Larry stared closely at the girl for a couple of seconds, then cleared his throat. "You related to Andrew MacKinnon?"

"Yessir. He's my daddy."

Larry knew Andrew had twin boys and that a girl had come along some years later. This must be that child. But heavens, she was a shrimp of a girl.

He'd heard the awful news about Andrew losing one of his workmen last week and personally knew how that sort of incident could play with a man's mind. When he'd been a young lad, one of his father's workers had died in the field. And more recently, just a couple of summers ago, there had been another incident in his fields that still haunted his memories.

Andrew MacKinnon was a friend, so seeing this girl was Andrew's daughter, Larry would try to find something she could do. Presently, he agreed with Rosie. She was too small to actually work in the barn.

He started racking his brain trying to come up with something. Lately, however, his brain had been doing double time trying to get a grip on developments that had taken most of his emotional energy and hadn't left much for anything else.

His wife, Ellen, had recently passed away. Leukemia had won that battle, and now he was left with a five-year-old daughter to care for on his own.

Presently he was searching for a full-time nanny for his daughter, Sarah, but so far, he was only able to find a local woman who could come a few hours a day. That left the rest of the day for him to care for the child and run a business. The word stress took on a new meaning.

He stood, then ran his hand along his chin. Thinking, apparently. He'd come up with something, but at the moment he was at a loss.

"Your daddy's a friend of mine, Clementine, so I'll see if we can't find some chores for you to do. I agree with Rosie, though, you might be a bit too small to work in the tobacco barn."

He removed his hat, scratched his head and nodded. "Actually, I can think of one job you might handle for me. That is if you will agree to it."

"I'll do whatever you need, Mr. Sutherland. I gotta show Daddy I can earn money, like he, James and Jeremy, and Mama do. He's always saying that everybody needs to be able to earn a dollar, pay their own way, and I need to learn how to do that. Like my brothers."

Larry smiled inwardly. *Yep, that sounds like something Andrew would say. The man doesn't know the meaning of the words "day off" or "vacation." He's a hardworking man and expects everyone else to be also. His boys worked for me a couple of summers. This child must have been a late-life baby for Andrew and Maggie. But she's here, presenting herself as if she were as big and tall as the other teenagers in the barn.*

"Come on, then. Wait in my office, then we'll go to the Tea House." He turned aside and addressed Rosie, who had stood quietly waiting for his instruction.

"Rosie, I think you're right. Clementine's too small to work in the barn. But, you know, she may be able to help me with Sarah while I'm still searching for a full-time woman to stay with her. She appears to have a quick mind and certainly seems willing to work at most anything. I can at least give her a try for a day or so."

"Yessuh. She probably could help with Sarah. That chile just needs someone to keep her safe, occupied and fed. That's 'bout all any five-year-old needs. And someone to play with her, 'course. I believe that's a good solution, Mr. Sutherland. And I'll be heah in the barn and keep a watch on 'em too. You can count on that. Ain't much goes on in the t'backy barn that Rosie don't know 'bout."

# 5

# *Just Watch Me!*

Two days before Clementine showed up at the tobacco barn, she'd decided on a plan of action. But implementing it might not be an easy task.

It was Saturday evening, and she stood outside the den door and listened for a moment before tiptoeing in. Several rooms had window fans going full blast due to the ungodly heat. But there was Daddy, sitting in his favorite recliner, with a blanket covering his lap.

"Daddy? Can I come in?"

Daddy didn't answer, just stared at her as if he didn't understand her question. She waited another moment, then walked closer and looked into his face. Dark circles hugged beneath his bloodshot eyes. She wondered for a moment if he was coming down with some illness, but intuitively knew his illness wasn't physical, but rather, mental and emotional.

Last week one of his workmen, a man called Skidder, had been struck by lightning and had died instantly. Since then, Daddy had barely spoken a word and had hibernated in this room. Clementine knew a bit about grieving, as they had just buried her Nana a few weeks ago. But, even then, Daddy hadn't sat motionless and certainly hadn't missed work. A week had passed since Skidder was killed, and still Daddy stayed in this room and grieved.

Clemmie waited another moment, then sat on the floor at his feet, where she sat most evenings when he would tell about his day in the woods and describe what kind of animals he had seen.

"Daddy? Can I ask you a question?"

He stared again for a moment, then nodded.

"I was just wondering. . . about something you always say to James and Jeremy. . .you know how you tell them, 'Everyone needs to learn to make a dollar?'"

Daddy nodded again, then quietly said, "Yes, everyone needs to learn to make a dollar, Clemmie."

"Well, if I can find a way to make a dollar would that be a good thing? Would you be proud of me?"

The first smile his face had allowed in a week began to slowly creep across his face. "Sure, Clemmie. But I'm already proud of you."

"I know, but I should learn to make a dollar, too."

Daddy closed his eyes then, and appeared to have said all he was going to say this night.

"Daddy?" When he didn't answer after a long minute, Clemmie tiptoed back out and hurried outside where twilight and fireflies were calling to her, and where she knew Mama would be sitting on the porch. As soon as she got there, Mama began a familiar tirade about the weather.

"The only good thing you can say regarding late August is that its relentless heat sometimes causes the Confederate Jasmine to bloom a second time. But I'll be glad to see fall," said Mama as she sat in her wicker rocker on the porch beneath the sweet-scented vines trailing overhead.

She watched as Clementine raced across the front lawn in pursuit of fireflies which were making their appearance.

"Gotcha!" Clementine squealed as she slammed the lid on her Mason jar.

"I got one, Mama. Wanna see?" She hurried to the porch to show her mother her captured victim. Mama smiled and returned to working on her needlepoint canvas. Clemmie released her catch and settled in the porch swing across from her mother.

"Do you know anything about fireflies, Mama?" she asked.

Mama put her needlework down in her lap. "Well, no. I don't suppose I do. The only thing I do know is they only come out at twilight.

"Well, actually they're interesting. There are more than two thousand species of fireflies. And they can be found everywhere. Except Antarctica."

"I suppose Antarctica is too cold for them?" Mama asked.

"Yeah. But the most interesting fact is how they use their flashes to attract a mate. The males flash a specific pattern while they fly, hoping a female will answer them. Flashing is how they communicate. But some of the females are dangerous. They send particular flashes to lure the male in. And then they trap him and eat him."

Mama smiled, "I see. Clemmie you might want to consider getting your nose out of your many books. Surely there's something more to do than just reading all the time."

"You mean like spending a week at the Wildlife Seminar for Kids in Savannah next week?"

Mama sighed, "We've been through this already, Clemmie. That seminar is for teens fourteen to eighteen years old. You're only eleven, so you can't go yet."

"But I know more than any of those fourteen-year-olds. And I'm bored. There's nothing to do except read and ride Missy."

“Clemmie, you’re going to have to develop a bit of patience. Not everything happens in the time frame you might like.”

Clementine rolled her eyes. “I hate being eleven. I wish I was older. Like James and Jeremy. Then I’d be able to do what I want to do. Go where I want to go.”

Mama sighed, “Don’t wish your life away so easily. One day you’ll look back on these years and realize how special they were.”

“Being young is no fun. And it will be years before I’m old enough to do the things I want to do,” cried Clementine.

“Sometimes being headstrong can be a good quality, Clementine. But it can also get you into trouble. It’s better to give something a decent measure of thought before you jump in with both feet. As I know you like to do,” Mama smiled, then picked up her needlework once again.

The next instant the shudder of an old truck's engine as it finally died had Clementine jumping to her feet. That sound meant James was here. And if James was here, then Abby would be with him.

She scooted out the back door and hurried over to James’ truck. She jerked the passenger’s door open and was greeted with a large, wet, pink tongue swiping across her cheek. Then the greeter hopped from the truck and placed her large paws on Clementine's shoulders.

Abby was a six-month-old pup, a mix of Border Collie and Australian Shepherd. James had gotten the fur ball from Mrs. Stoutamire, an older lady down in Blue Creek whose Border Collie had recently littered five pups.

"Abby, you're going to be quite a large lady one day,” Clementine giggled as she struggled to stand with Abby’s two huge paws planted on her small shoulders. She removed Abby's paws, reached into the pocket of her shorts, and pulled out a doggie treat, which Abby devoured almost before Clementine took her hand away.

"That's more than I can say for you, runt," James laughed as he pulled Clementine close and put her in a headlock. His version of a hug.

As for calling her runt, that had begun years ago, and Clementine had never minded it until recently, as it was becoming apparent that perhaps that was all she was ever going to be. A runt of a girl.

She pulled away from James and looked closely at him. "What happened to your eye? It's all purple underneath. And swollen."

"Aw, a limb slapped me when I tried to break it. Working in the woods with Daddy has its problems."

Clemmie shrugged, "Huh. I guess so." Then she called to the pup, "C'mon, Abby. Let's go to the barn. I'll get a brush and work on your coat. Looks like James never does."

James entered in the back door, grabbed a Coca-Cola from the Frigidaire and strolled to the front porch. "Hey, Mama, what's going on with you? Where's Daddy?" he asked as he settled in the swing at the end of the porch.

Before she answered, she, too, observed his bruised, swollen eye. "James, what happened to your eye? Here. Let me take a closer look," Mama said as she lay her canvas needle work aside and approached him.

But he pulled away. "It's nothing, Mama. Just a limb that struck me when I was working last week."

Mama lifted her eyebrows. "A limb you say? Are you sure about that?" This wasn't the first incident with a "limb" or other object getting in his way.

He sighed, "Look. It was just a misunderstanding with one of the workmen. We had a difference of opinion and got a bit carried away. That's all."

"Who was it?"

"Just one of the black workmen. A fellow called Hercules. A nickname he tries to live up to I guess."

"Your daddy will take you to task on this, James. You know how he feels about this racial problem. And you getting into a quarrel with one of the black workmen feeds right into that issue."

"Well, I'll not sit by and let one of them call me honky and not respond. This racial issue isn't one sided, Mama. You never worked with any blacks and don't know how things are right now. A couple of the other white men had words with him too."

"Still, your Daddy is gonna be all over you for this. He expects you to set an example for how we treat others. And that includes the black workers as well. He'll..."

Just then Clementine came up on the porch, Abby close on her heels. As always she began to chatter away. "I think Daddy's still feeling bad, Mama. He didn't want to talk much. But he did say I could learn to make a dollar."

James smiled at this remark. "Yep. He's told me that a hundred times." He then looked over to Mama. "That business with Skidder still got him upset?"

"Yes. His mind keeps replaying the scene of the lightning, discovering Skidder's body, and then going to see Corina. And attending the funeral. He's having nightmares and hasn't slept in days. He's going to have to work through it, but it'll take time."

Clementine began to work on the tangles in Abby's fur which was matted in a number of places. "James, why did you name her Abby? Seems like a strange name for a dog."

"Abby was my first girlfriend. In fifth grade. She had a sprinkling of freckles across her nose that looked like the spots on Abby's coat. The name seemed to fit," James replied as he took a swig from his Coca-Cola, downing half of it in one long swallow.

Abby stood perfectly still as Clementine brushed gingerly, removing one tangle at a time.

Clementine glanced over to her brother. "Do you know why Abby's got one blue eye and one brown one?"

"No, but I'm sure you're gonna tell me, runt," James responded, grinning broadly.

"Well, according to my Encyclopedia Britannica, Border Collies often have a *merle* gene, which means they might have coats with streaks or splotches of darker colors and may have blue eyes. Or, like Abby, one eye may be blue and the other brown, or maybe even amber."

"Is that right?" James smiled and nodded, "Now, who would have known such information?"

"When I become a vet, I'll know a lot more than I do now. Maybe I'll even have a dog like Abby, too."

James sighed, "Listen, runt, you can't be a veterinarian. First of all, you're a girl and girls aren't vets. Second, even when you finally do grow up, you'll be too small. Look at you now. You're gonna be just like Nana MacKinnon, who wasn't even five feet tall and weighed a hundred pounds when soaking wet. Vets have to be strong and big. Only men can do that kind of work. If you're determined to have some kind of career, you should to be a teacher, like Mama. Or maybe a nurse."

Clementine stood, threw the grooming brush at him and started for the screen door leading into the house. She yelled to her brother then, "You don't know everything, James. Granddaddy says I can be anything I want to be!"

Her voice was one second from becoming a sob, and she was not going to let James hear her cry. She slapped the screen door closed as she fled, causing it to rattle on its hinges.

Right on cue, her mother called from the porch, "Clemmie, that's no way for a young lady to behave."

Mama's words were delivered in her soft, mellow, voice and floated through the hot August air. Air so humidity-laden that Clemmie's towhead curls were even more rebellious than usual. Mama usually fashioned Clementine's hair in a long braid, but somehow it always managed to escape its confines and riotous wisps sprigged everywhere.

Granddaddy MacKinnon always teased her, "Clemmie, those curls are just like you. Determined to go their own way." Then he'd laugh at his own joke.

The twins were nine years older than Clementine, and like James, Jeremy was also prone to teasing Clementine. But he'd gotten a scholarship to the state university and was away studying to become a forest ranger. Clementine was glad he was gone. At least there was one less brother to aggravate her. She was aware she was rather small for her age and didn't need those two reminding her.

Frustrated and irritated, she returned to the porch and stood in front of James—hands on hips—and stared at his grinning face.

"You're wrong, James. It's 1955 and things are changing. Women can become vets now. And I will. You just watch me. And I'll learn to make a dollar, too!" Then she disappeared back inside rather than let James see her cry.

Mama put her needlepoint down again. "Leave her alone, James. Clemmie wants to be as grownup as you and Jeremy. Don't tease her so; she worships you both, you know. But, I'm afraid you're right. She does appear to have Nana MacKinnon's small frame and will likely be rather small even as an adult. And, truth be told, it seems she may have inherited Nana's independent streak as well."

The two shared a smile at that comment as Nana had been much loved, but did have an independent spirit which meant she would voice her opinion. Even if it wasn't always wanted!

6

# Prelude to the Second Coming

When Clemmie tiptoed from the den, her daddy sighed. He just didn't have the energy to engage her today. Presently, Andrew's mind was re-running the scene once again—as it had for a week—and he could feel his pulse begin to race.

When the mental images began once more, it was like watching a movie. Images of himself standing there, looking down at the body. The body of his friend. A friend who was no longer a part of this world. A dead friend.

The next image revealed that he was no longer standing. Instead, he fell to his knees. Tears streamed down his face. His head was bowed and his shoulders crumpled into his body. And even though he was quite tall and well-built, he now appeared to be smaller, without strength to hold himself upright.

This scene wouldn't have seemed incongruous but for one small, but relevant, detail. Since when did a white man shed tears for a black man?

The images now showed that before this great calamity, this death, all was quiet but for the steady, slow-dripping but incessant rain that had soaked the ground for more than a week.

But today, without warning, the sky reverberated with earth-shattering bolts of scorching fire ripping across it. Forked and jagged. Menacing. It was like someone, maybe one of the Greek gods, or Almighty God himself, was hell-bent on releasing his wrath in a spectacle of unbridled anger. Seeking something—or someone—on which to visit this wicked vortex.

After what seemed an eternity, but was only seconds, a distant, protracted rumbling of thunder heralded the termination of this fury and the beginning of an even more fearsome event.

When the first bolt of white-hot lightning slashed across the sky, Andrew could only watch in awe at such an unexpected exhibition of Mother Nature's power.

"Holy Mother of God!" he muttered as he scurried from beneath the tall pines, trying to get to his truck. He knew the best thing to do in a lightning storm was to get inside your vehicle where the metal could protect you. But before he got halfway across the path, a second blistering bolt came spiraling down, scorching the ground near his feet.

"What the hell? Is this the prelude to the second coming?" he yelled as he dashed the last few yards, then jerked the truck door open, scraping his shin as he struggled to get to safety.

He glanced over where Skidder, one of his workmen, was sitting atop a tractor. Ready to complete a small task before leaving for the day. Andrew prayed the metal cab of the tractor would provide some measure of safety for him. That was his thought as yet another flaming ball of fire came screaming down, singeing the earth near his truck.

Andrew was no stranger to lightning, especially in these woods filled with tall pines of various species. Even so, this terrifying exhibition of outrage was unlike any he'd ever experienced. The lightning was like a living, breathing, entity.

He felt static electricity running up his arm and the very air sizzled for several moments after the initial strike.

When the lightning storm abated, Andrew sat still, trying to get his bearings. During the hellacious event, he had floundered about, squinting his eyes in order to escape the harsh, blinding brightness that enveloped everything in its path.

"Don't believe I want to go through another hair-raising show like that one. Bet it scared Skidder and the other men half to death. Just like it did me."

He spoke aloud as if verbalizing the event would reduce some of the anxiety that had coursed through his veins and continued to have his skin crawling like he'd been stung by one of the small, Southern Devil scorpions that made their home in these woods.

When he climbed down from his long-bed logging truck, empty now since they could not load logs in this knee-deep mud, the first thing Andrew noted was an eerie silence following the ear-shattering, deafening, moments he'd just survived. Gone was the usual cawing of the black crows, the twittering of brown thrashers, the raspy "*sklit-sklit-sklit*" call of the red-cockaded woodpeckers, and the screech of red-shouldered hawks that haunted these forests.

With his faculties seemingly in working order, he looked about. A tall, longleaf pine tree lay sprawled in front of his truck which was parked across the path from Skidder's tractor. Apparently, the tree had been struck by one of the cracking bolts and had toppled over, split open down the middle, it branches splaying the ground when they should have been stretching to the heavens.

Where was Skidder? He'd been sitting on his tractor but wasn't there now. Did he jump off when the lightning Kabuki dance started? Perhaps he ran for a ditch. He would have known not to go into the forest during a lightning storm.

"Skidder? Skidder?" Andrew called as he hurried over to the downed tree, trampling on the low-lying branches, stumbling. Now on his knees. When he pulled a long branch away from the tree trunk, a navy-blue workman's cap lay crumpled beneath. Andrew's heart pumped wildly as he pulled first one branch then another, searching for what he hoped *not* to find. Skidder. His erratic breathing made his task even more difficult, and he found himself hyperventilating because some intuitive, unnamed sense knew what he refused to acknowledge.

As he jerked away one last branch, one with seared edges, Skidder's face came into view. "Oh, no. Not this. No. God in heaven please tell me I'm dreaming!" Andrew called out, his voice getting louder with each word.

Skidder's body lay in repose as if he had decided to take a short rest before completing his work. Closer inspection revealed a jagged line of charred skin and clothing running across his upper torso leading down to his right leg. His facial expression was the same as always. Almost smiling as if he knew something you didn't. And even though he had to be about forty years old, he still looked the same as when Andrew hired him some twenty-odd years ago.

Andrew was familiar with the devastation that resulted when lightning struck a tree and was sure the sheer amount of electricity that had coursed through Skidder's body would have caused his heart to cease functioning. The blood oozing from Skidder's right ear indicated his eardrum had ruptured as well. Curling ribbons of smoke rose from his blue chambray shirt, and Andrew found himself trying to smother them, to stamp them out with his hands. And though he knew there was no need, he put his hand on Skidder's neck and checked for a pulse.

He continued to kneel as he couldn't seem to find his legs. Maybe it was a way to console himself as Skidder was past consoling. Or perhaps it was just easier to remain in this kneeling position. To utter a prayer for someone. Skidder. Himself. Someone. Surely prayer was needed.

When his tears began, they were like the rain. Continuous with no letup in sight.

# 7

# Real Men Do Cry

Skidder's death was a tragic event that would forever haunt Andrew. And he wasn't the only person whose life would be changed as result of Mother Nature throwing a temper tantrum.

Skidder, Toby, and Jesse often rode to their work sites together. And the morning of the lightning storm, Skidder had asked Toby to drop him at the edge of the forest, stating he would walk from there to his tractor. He'd said, "Should be finished in about half an hour at most. Wait for me here at the edge of the woods. No point in getting your truck stuck in that mud again. I'll hike out of there and meet you as soon as I'm done. Then we can head to the Hollow."

"All right. Be waitin' on you. You're right. Don't want to chance getting stuck in that mud again. Mr. Mac already had to pull me out yesterday morning."

Toby had been standing next to his truck talking with his brother, Jesse, when the lightning blitzkrieg had begun. The brothers crawled inside the truck and watched with awe as the flashing spectacle of light lit up the woods.

A short while later Toby was getting antsy. Worried. "Jesse, I think we should check on Skidder. Could be that a tree fell across the pathway. That happens sometimes following a lightning storm. He might need help." Jesse agreed and they sprinted down to the area where Skidder was to have moved some cut logs on to one of the large trucks.

When they got to Skidder's tractor, both men stopped abruptly. There was indeed a downed tree, but that wasn't what got their attention initially. Rather, the odor of seared flesh—nauseating and putrid—caused their nostrils to flare. Both men had heard it said that you never really get the smell of burning flesh out of your nose entirely. No matter how long you live.

Toby straightened his massive shoulders and walked forward slowly. Jesse then stood back, letting Toby walk alone toward the impossible scene that lay before them.

Toby slowed his steps as he saw his friend lying on his back, his eyes wide open with a vacant stare that told the story better than any words might have. The fabric of his shirt had melted into his chest and tendrils of wispy smoke still drifted upward.

Toby's first response was the same knee-jerk reaction one always has when disaster strikes. Denial of the situation. And yet, one of Toby's greatest strengths was his ability to face problems head-on. No procrastinating. No wishing some situation was otherwise. He'd just deal with it. But today's situation might be difficult.

He came closer and looked down. Then cried out, "No! That can't be you, Skidder. That body looks lifeless. It can't be you. You can't be dead!"

When he tore his eyes from Skidder's body, he turned to see Mr. Mac, Andrew, his employer, kneeling. Tears streaming down his face.

Toby's brain was issuing orders, commands, to get to his friend. To his employer. To help them. But his feet were having difficulty executing these commands. They simply refused to move. Probably because that same unnamed sense that told Andrew what he didn't want to know, was at work in

Toby's mind as well . . . and that unnamed sense kept insisting that what it whispered was true.

When he did get his feet to comply with his brain's commands, he walked toward the two. And then he, too, found himself on his knees. He placed his hand on Skidder's arm.

"Aw, no. Not you. Skidder, you can't leave us like this!" His voice caught in his throat, and he wanted to lay down next to his friend. To hold him close. To ease his pain. But Skidder wasn't in pain. Toby was.

Then he turned and gently lay his hand on Andrew's shoulder. "Mr. Mac? You all right, Mr. Mac?"

Andrew looked up at Toby, but no words came out. He just stared, then nodded. After a long moment, Toby took a deep breath and stood. He'd never known Mr. Mac to not be completely in charge of any situation, even dire ones. At this moment he was staring at Skidder's body, his dark eyes so full of grief Toby had to look away. To see Mr. Mac here, unable to do anything except stare and remain in this kneeling position was discomforting. Actually, maybe even frightening.

Toby and Skidder were the best of friends, and Toby was aware that Skidder and Mr. Mac had a very unusual relationship. More than just employee and employer. They were friends no matter how you looked at it. And the fact that one was black and the other white never seemed to be important. Lately, though, with racial tensions beginning to heat up across the South, Toby wondered not if, but how this friendship would be affected.

Then, lifting Andrew to his feet and leading him away from Skidder's body, Toby took control of the situation. "Come on, Mr. Mac. We need to go now. Let's get you home and I'll come back down here to take care of Skidder. Come on now. It's time to leave." Toby fought to keep his own tears from joining those that continued to make a path down Andrew's face.

Andrew stood and began walking ever so slowly, as if his legs still weren't committed to supporting him. Then he stopped and turned to Toby, "I'd just said, 'Let's call it a day, Skidder. This damn rain has saturated the ground to the point the men can't get the trucks to the logs that are already cut. We'll wait 'til the ground dries up a bit. Then we'll try to retrieve the cut timber and get it to the mill.'

"And he said, 'Yessir, Mr. Mac. I can get my tractor in those low places better than the trucks. I'll just clear the path so when we come back the men can get right to work.'"

"Sounds good," I told him. "Then I'll tell the men to go on home. And you finish up and take yourself home, too."

"Yessir," he said. "You'll pass Toby up at the edge of the woods. Tell him I'll only be a few more minutes. Then I'll ride with him to the Hollow. Lordy, but this rain has gotta stop."

"That's what he said. 'This rain has gotta stop.'"

Toby then spoke to Jesse, who had come closer but had yet to say a word. "Jesse, take Mr. Mac home. I'll take care of the situation here in the woods."

This task, taking Skidder's body to the undertaker to ready him for burial, would be one Toby wouldn't pass on to anyone else. This would be his last act of friendship for Skidder.

As Jesse escorted Andrew down the logging path, Toby's thoughts scurried back to wondering about the friendship between Skidder and Mr. Mac. A friendship that had been clear to all, if not understood.

Toby was aware Mr. Mac looked to Skidder to keep him abreast of any problems in the black community. But Toby knew how quickly situations can change. Skidder was the leader of that community. Of Smokey Hollow. Or had been. And now, with him gone, there would no doubt be changes that may have unwanted consequences.

Skidder was a bit older than Toby and had taught him so much that Toby often wondered why Skidder had bothered as he could often be a thorn in everyone's side. Even last evening, at a meeting of the men in the Hollow, Toby had been one of the outspoken ones who were incensed by an article that had appeared in the local newspaper yesterday.

The article gave the gory details of the death of a young black man who had been kidnapped and murdered in Mississippi. The reporter had further stated that this man, this Emmett Till, was a "born troublemaker" and was working to "fire up the blacks in Mississippi" by encouraging them to march with him and others who were working for racial reform in that state.

This murder was preceded by another event this same year, 1955. A black lady named Rosa Parks had made headlines when she refused to give up her seat in the "white" section of a city bus in Montgomery, Alabama. That event had brought about a boycott of the Transportation Authority, a boycott led by a man whose name would become synonymous with racial reform. Dr. Martin Luther King, Jr.

There had been quite a heated discussion last night, and Toby and a couple of other younger men were all for making placards and marching down Main Street with their feelings exposed for the whole community to see. Skidder, in his usual composed manner, had simply made one statement:

"Toby, and you others who are determined to march, I understand your anger. I want nothing more than for my children to have the same good schools, the same good teachers, the same freedoms and choices that the white children have. But I would remind you that most of us here in this community of Harper's Mill have decent jobs. And in the case of those of us who work for Mr. MacKinnon—and many of us do—we receive the same pay as his white men. I know. I deliver their wages. Part of my job.

"And, yeah, I know not every white man is as respectful of us black folk as Mr. Mac. But how he treats us is known in this community. He sets a good example.

"I agree it's long past time for change. I do. I believe we should do our part to make life better for all of us. For our people. But we should make sure we don't cut off our nose to spite our face. I say let's talk with Mr. Mac. See what his thoughts are concerning us marching. He's not the enemy. It wasn't his fault he was born white. And he's told me more than once that he can't right the wrongs of the world, but he's nothing if not fair in any dealings I ever had with him.

"I read the article about the death of the young man in Mississippi and the racial protests in other places. Dr. King is an intelligent leader. And he may be the one who actually brings about change for us. He talks about "non-violence" in these marches, but from what I've read, there's always some who can't abide by that vision and people end up getting hurt. In some cases, dead. And I don't want that to happen to any of us."

Toby spoke up then, "Not everyone has your experience, Skidder. Having a white man for a friend. One that I notice you still say "yessir" to when you talk," he continued.

Next to speak was Gabriel, a twenty-three-year-old, and the youngest man there. He was also an exceptionally handsome young man. And the most rebellious one of all. He stood up and looked around the room. Then he made his point, "Freedom has to be demanded. It's never free. And civil rights ain't always civil."

Toby nodded in agreement and took the floor again. "I know what you say is true, Skidder. Mr. Mac is a fair man. But, do you think he would agree with us when it comes to marching?"

Skidder looked up to the ceiling. Perhaps seeking heavenly help for a response to Toby's question.

"You're right, Toby. I do say "yessir" to him. First of all, he's older than I am. And secondly, he's my employer as well as my friend. And for the record, I also say "yessir" to old Theodore, the janitor in our church. It's called "respect," Toby. Do I think everything about this friendship is perfect? The way I wish it was? No, but it's a start. A start to perhaps a time when the color of a man's skin takes backseat to the color of his heart. And remember this: If we work together, we can accomplish much. If we work alone, it takes twice as long, and we still may not get where we want to go.

"Me and Mr. Mac share our thoughts and sometimes our hopes. And most times they're the same. All I'm sayin' is let's talk with him. If you'll let yourselves give it a try, you might find he's not so concerned with a man's skin color as he is with what's inside the man. What he values. What he believes in."

Toby sighed. "Well, I hear you. But no matter how you look at it, Mr. Mac's white and there's no way he can relate to how we all feel. How tired we are of being second class citizens. But, all right. I'll try this approach, but I've got my own ideas about how to proceed if your suggestion fails to bring a satisfactory outcome."

Skidder nodded. With the meeting coming to a close, he started for the door. He turned back to the group, "What I do believe is this: It's time to give Jim Crow and his laws a decent burial." That brought much-needed laughter and several *amens* to boot.

But that was yesterday. A lifetime ago. Toby shook his head. Somehow the conversations of last night, heated at times, seemed unimportant. Skidder was dead. Did any of those issues matter now? Marching? Telling the world how angry you are that a young black man was murdered by a group of whites? That you demand social change?

As he returned to the logging path after delivering Mr. Mac into Jesse's capable hands and retrieving a blanket from his truck, he peered down into the face of his friend. His mentor.

He refused to call an ambulance. He wept within as he knelt and gingerly wrapped Skidder in the blanket. But he'd not shed tears today. Maybe tomorrow. Today he'd clutch his grief inside and make sure Skidder was cared for in death as he'd cared for others in life.

Skidder was tall and lean. Toby was the opposite. A short, stocky man with tremendous shoulders that routinely popped off his shirt buttons. Today he used these massive shoulders as he carefully lifted Skidder's body, cradling him as he might a child, close to his chest. He sighed deeply and spoke to Skidder as if he were alive. As if he could hear every word.

"I don't know how successful we'll be in our efforts to bury Jim Crow and his laws, Skidder, but I'll see to it you receive a fine send-off. One that will take you to the Pearly Gates as I'm sure St. Peter will have reserved a special seat for you in that place. And it occurs to me that he may have a cold bottle of Pabst Blue Ribbon waitin' for you."

## 8

# Rebel With a Cause

While waiting in Mr. Sutherland's office as instructed, Clementine's mind was beginning to send her messages she didn't particularly want to receive. Messages that had her questioning her decision to come to the tobacco barn.

These messages were simply Nana MacKinnon's warnings that seemed to have a way of running through her head when they were most needed. "*There are consequences for acting before thinking, my lass.*" How many times had Nana said that! Well, Clementine had given her plan a bit of thought, but perhaps not quite enough. And she actually hadn't told a lie. Daddy did say she could "learn to make a dollar." And after those heated words with James, she had been more determined than ever to show him and her family how capable she was.

Before she left on Sunday morning, Mama had said, "I'm going to Brunswick for a couple of days to check on Aunt Alice. She's alone now that Uncle John passed on. While I'm gone, you take care of Daddy. He's all right, but he's grieving for his friend. So, you be sure to stay close by in case he needs something."

Knowing that Mama would be gone on Monday morning made Clemmie's plan much easier to execute. So, very early this morning, Monday, she'd peddled her bicycle to the post office where she parked it behind the tall shrubs. She then hurried to stand at the rear of a line of young people, both black and white, waiting for the bus to take them to the tobacco barn.

Now, in the early morning light, the sun still not yet peeking its head fully above the horizon, she was already questioning whether her plan was a good idea. In fact, she was pretty sure it wasn't.

Clemmie was aware that the death of Skidder, something that happened in a matter of seconds, had rocked Daddy to his core. He'd worked these timber forests all his life and had never lost one of his men.

But Saturday evening when she'd asked him for his permission to "learn to make a dollar," he'd nodded and said, "Sure, Clemmie. Everyone needs to learn how to make a dollar." Well . . . that meant she could go to the tobacco barn . . . didn't it?

Actually, she wasn't even sure Daddy had understood what she had said. When she had approached him with her questions, he'd just stared at his feet, clad in workman's boots heavily splattered with pine sap from his days of clearing, cutting, and dragging trees from the forest.

Clementine was quite sure Mama would never have allowed her current escapade, but her brothers had worked at the tobacco barn during their summers, and she couldn't see any reason she shouldn't. And Daddy seemed so distant at the moment that she wasn't sure what he would think. But she knew Mama would be angry that she'd "fudged" the truth, would give her a tongue lashing, and for sure would take away her riding privileges. If all else failed though, she knew

Grandaddy would take her side. He always had a soft spot for her and she could always count on him to help her out of a tricky situation.

At 6:00 a.m. on the dot, the old bus that would take the young workers to the tobacco barn pulled into a dirt lane next to Hardee's Pool Hall. The young people climbed in and Clementine took a seat on the first bench behind the driver, across the aisle from where a couple of black boys sat. Like the black riders, she thought it might be the safest seat. Plus, she recognized a couple of older boys in the rear of the bus and knew they delighted in taunting anyone they could. There were a couple of teenage girls, too, but they kept to themselves.

Bennett, the bus driver, was a young man in his thirties who was employed by Sutherland Tobacco Inc. to bring the young workers from Harper's Mill to the tobacco barn each morning. This morning he strolled down the aisle of the bus, counting heads and stopping long enough to instill a dab of fear into a couple of rowdy boys who always tried his patience.

He got to the last bench and stopped. "Wayne. Jimmy. I ain't gonna tell you boys but once. Leave them girls alone, or I'll kick your sweet asses off my bus in a heartbeat. You got that?"

Wayne smiled and Jimmy saluted, "Got it, Bennett."

"That's Mr. Bennett to you, Jimmy," instructed Bennett. Dealing with these boys was a pain in the rear. Of course, Bennett recognized himself in those two. He'd been a bigger headache than either of them when he was their age. As time passed, however, he'd managed to leave some of his juvenile antics behind, and had become a responsible adult who cared about his community. But, the one thing that hadn't undergone reformation was his penchant for colorful language, and he still retained a salty tongue that he had to keep in check.

Bennett took his place behind the wheel and started the engine. Then he checked his rearview mirror and saw both Wayne and Jimmy standing in the aisle.

He yelled loudly, "All right, you boys. Yeah. You two in the last seat. Sit down and keep it to a dull roar. I can't watch you every minute. And don't forget what I told you."

Clementine stared out the window as the bus made its way along the street, passing by a scattering of clapboard houses and a couple of open fields where cows wandered about hoping to find a bit of ryegrass or maybe some sweet clover on which to munch.

As the bus moved on, she spied a deserted building with the windows broken out, where tall weeds and dog fennel crowded through the doorway. Clemmie thought it had been a cotton mill many decades ago, but today it was just a place that provided hidey holes for field mice and rabbits.

Next, they cruised by the First Methodist Church where Clemmie and her family attended worship every Sunday. Well, she and Mama did. Daddy often stayed home. He had his own ideas relating to worship, and they weren't the same as Mama's. An issue that had been put to bed long ago.

As the bus approached the railroad tracks, Bennett braked heavily. Once across the tracks, he turned right on Main Street, where Dorothy's Beauty Salon, Sam's Barber Shop, Strickland's Grocery, and Jackson's Auto Repair were all aligned side by side like toy soldiers.

Across the street was the Purina Feed Store owned by Mr. Hawkins, an elderly gentleman who sat in the pew in front of Clementine's family at church. He had always been one of her favorite people, but he had become so hard of hearing that Clemmie had to stand on tiptoe and yell into his ear. Something Nana had suggested.

The bus stopped at the traffic light—the only one in town—that marked the crossroads, then Bennett made a sharp left turn and they were headed north. A large, peeling, billboard proclaiming "*Jesus is Coming*" stood in the open field that flanked the right side of the highway. This warning would be the first thing a visitor would see when coming to Harper's Mill, and the last thing when they left.

Clemmie had once asked Nana MacKinnon about the message on the billboard and Nana said, "Uh-huh. Jesus is coming. But I don't think it'll be today."

Taking a peek in his rearview mirror once more, Bennett spied Dicky Stanley tossing a ball of paper at one of the teenage girls. Dicky didn't usually cause problems, but today he might be seeing how far he could push the driver.

In a loud voice Bennett called, 'Dicky, if you don't want to walk to the tobacco barn, then I suggest you keep yourself seated and drop them balls of paper."

When the bus left the edge of town, they were traveling through piney woods where wiregrass grew in dense, spreading tufts that covered the ground beneath longleaf pines. Woods where Clementine had wandered looking for coveys of quail, red-tailed hawks, pileated woodpeckers, and swamp rabbits. Where Granddaddy had taken her walking since she was small and where she could name every species of tree and brush.

It was close to 6:30 a.m. now, and the first rose-colored fingers of dawn nipped at the darkness, offering to lift the smothering blanket and replace it with the promise of a sun-filled day. Something everyone hoped for. It had rained for six days running, and that, too, probably put Daddy in a dark mood. Rain meant work would be slow, if at all, and Daddy's workmen often struggled from one paycheck to the next.

The dilapidated bus jostled along, creaking and spitting a plume of dark smoke and fumes from the exhaust. The windows had long ago been broken out, probably by the same mischievous boys sitting in the back today. The air coming through the open windows gently teased Clementine's hair as she leaned her head close to the opening.

For the second time this morning, she questioned her decision to go to the tobacco barn, but it was too late now. In about thirty minutes they would arrive at the barn, and she had no way of getting home until the bus returned in the afternoon.

Bennett was pushing the bus at top speed now, roughly forty-five miles per hour. In another fifteen minutes, he let up on the accelerator and slowed to a snail's pace, barely creeping along.

"Damn that lousy Department of Transportation. One day this excuse of a bridge is gonna drop right out from under this rattletrap bus and I'm gonna find my scrawny ass floating down the Appahoochee," Bennett muttered.

He'd made this trip many times and knew this particular spot was the one place where speed could get him into trouble. The weather-beaten, rusted sign by the road read: *Appahoochee River*. At least that's what it originally read. Today it read *App hoo  ee Ri er*. Just a few letters missing. Sorta like the bridge itself, where several wooden planks were missing from the base. But if you were careful, you could make it across.

Today the water was high. Locals would have said "swollen." Barely a few inches from touching the underside of the bridge. The river was wide at this point, and crossing it took several minutes. In earlier times, the fact that the river was wide had made it ideal for transporting goods such as tobacco and cotton to ports where it would be shipped to dealers up in Savannah and Charleston.

On this day, one lone truss standing on the left side indicated this had been a covered bridge at one time. Long ago for sure. Bennett carefully maneuvered the old windowless, belching vehicle closer to the one standing truss, avoiding the area of the missing planks. "This could be the damn river Styx for all I know," Bennett said to himself. He always breathed a bit easier once he got to the other side.

Clementine stuck her head farther out the window. After craning her head, she saw the swiftly moving water thrashing around the pilings of the bridge. Small limbs rushed by leaving bits of bark and leaves trailing in their wake. She heard the call of a barn owl as he voiced his complaints about the day beginning. He much preferred the night.

They stopped at a second railroad crossing at the junction of two roads. Bennett brought his lumbering transport to a halt, looked both ways, then proceeded.

Clementine had walked this railroad track all the way to the trestle where—if you were brave enough—you could look down below and see the large rocks which appeared to be small pebbles from that height. The first time she had crossed the highest part, Granddaddy had held her hand. But she'd still shivered with fear.

The boys in the rear of the bus were singing a ditty, something about a lady named O'Leary, but they couldn't remember the words so laughed it off and started one they did know. One about old MacDonald. Clementine sat with her back rigid, feeling more anxious as they got closer to the tobacco barn.

The sun peeked its head higher now and sent rays of light through longleaf pine needles which shone like silver threads woven through a forest of lush green woods. Clementine spotted a red-shouldered hawk perched upon a limb of a large sweet gum tree at the edge of the road.

There were no houses along this section, so it was either government-owned property, or more likely, land owned by Sutherland Tobacco Incorporated.

The bus slowed down now, wheels turning ever so slowly. They had reached the rutted path, Tea House Lane, that led to the tobacco barn, and the belly of the old bus scraped against the scrappy wiregrass growing in the middle. Another hundred yards and Bennett brought the bus to a halt.

"All right then. Outta here with you. I'll be back here at five sharp, and I'll pull out at five fifteen. If you ain't here, that's your problem. Them's the rules."

He flicked the last inch of his cigarette out the window and lighted another immediately. Despite his authoritative manner and his salty tongue, Bennett was a most likeable fellow with an engaging personality. He was one of the few people who could cause Mrs. Watson (the local school principal) to smile, and that was a real accomplishment. He could be counted on to do his part in any undertaking, and he believed in being punctual. As his mother had taught him. So, if he said the bus would leave at five fifteen, then that's when it would leave.

# 9

# *Gone . . . not Forgotten*

Jesse had left Andrew sitting on the porch. Staring into space. Never uttering a word. Not aloud, anyway. Within, however, he wrestled with what he needed to do, but couldn't seem to act on.

*I gotta get up. I gotta go tell Corina. But I don't know what to say. If Norah was here, she might suggest some words. Or Nana. She'd have something to say that would bring some understanding. But for the life of me I don't know any words that will explain such a heartbreaking event. I feel like I've stepped into a horror story and there's no way out.*

With some effort, he stood and went to the kitchen where he downed a couple of shots of Jack Daniel's whiskey, shuddering as the amber liquid burned its way down his throat.

*Somehow, I don't think that liquid courage is going to help. I gotta get myself together. I've got a job to do. Seeing Corina is the only thing that's important right now.*

He tucked his shirttail in, grabbed his workman's cap and headed to his pickup truck. He sat behind the wheel a couple of minutes, then started the engine.

Knowing this was the most difficult task he'd ever had, or would ever have again, he drove to Smokey Hollow, pulled off the dirt road and parked his truck under a giant oak tree in front of Skidder's home. He stood quietly for a moment, then walked to the front door where he removed his cap and knocked lightly. Corina opened the door to him, a smile on her face.

"Mr. Mac? What you doin' here in the middle of the morning? Don't tell me Skidder sent you for his lunch pail. He left it sitting on the counter this morning. Wait. I'll fetch . . ."

Andrew reached out and lay his hand on her arm, "No, Corina. I didn't come for Skidder's lunch."

"Oh, then come on in. Now what's got you coming all the way to the Hollow?"

Andrew sat in the small, ladderback chair she indicated. Around the kitchen table.

"I've got a fresh loaf of raisin bread, Mr. Mac. You care for a slice?"

"No. Corina. I'm fine." He struggled for a few moments before he finally found his tongue and uttered words that sounded so lame. So unreal. So impossible.

"Skidder's had an accident, Corina."

She looked quizzically at him, "What kind of accident, Mr. Mac? He's not in the hospital, is he?" She clasped her hands together beneath her chin. In prayerlike fashion.

"No, Corina. He's not in the hospital."

She sighed, "Oh, that's good then. He's a strong man. Takes a lot to get the better of him."

Andrew then reached forward and took both her hands in his, praying his errant tongue wouldn't betray him again.

"He's gone, Corina."

"What you mean, gone?"

"He's . . . he's dead."

She stared at Andrew for a long moment. Then she leaped from her chair, causing it to topple and land on the floor with a thud.

"What? What did you say? He can't be dead. Mr. Mac, that can't be."

She took a step back and shook her head back and forth. Then she leaned in closer, searching Andrew's face for some sign that he'd misspoken. That he'd made some horrible error in his choice of words.

But all she found was the same dark, grief-filled eyes that Toby had turned away from. The pain she saw in Andrew's face couldn't be denied. The hurt displayed in those dark orbs left no room for doubting his words.

The soul-wrenching keening that Corina let loose tore into Andrew's heart, ripping it apart as if it were made of tissue paper. Her bones appeared to turn to liquid, and she melted to the floor. Andrew gathered her in his arms and held her as he would have held his own wife were she in such pain.

If someone standing outside witnessed this emotion-filled scene, a white man holding a black woman, then so be it. Skin color had no place in this situation.

# 10

# Funerals are for the Living

Dark suit. Crisp white shirt. Subdued tie. Polished shoes. Fresh hanky in pocket. And most important of all, his emotions wrapped tight as a silkworm in a cocoon.

Andrew, a ruggedly handsome, middle-aged man with a thick thatch of dark hair beginning to gray at the temples, was unaccustomed to feeling such loss of control. Presently, he needed to adjust his tie but he refused to look into the mirror. Didn't want to see his face. His eyes. Eyes that could read a man's face and know a lie before it snuck in. Eyes that could shed a tear as easily as any woman. Eyes that were so filled with pain Toby had turned away from them on that fateful day. He jerked at his tie one last time.

"I guess I'm ready. But God help me, I don't know if I can do this, Norah."

Norah held him close. There was nothing to say she hadn't already said. This strong man, her man, was a fighter. Would stand toe-to-toe with anyone he thought was in the wrong. Would fight to the finish for his beliefs.

But the death of his friend had thrown him into an abyss of grief. Grief that felt like an enemy in its determination to overpower him. How do you arm yourself for a fight with such a faceless foe?

When his mother had passed away several weeks ago, Andrew had become acquainted with a new level of pain. Pain that comes when a loved one leaves you. A kind of pain he would gladly have remained unfamiliar with.

He took a deep breath, "Today I've learned that pain cares less if it's the death of a family member or a friend. It still weaves its fingers around your heart and has you praying for its release.

"But as painful as Mother's death was, I understand it. Dying is part of living. She had a full life. Lived to be seventy-eight. And she didn't suffer; she just went to sleep one night and didn't wake the next morning. But this funeral today—for a man in the prime of his life with a wife and two small children—this death feels like something you'd read in a novel. A scene some fanciful writer might have dreamed up. But it's not a dream, Norah. It's all too real.

"Mother once told me funerals are for the living, not the dead. She was right. Skidder won't witness the crushing grief his friends will be feeling when they parade past his casket. He won't hear the sobs, the soft weeping and sniffling coming from the pews. Won't see how difficult it is for Toby and Jesse to keep their emotions in check. Won't see the glorious bouquets of flowers and inhale the scent of lilies, which always finds its way to funerals. He won't hear the church bells ringing out their message or the choir singing their sad verses. Won't see how Corina is suffering as she gathers her children close when they look upon their father's face for the last time.

"But I will, Norah. I'll see it all. I'll hear it all. I'll smell those sickly-sweet lilies. And the sights, sounds, and scents will stay with me."

~ ~ ~

On the morning of Skidder's death, the morning following the meeting of the men in the Hollow, Andrew and Skidder had stood together, leaning on Andrew's truck, discussing the troubles in Mississippi—the death of Emmett Till.

Skidder sighed, "The death of that young black man, Emmett Till, is weighing heavy on the men in the Hollow. You and me both gotta know change is coming, and we both are gonna be tried.

"Gabriel, one of the younger men, is smart, full of passion, and he's raring to become part of the 'fight for freedom' as he calls it. And Toby. Well, at least he's inclined to think first, and he's all for raising cane if he thinks it will help Dr. King's push for racial equality."

Andrew nodded, "This death and its ramifications are a problem for us whites too, Skidder. We got a few young men who are as hard to deal with as Gabriel. And a couple of 'em have a mean streak as wide as the Appahoochee River running through them. They'd like nothing better than to start trouble.

"And, truth be told, my own son, James, has a quick temper. He's young, so I have hopes he'll learn to conquer that temper and think things through before acting. But I don't know. He's got a lot of characteristics that my brother, Colin, had. And he never did learn to look at both sides of any difficult issues.

"When Colin was a teenager, he and Daddy had problems. He decided he couldn't abide by the MacKinnon rules, so he left. That was years ago. He's in Texas somewhere. But we don't see him often. Maybe at Christmas. I just hope James doesn't follow in Colin's footsteps.

"And you're right, Skidder, we're all going to be tried. America was founded on a set of beliefs. Among them was the idea that all people are created equal whether European, Native American or African American. Our nation is one to be proud of in many ways and our forefathers fought endless battles to overcome the oppressions of a king. Many lost their lives trying to create a country where every man is entitled to certain rights. Freedom of speech. Freedom to worship as we please. Due process of law. Freedom of assembly. And some others, but I can't recall all of them.

"Many of those aspirations and dreams are fairly well founded in America. But now, almost two hundred years later, we're still struggling as a nation to uphold these beliefs and rights. And from the beginning of the country, the black man, your people, have never been treated as equal. In her defense, America is a very young country and as all young countries, she has much to learn.

"I didn't go on to college as Mother wanted, but I've read a lot about slavery and that terrifying time. And there's no way I can ever know the pain that your people have endured. No way I can change the past."

Andrew rubbed his hand across the back of his neck, "Ah, Skidder, as I always tell you, I can't right the wrongs of the world, and I can't undo what my ancestors did. I believe all men have self-worth and should be treated accordingly. That's another right as far as I'm concerned.

"So, like it or not, some difficult days are coming. But I hope by working together we can keep our community from letting these incidents of hatred and violence rule the day."

~ ~ ~

Now, four days later, Andrew was headed to Smokey Hollow again. Skidder was being laid to rest. He prayed that his presence, the presence of a white man at such an emotion-laden event, wouldn't cause a stir.

Just for today, Andrew hoped any such issues would be left outside the church. Today he simply wanted . . . no that's not right . . . he *needed* to pay his respects to his friend.

He arrived at the church and parked his truck next to Toby's around the side of the building. Thinking to sneak in and slide into one of the pews in the rear, he quietly opened the church door. Before he could get seated, however, Toby appeared at his side.

"Mr. Mac, Corina would like you to sit with her. In her pew. She ain't got family here. They all live in South Carolina somewhere. She would like you to be with her."

Andrew swallowed. "Of course, Toby. If that's what she wants."

Andrew had been to many funerals, but this one would be etched into his memory. And all the worries he'd had? Those concerns he'd expressed to Norah this morning? He was all wrong about those.

He'd thought Skidder's funeral would be a sad, mournful affair, with loud crying and wailing. And he'd dreaded going. But, not so. These folks showed him how a funeral should be conducted.

The small, unpainted wooden church was adorned with fresh flowers, and soft piano music played quietly in the background. A rotund, white-robed minister—an older gentleman without a sprig of hair on his shiny head—read a short bit of scripture from a battered, old Bible and mumbled some kind words regarding Skidder. Then a long line of friends marched to the podium to give testimony to the fine person Skidder had been.

Andrew hadn't thought of that. Would he be expected to speak, too? If so, he wasn't sure he could manage such as that painful lump in his throat still refused to budge. He was breathing, but anything more was unbearable. He hadn't even been able to tell Norah everything. It was as though he must keep this painful experience to himself. It wasn't something he could or even wanted to share.

When Toby went forward, Andrew held his breath. Toby and Skidder had been friends for a lifetime. Toby stood at the podium, straightened his huge shoulders, and fingered the paper he held, his large hands pulling at the edges. He flipped the paper over. Then flipped it over again. Finally, he placed it face down on the podium.

He cleared his throat and began, "We're here today to honor Floyd Leroy Sanderson. Floyd? He was Skidder so long I guess I forgot his real name. I told him we would give him a fine send-off. One that will get him to the Pearly Gates. So y'all gotta help me do that. I was gonna read my testimony to you, 'cause I thought that would be better. But now I'm here, standing in front of Skidder, with him lying there in his satin-lined casket probably laughin' at me, I think I'll just tell you what's in my heart.

"Skidder was like an older brother. He saved my hide from more beatings than I want to recall. 'Course, my mother probably knew he was covering for me with his little fibs, but if so, she never let on. More than anything, Skidder taught me how a man, a real man, behaves. Sometimes I seem to forget what he taught me, but I could always count on him reminding me. I couldn't have had a better teacher. Or friend."

His voice cracked on the last comment, so he stopped with one last statement. "I'll miss him every day."

All was quiet for a long minute. Then, suddenly, a voice emanating from the rear of the church—a voice Andrew was sure must have been Mahalia Jackson—sang out loudly, the strong, rich, contralto tones sending chills spiraling up his spine. He'd never thought the word "hallelujah" was particularly special, but when this woman sang it, it took on new meaning.

Then the most harmonious, uplifting voices he'd ever heard joined in, and Andrew was sure the rafters in the old church were rising to accommodate them. The voices grew stronger and louder as the purple-robed choir came forward down the aisle, their hands lifted above their heads. This choir needed no musical accompaniment. They brought a special kind of excitement in the old *a capella* shouting style of singing that originated with their Gullah/Geechee ancestors in their *praise houses*. It was simply a part of their soul.

*Hallelujah! Hallelujah!*
*He's gone home.*
*Yes, he's gone home.*
*Hallelujah! Hallelujah!*
*He's gone to be with his Lord.*
*Hallelujah! Hallelujah!*

Their voices were so filled with glee that Andrew's heart—the one that had been ripped to shreds—rejoiced listening to their wild, abandoned, expressions of joy for one gone to be with his Lord. This was not a funeral. It was a celebration of life. A celebration of and for a special man named Skidder.

# 11

# Tea House Lane

Rosie lived a mile down the lane from the tobacco barn on the edge of a small creek that branched off the Appahoochee River. Her cottage had been built upon stilts, the same as all the cottages "Old" Mr. Thomas Sutherland had constructed for his workers. Being on stilts allowed air to flow beneath the houses and should the creek ever rise, their homes wouldn't be flooded.

The cottage was truly hers as *Keke* had taken steps to make sure her name was on the deed. Larry's grandfather had been the kind soul who had deeded the small wooden cottage to *Keke* for his "years of dedicated service" he'd said.

Thanks to the original "Lady" Sutherland, Rosie's home had a street address: 16 Tea House Lane. The first Mrs. Sutherland, a "lady" from England, was not impressed that her big Georgia mansion had a rural route as the address. So, at her insistence, the local authorities agreed to change the address to 15 Tea House Lane. She further insisted that all the cottages on the property have an address as well, rather than the usual rural route and box number.

"Of course the cottages will have an address," she'd said. "Everyone deserves the dignity of having a particular place they call home. That's quite important."

Rosie could remember *Keke* and old Mr. Sutherland chatting like two magpies, and she wondered how they had developed their relationship. Black and white didn't often mix in those days. Nor now either.

Old Mr. Sutherland would saunter up to the steps of *Keke's* porch but would never come inside. Instead, *Keke* would come out and the two would sit on the steps and the discussions would commence. And the fact that *Keke* was an avid reader was of importance. They could discuss many topics.

Mr. Sutherland would usually begin the conversation. "Barrie, I tell you I don't know what's going to become of this country. We seem to drift from one problem to the next. Now we're in a flap with some of the European nations concerning the price of tobacco!" He'd shake his head and rub his chin.

Barrie (*Keke*) would smile, "Uh huh. No surprise, though, Mr. Sutherland. The world has always had problems and I imagine it always will."

"Seems to be that way. Yes, it does seem to be that way. And what do you think of this new generation? They might be more educated, but I'm not sure one of them can put in a day's work that will come close to what you and I have done in our time."

Then they'd both laugh. They were just two old men spending time with each other. Both were widowed and that fact alone—the sharing of grief—cleared an easy path to friendship.

Then *Keke* would pour a small taste of Cooter's homemade brew into a cup for each—maybe a thumb or so—and they'd talk on a few more minutes. Then they would say their goodbyes as the sun sent its final sparks of light through the tall piney woods.

*Keke* not only passed on his love of books and reading to Rosie, he also passed on the tradition of telling the stories of his ancestors in Sierra Leone that his grandmother had told him about. Particularly the stories of a special woman called "Kadie."

"Rosie, you gotta keep this tradition of storytelling. Else our story will be lost. So listen carefully when I tell them to you." *Keke* would say each time he repeated one of the stories.

*Keke* was an artist of sorts and spent his evenings sketching birds, deer, chickens and other wildlife they were surrounded by in those piney woods. His drawings of people were breathtaking, and he captured their emotions simply by making a few marks on the paper with his small piece of charcoal.

He hadn't passed his artistic talent on to Rosie, but his great-grandson, Dean, was already showing promise in that area. He was fourteen now and had been drawing for several years, his sketches being every bit as full of expression as his great-grandpa's had been.

Rosie was still telling the stories to Dean. He often pretended he wasn't interested, but when she saw some of his drawings, she could tell he had heard every word, and his charcoal drawings of their people of long ago brought life to the stories.

12

# Mansion on the Hilltop

Larry Sutherland had too many issues on his plate. But, with Clementine agreeing to occupy Sarah for part of the day, his plate was a bit lighter. He stood and nodded to Clemmie who was still sitting on Rosie's stool.

"Come on, little lady. Let's head to the Tea House." He took Clementine by the hand and led her from the barn up the hill leading to the Tea House, which was what the large Grecian Colonial house at the top of the hill was called.

"Geez. That's a big house, Mr. Sutherland," said Clementine as she saw the house in the distance.

"Yeah. It is for sure. It was built in the 1800s and my great-grandfather bought it sometime later. For his new wife. A young woman he met in England when he went abroad to get a firsthand view of the tobacco fields and cigar factories in England and Scotland."

"Your great-grandmother was from England?" Clementine asked, hurrying to keep pace with him.

"That's right. From London, actually. You see, old Grandpa was certain his new wife would never be happy in a simple piney-woods cottage like the one he'd grown up in. So, as he'd done well in the tobacco industry and could afford to keep her in the style she was accustomed to, he bought the house on the top of this hill which wasn't far from his tobacco fields.

"Sutherland Tobacco Inc. employed a large number of folks from around the area where the tobacco barn was located. That being the case, it didn't take long for the locals to learn Grandpa Thomas had returned from England with a new wife in tow, and that she'd come from a well-to-do family. Rumor was that she was a "lady" in England.

"A lady like I read about in some of my books?"

Larry smiled. "Just so. Lady Camilla Sutherland was taken with this tobacco baron, this American, with his blue eyes, his sandy hair pulled back in a queue, and an easy way of talking that put her at ease immediately. So, when he left England, she was at his side.

"Grandpa liked to tell tales of his new wife, Lady Camilla, and how in a short while after coming to the Georgian mansion, it was not uncommon to see her traipsing down the hill in her fine dresses, headed to the tobacco barn. And Jinks, a house servant, would be on her heels carrying a tray of sandwiches, sliced cakes, and fresh fruit. So, with little effort, she worked her way into the hearts of the field hands.

"If one of the workers was ailing, my grandmother's instructions were to bring him or her to the house where they would be ushered by Jinks to the "day" room. She'd bring freshly brewed English tea and cakes, and though she had no medical training, she had an ear for listening. She believed that giving someone a cup of tea and listening to their problems sometimes gave them an outlet for expressing their worries. The place became the Tea House from then on.

"She called it 'sharing the load.' This was how she learned the ins and outs of the workers' lives, and she often shared her memories of life in what the locals called a foreign land.

"She discovered that these moments of sharing tea and a bit of conversation were healing for both the worker and herself. Something I try to remember even today."

# 13

# Read to Me

Mr. Sutherland moved along at a brisk pace with Clementine hurrying beside him as they trudged straight up the steep hill. When they got closer, they crossed over a lengthy, arched footbridge below which a swiftly flowing stream ran.

In another few minutes they came to the top of the hill where the large, white house with tall columns stood. Imposing and magnificent at the same time.

As they approached the front door, an older black man—resplendent in his black jacket and matching string tie—opened it wide and greeted them. Even in his older years, he had a head full of grey curls that he kept close-clipped. As Mrs. Sutherland had suggested.

"Morning suh. Miss Sarah's been waiting for you. She's in the parlor with Miz Jefferson."

"Thank you, Jeremiah."

Larry walked in and Clementine followed. They entered a long hallway with mahogany floors that gleamed in the sunlight, and the Tabriz runner that ran down the middle of the hall was stunning with designs Clementine had never seen.

She stared at the paintings that lined both walls. Some were of people—she guessed ancestors—but a few were of scenes familiar to her. Horses grazing in a field. A covey of quail skittering along the edge of the forest. And one she particularly liked, a simple vase with a sprig of honeysuckle.

A high-pitched peal of laughter got her attention, and she hurried to stay close with Mr. Sutherland.

"Daddy! I thought you'd never get here. Mrs. Jefferson has to leave early today," called a small girl skipping down the hallway.

Larry bent down and embraced her. "I know. Couldn't be helped." He released her and turned to Clementine, who stood close behind him.

"Sarah, this is Clementine. She's going to take care of you in the afternoons when Mrs. Jefferson leaves."

The two girls couldn't be more different. Sarah had straight, dark hair and brown eyes, whereas the young girl before her was blue-eyed and fair haired.

"Clementine, this is Sarah. My special girl."

Clementine nodded but said nothing. She had expected to work in the tobacco barn, but here she was being called on to babysit. She wasn't sure she liked the idea, but if it would make a dollar, then she'd accept the position.

Larry watched the two as they looked each other over openly—without concern for being polite—and decided to give them a few minutes to get better acquainted.

"Sarah, take Clementine to your room. Show her your collection of Madame Alexander dolls. Go now. I'll come up in a few minutes. I've got to pay Mrs. Jefferson."

"Clementine. That's a funny name," said Sarah. She stared for another moment. Then in a natural, childlike way grabbed Clementine's hand and started to climb the staircase.

"Come on. I've got five now. Five Madame Alexander dolls. Mama always gave me one on my birthday. But she's gone now, so I may not get any more. How many dolls do you have?"

By the time Larry climbed the stairs a few minutes later, the girls were chatting away like old friends. Exactly what he'd hoped for. When he entered the room, they were sitting in a corner with an audience of Madame Alexander dolls arranged in a circle, and Clementine was reading a book to Sarah.

"What are you girls reading?" Larry asked as he sat down on the floor next to the two.

"Daddy, it's a book about a little boy named Mowgli, and he lives in the jungle with his friends. And his friends are animals."

Larry reached for the book, checked the title, then handed it back to Clementine. He was a bit surprised to see she was reading Rudyard Kipling's *The Jungle Book* to Sarah. He'd have thought it was beyond her reading ability and comprehension.

"*The Jungle Book*, huh?"

Clementine nodded, "It's my favorite. Well, except for *The Secret Garden*, that is. Mama says I need to increase my vocabulary by reading other books, but I still like these. Mama's reading *Gone with the Wind.* But it's quite long."

"All right then. I've got to get to the barn. Clementine, find your way around the kitchen and be sure to be at the barn by five o'clock. The bus leaves at five fifteen, so you don't want to miss it. Bring Sarah down with you. If I'm not there, Rosie will watch after her until I return."

"Yessir. I'll take good care of her. I'm sure she won't be any trouble."

"Never has been. But, a warning. She can be a stubborn child at times. You gotta be firm with her."

Clementine smiled. She'd heard those same comments about herself. "Yessir. I can make sandwiches and tea, too."

"Good. A lot of tea has been made in this house. It's a soothing drink, and Mother never let a day go by without brewing at least one pot. That's how the place got its name. But better not make any just yet. Don't want to have a fire. You two stick to drinking Coca-Cola. There's some in the pantry."

"Yessir. We'll have Coke."

"All right, then. See you two around five o'clock."

He kissed Sarah on the forehead and hurried to the front door. Jeremiah handed him his hat as he left, and then the old gentleman continued with his chores. Which were minimal.

Jeremiah's days started at 6:00 a.m. and ended at 1:00 p.m. After that he would make his way to his cabin down the road near the dilapidated chicken house that was long ago abandoned but still smelled "fowl," feathers being the only thing that held the old hut together.

Jeremiah was aware Mr. Sutherland kept him on as an employee as a gesture of kindness. But even so, he was glad to have a place to go each day. He had a purpose. Even if he did nothing but make coffee, open doors, hang Mr. Sutherland's hats, and sweep the long, brick walkway each morning. He was still needed.

After Larry left, Clementine read on. "*There-there! That was worth a little bruise," said the Brown Bear, tenderly. "Someday thou wilt remember me." Then he turned aside to tell Bagheera how he had begged the Master Words from Hathi, the Wild Elephant, who knows all about these things, and how Hathi had taken Mowgli down to a pool to get the Snake Word from a water-snake because Baloo could not pronounce it, and how Mowgli was now reasonably safe against all accidents in the jungle because neither snake, bird, nor beast would hurt him.*"

"So, nothing in the jungle can hurt Mowgli?" Sarah asked, twisting the end of her ponytail around her index finger."

"That's right. Nothing. Okay, we'll stop here for today," said Clementine as she closed the book.

Sarah jumped up, putting her hands on her hips. "No, I don't want to stop. Read some more. The part where the Wild Elephant talks."

"No, we need to get a snack and go down to see Rosie at the barn."

"No! I'm not going. Read some more!"

This was Clementine's first exposure to the "stubborn child" Mr. Sutherland had alluded to. Well, he'd said to be firm, so she would try that tactic.

"Let's put the dolls away and go to the kitchen. I'll fix us a peanut butter and jelly sandwich, and we'll get a Coke from the pantry."

Sarah stood, a frown on her face. She watched as Clementine put the book in the bookcase, totally ignoring her wishes. She pouted another moment, but something within urged her to not make a scene. At least not this time.

"Okay, but I only want jelly on my sandwich. I don't like peanut butter."

The kitchen was huge. The black and white tiled floor was sparkling clean and the pantry was organized. Spices lined up in a row, bags of rice on another shelf, and numerous jars of homemade canned goods such as peaches, blackberry jam, and tomatoes with okra in the same jar.

"Where do you keep the plates, the small plates, for our sandwiches?"

"I'm not sure, but I think they may be in the tall cabinets above the stove."

Clementine pulled a chair from the corner, stood on it and reached the tall cabinet. There were stacks and stacks of plates and cups, but no glasses. She chose two small plates and two cups and placed them on the counter.

After they finished their snack, Clementine rinsed the plates in the sink. As she wiped the plates, she read the inscription on the back: *Royal Albert.* Looked like she had selected some of the finest china for their snacks and Cokes. She carefully placed each piece in the tall cabinet and closed the door.

"Done. Let's get down to the barn. I want to watch Rosie as she strings the tobacco leaves. That still looks like something I could do."

"Okay. And I'm gonna take Miss Ellen, my newest Madame Alexander doll, and show her to Rosie. I had named her Geraldine, but I changed her name to Ellen. Mama's name."

Sarah was outfitted in a sundress with yellow and white daisies dancing across the green fabric, and Mrs. Jefferson had tied a matching green ribbon around her ponytail. Her shoes were black patent leather. What Clementine's mama called Mary Janes. Clementine had a pair like them that she wore to church on Sundays, but not during the week.

Today she wore her oldest gym shoes, which had holes at the toe. She had pulled on a pair of dungarees, rolled them up to her knees, and put on her favorite YMCA tee shirt, long ago relinquished to "play or work" clothes status.

She was quite sure Mama would have approved of her choice of clothing, if not her decision to work in the tobacco barn. But Mama would stay with Aunt Alice in Brunswick for a few days, so Clementine wasn't too worried that she'd know anything. Yet.

"Can you walk that far?" Clementine asked.

"Uh-huh. I go to the barn with Daddy most every day. But Mrs. Jefferson will be mad if I get my shoes dirty. She says young girls should stay inside, not go outside in the elements. Do you know what elements are?"

"She just means you should keep out of the hot sun, and if it's cold, you should stay inside."

"Oh. Then I'll go with you. Maybe if I'm careful my shoes won't get mussed."

"Who watches you when Mrs. Jefferson isn't here?"

"Rosie watches me if Daddy has to leave. But sometimes she's so busy I think I should go back to the Tea House."

Clementine nodded. "Let's go down toward the barn. I saw some wild violets growing near that stream halfway up the hill. Mama likes violets, so I'll take some to the house and put them in a vase of water."

As they approached the stream, which was actually a branch off Willow Creek, Clementine stopped and looked around. Being this close to the Appahoochee, creeks and streams ran through the woods all along the riverbank. Earlier, when she walked the long hill with Mr. Sutherland, she'd noticed the violets clustered next to the long, arched, wooden footbridge they'd had to cross to get to the Tea House. But now they were no longer in sight.

"I guess I was wrong. Don't see any here. Maybe they're farther down the hill."

The girls crossed the footbridge, and Clementine began pointing out the various plants and trees as they moved along.

"This is a loblolly pine, and this bush is called Catesby's lily. When it blooms, the flower is kinda pretty. A bright orange color."

She pointed to another bush a few feet beyond the bridge. "And that's one plant you should avoid. It bites."

"Which one?"

"That one there. The one with the fan-shaped leaves. It's called saw palmetto, and its fronds are sharp and will rip your hands if you're not careful."

Sarah listened, in awe of this new friend who seemed to know everything. "How come you know so much?"

Clementine smiled. "I don't know much at all. Except for plants and flowers. And a little about animals. When I was your age, Granddaddy and Daddy took me hiking through the woods a lot. And every time I went, I would learn a new plant or bush. Sometimes we saw animals too."

"My daddy is too busy to take me hiking. Just like Rosie. And Jeremiah's too old to walk anywhere."

"Maybe Mrs. Jefferson could take you on a walk when she's here."

"No. She's afraid of snakes and won't even go to the tree near the back flower garden to see the bird nest. Daddy says it's a cardinal's home. I'm not to touch it."

They wandered close to the stream, Clementine still pointing out items of interest. At least to her.

"See that small rock next to the stream? The one that's covered with green moss? That's called lichen. It grows everywhere. But it's not a plant. It's called algae. Nana once told me that the fairies, the little people that live deep in the forest, make their homes in beds of lichen."

Sarah laughed at that remark, and Clementine grinned at her. Maybe this job would be all right. So far it was like playing with a younger sister, which she would never have. She leaned closer to the stream and smiled.

"Hey, see here. A pollywog. A lot of pollywogs."

"What's a pollywog?" asked Sarah as she squatted down, holding Miss Ellen to her chest, careful to not step into the water and muddy her shoes.

"You don't know what a pollywog is?"

"Is it a flower?"

Clementine laughed. "No, silly. Come closer."

"Okay."

"See those critters swimming back and forth across the stream?"

Sarah nodded and watched, never blinking an eye in case she might miss seeing this pollywog. Whatever that was.

"Another word for pollywog is tadpole. I'm sure you've heard that word before."

"I don't think so. But if it's in the water, then it must be some kind of fish."

Clementine laughed again. "Not exactly. A pollywog, or tadpole, is a stage the critter goes through before he's grown. Guess what he is when he grows up?"

Sarah said nothing but remained spellbound by Clementine's knowledge. Her mother never even talked this much.

"What?"

"He becomes a frog. Isn't that funny?"

"A frog? I know what a frog is. They hop around the kitchen door at night and sometimes Mrs. Jefferson steps on one when she comes in. She screams every time that happens. But I don't understand how a pollywog can become a frog."

"Well, neither do I. But it does. Some things we have to accept whether we understand them or not. That's what Daddy says."

A loud clanging noise coming from the barn had Clementine turning in that direction. She'd seen the huge bell on the pole next to the water trough when she entered the barn this morning. It now sent out a message that refused to be ignored.

She looked down the hill. People were rushing in all directions, calling to each other as they ran. She was too far away to understand the words, but something inside urged her to hurry down there. The clanging continued, and the closer the two girls got to the barn, the louder the sound became.

"Hurry, Sarah. We've got to run. Fast now!"

Clementine fled down the hill, quickly leaving Sarah far behind. When she was halfway down the steep hill, she stopped.

*"Oh no. I did what Mama says I always do. Take off before I realize what I'm doing. Not thinking of others.*

She stopped, caught her breath, then ran back the way from which she had come.

*I've got to stay with her. She's my responsibility now. This is my job.*

She grabbed Sarah's hand and pulled her along, all but dragging the child in the process. No doubt her patent-leather shoes were getting mussed for sure.

"Clementine, I can't go so fast. Please slow down," pleaded Sarah, reaching down to brush the dirt from her shoes and struggling to hold on to Miss Ellen.

Then a long blast from a whistle tore at Clementine's ears, causing her to cover them in an effort to withstand the painful noise. That blast was followed by two more short ones.

By now they had reached an old well, long out of use and boarded over, but with the well sweep still in place. Clementine stopped and grabbed Sarah, taking her by the shoulders.

"Stay here. Right here. Don't move. You understand?"

Sarah nodded, too frightened to say a word and without even a wish to move.

The closer Clementine got to the barn, the more confusing the scene became. Young men were running in one direction, while the older women were screaming and crying and fleeing in all directions. She didn't see Rosie anywhere. Finally, she reached the rear door of the tobacco barn and stopped before entering. Afraid to go inside. What would she find?

At home in Harper's Mill blasts from the sawmill whistle were the signal to everyone that a catastrophe had happened or was happening at the moment. So when she heard the clanging of the bell, then one long whistle blast followed by two short ones, Clementine knew something terrible had occurred somewhere.

Mustering enough courage to cross the threshold, she took off at a run when she spotted a small bit of color at the other end of the barn. A long, pale, blue ribbon flapping in the wind, having been dislodged from Rosie's "always-just-right" bun.

"Rosie! Rosie!"

"Heah, chile. Come heah. Hurry now!"

Clementine rushed forward, and the minute she reached her, Rosie's thin arms embraced her with such intensity she could barely breathe.

"What's happened, Rosie? Why is everyone crying and scattering everywhere?"

Rosie appeared not to hear her questions and began asking her own. "Where's Sarah? You didn't leave her by herself at the Tea House, did you?"

Clementine shook her head. "No, ma'am. She's outside. By the well. She promised to stay right there."

"Oh, thank the Lawd. We don't need anything else to go wrong." She released Clementine and stood tall. "Go fetch Sarah and bring her to me. Go, now. We got some situations to work through."

She then carefully threaded the blue, satin ribbon through her bun and began to work on a plan. Or not. Her brain appeared unable to get past what had just occurred. But she knew there was more to come.

"Please, Lawd. Put yo' arms around us," she whispered under her breath.

## 14

# Sounds Like Trouble

When Larry left Clemmie and Sarah at the Tea House he headed to the barn. Several of the workmen were gathered there preparing new slats and cheesecloth to replace the worn ones on a couple of areas in the tobacco field.

To his delight, his truck cranked right away and Larry threw up his hand as he pulled away from the tobacco barn. "See you fellas later. Looks like rain again. Can't take much more of this. The ground is saturated already. Careful in your work today."

Three of the workers acknowledged Larry's departure with a wave of their hands, but the two younger ones, new hires from McRae, looked off in the other direction. A gesture that was not lost on Larry. But at the moment, he had a more pressing problem to address.

The International Harvester flatbed truck was nearly as old as Larry Sutherland himself. Well, maybe not quite that old, but the battered truck had so many dents, scrapes, and rusted patches that Larry was careful when he placed anything in the bed.

His chore today was to get down to Harper's Mill and talk with the principal at the local school. If he could talk her into letting Sarah start school in the fall, that would solve a lot of his problems. He'd not need to find someone to stay with her during the day. Sarah was only five, but Ellen had spent a lot of time reading to her, teaching her to count, and had employed a piano instructor to come once a week for piano lessons. She couldn't read yet, but did know the alphabet and was intelligent and eager to learn.

When he got to the crossroads, he stopped at the Gulf Station. The large metal “Gulf” sign was hanging by a small rusted chain on one side and the other side was flailing in the wind. He got out as the attendant rushed over.

“Morning, Winston. Fill’er up and check the oil.”

“Yessir. Will do.”

The attendant would take care of the gas, clean the windshield, use his swish broom on the floor mats, and check the oil. Larry was quite sure he'd need a quart. The flatbed was a greedy ol ’gal when it came to oil.

He opened the screen door and entered the station. "Hey, Sheila. Everything all right with you?"

"Hey, Larry. Yep. No complaints. Randall’s arthritis is bothering him again, else I'd be at home today. Got to do something with that hamper of peas sitting in my kitchen. They'll sour if I don't get to 'em soon now."

Larry nodded and smiled at her. Shelia was in her sixties, but the beauty she was as a young woman was still apparent today. She dressed like she always had. Tight-fitting slacks and a blouse that threatened to burst open across her ample bosom. She was a fixture in the small village, and he'd known her for years.

He'd heard a rumor long ago that suggested his father, Thomas, may have had a "relationship" with Shelia. But his mother assured him that was simply loose gossip, and he should ignore it. So he had. Of course, his mother always did just that. Refused to believe anything that suggested his father was anything less than the perfect husband, father, and most of all, gentleman she married.

"You hear about Floyd Sanderson? Him getting struck by lightning?" Shelia asked as she closed her cash register.

"Floyd?"

"You know, Skidder. Skidder Sanderson. Works, or worked, for Andrew MacKinnon."

"Oh, yeah, but didn't know Floyd was his name. He's always been Skidder. That's a heartache for his family and this community as well. Guess his wife will have a hard time of it now. Hope she's got some family to help her."

"I'm more worried about Andrew. He's taking the death of his number one man quite hard. Word is he's pretty down in the dumps. Missed work last week is what I heard. He usually comes in at least a couple of times a week, but I ain't seen him since the accident."

"I see. I'll go by and check on him. Unlike him to not be working. He's as dependable as the sun rising in the morning." He paid for the gas and sauntered out, the screen door slapping him in his rear as he left.

Sheila laughed. "Sorry 'bout that. Randall's gonna fix it one day."

Larry grinned, threw up his hand and went on, with a new errand to add to this day's list. A visit with Andrew MacKinnon.

He'd make a quick stop at Andrew's place before he went to the school to talk with Mrs. Watson. She'd been selected as principal following old man Tolar. He'd operated the school with an iron fist, and Larry felt sure his chances of getting Sarah enrolled early were much better with her than they would have been with Tolar.

A mile east of the Gulf Station, Larry wheeled the flatbed across the railroad tracks, trucked a couple of miles north, made a left turn, and ambled down a long, dirt lane thickly padded with pine straw and an occasional equine patty, compliments of Clementine's pony, Missy.

The lane was hedged on either side by a row of crape myrtle trees as thick as summertime mosquitoes, and this time of year they were heavy with white blossoms that inevitably found their way to the ground, blanketing it with wispy, crinkled petals that flittered about with each change of the wind.

The house at the end of the lane was not elegant like the Tea House; nonetheless, the white, two-story clapboard was inviting, its mint green shutters lending an air of gentility. Very crisp and clean, with a wrap-around porch that begged one to sit awhile. Like the Tea House, its walls held stories and secrets of more than one generation of folk.

Larry removed his hat, a deep brown fedora that was worn and ragged at the brim. He stepped up on the porch, and as he raised his hand to knock, Andrew came slowly strolling in from the side of the house.

Andrew, tall and muscular like all the MacKinnons, was graying about the temples, but he still had a full head of dark hair that Larry wished he'd share. He, himself, was getting thin at the crown.

Andrew's head was hung low and he appeared lost in thought. When Larry cleared his throat, Andrew looked up, surprised to see his friend.

"Morning, Larry. Didn't think to see you today," Andrew said, reaching out his hand.

"Andrew." The two shook hands as was the customary greeting from a friend you didn't see every day.

"Thought I'd stop by for a couple of minutes. I heard about Skidder's accident. Know that's gotta be hard on his family. And you, too."

"Ah, Larry. It's driving me mad. Skidder wasn't only one of my workmen, he was a friend, too. Can't replace him."

He flicked his hands at the beggar's lice that had taken up residence on his pants as he walked in the south pasture early that morning. He'd strolled through the tall pines, treading softly on the wiregrass beneath his feet, trying to make sense of a senseless event. The pines whispered as they always did, and Andrew often thought if he listened hard enough, he might learn their language.

"I had the pleasure of meeting Clementine this morning," Larry began. "She's quite a girl."

"Oh? She was here when you arrived? I haven't seen her this morning. Guess she took Missy out already. She rides every day, usually early. You run across her on the path?" He gave up on removing the beggar lice. Hopefully, Norah would take care of them.

"No, not on the path. She came to the tobacco barn this morning. Rode the bus with the other kids from down this way."

"What? She took the bus to your barn? Now, why would she do that?" His faced revealed his surprise.

"She said you told her learning to make a dollar is a good thing." Larry grinned at Andrew.

"And I agree with you. Everybody does need to know how to make a dollar."

Andrew stared at Larry. "That girl knows not to go traipsing off without permission."

"Not to worry, Andrew. She's a bit small for actually working in the barn, but I put her to work babysitting my Sarah. You know, with Ellen no longer with me, I'm struggling to find someone to take care of her. So, if you don't mind, if Clementine could stay on a couple of weeks, until school starts, I'd appreciate it.

"I'm headed to the elementary school to try to talk the principal into letting Sarah start first grade early. I know the law says a student must be six by September first to enroll, but she'll be six in December. Surely that's close enough. Otherwise, she can't start until a year from now.

"If she could start this fall, she could go to school all day, and then it would be late afternoon when she gets home, and Rosie will keep an eye out for her for a short while until I can take her to the Tea House."

"I see. Well, if you think Clemmie can help, that's all right by me. But Norah is going to skin both Clemmie and me. I'll never live this one down. All right then. But make sure she—"

Andrew was cut short by a screeching blast from the whistle at the sawmill. The sound shattered the quiet air in this wooded acreage, and the two men stood still. Listening. For what they were dreading would come next. Two short blasts from the same whistle.

When the blasts came, nothing needed to be said. The two jumped into Larry's old flatbed. It groaned as Larry shifted into first gear and headed to the sawmill where they hoped to find someone who could enlighten them. Their imaginations were conjuring scenes they wouldn't think of voicing to each other.

If nothing else positive came of this event, at least it forced Andrew to swallow his grief, crawl out of that shell he'd been hiding in, and turn his mind in a new direction.

# 15

# Tower of Babel

Clementine scurried through the barn and halfway up the hill to the dilapidated well. Sarah was still where she'd left her. She'd removed the ribbon from her ponytail and was twisting a lock of hair around her index finger. She needed something to hold on to, and her long, dark tresses were always handy.

"Come on, Sarah. We've got to get down to the barn. Rosie says we got to hurry."

Even at her young age, Sarah knew something had happened. She could feel waves of anxiety coming from Clementine.

"No, I want to go home. Daddy will come for me." Then, with a last look at Clementine, she started toward the Tea House.

"No, Sarah. You've got to come with me. Come on now. Rosie's waiting for us." Clemmie pleaded with her.

"No. I want Daddy. Daddy will come for me!"

She plopped to the ground as if her small legs would no longer hold her, and then the tears came. The last time she had cried was when Mama had gone away, never to return. And she hadn't understood that either.

She looked up at Clementine. "Has someone died? Like Mama?"

"No. I don't think so. I don't know. But we're going to the barn. We have to go, Sarah."

The child stood, then took the hand Clementine offered. Anything to anchor her as she felt she was floating without a tether of any kind. Like the balloons she'd released on her birthday to watch them float away to the sky. Where she thought they may encounter her mother.

Rosie was waiting at the barn door when the two girls came rushing in. She got to her knees and took Sarah by the shoulders, looking her in the eyes.

"Sarah, you stay right close here with Rosie and Clementine. You heah me now?"

Sarah nodded. "Is Daddy coming for me?"

"No. Not right away. There's some trouble, and I know yo' daddy will be down in Harper's Mill trying to help get everything under control."

Clementine then asked the pertinent question, even though part of her wanted to close her ears. To shut them tight like she did her eyes when she wished to escape from a frightening sight.

"What's happened, Rosie? When the whistle blows down at home it means something bad has happened."

"It means the same thing here. Young Cooter come by. Old Cooter's son. He's the one that delivers feed for Mr. Sutherland's horses and mules. He said we all need to get to higher ground. The River Junction Dam has done broke. You know, where them three rivers come together? He says that dam just came a-tumbling down, like the Tower of Babel in the Good Book. That means anything down below it will be flooded. And soon. This barn sits mighty close to that stream that runs beneath the footbridge back up the hill. And that stream is just a branch coming from Willow Creek. That means in a short while that stream will come flooding through this barn where we standing."

"But I've got to catch the bus, Rosie. I've got to get home," Clementine wailed.

"Oh, girl, you done missed that bus. You know that driver. He leaves at five-fifteen no matter what, and if you ain't on the bus, then you got to find yo' own way home."

Clementine had no idea it was so late. She'd been so busy making sandwiches and reading to Sarah that time had flown by.

"Then I better call my daddy to come for me. He'll be awful mad. But he'll come anyway."

"You can't call him. Cooter said all lines comin' from that way are down. No 'lectricity, no telephone. Nothin'."

"But I have to go home, Rosie."

"Now you two girls listen to Rosie. The Tea House sits on much higher ground than this barn. We gonna get ourselves up there and wait. We'll be all right. And when he can, Mr. Sutherland will make his way home."

"So, he'll be here soon?" asked Clementine, her mind only now beginning to process the repercussions of the dam breaking.

"I don't know how long. If the floodwaters are strong, then most of the bridges in the area will be flooded. Maybe even washed away. I been through a flood when I was a girl, 'bout yo' age. And that old bridge over the Appahoochee might not hold this time. It near 'bout was washed away that time. But maybe they repaired it, and it'll hold together this time."

Clementine remembered seeing that bridge this morning. The river was much wider than she'd thought it would be. And that bridge was ancient—with its one truss the only thing standing—and missing planks in the deck. The bus driver had carefully avoided those areas where the planks were missing. She didn't have to be told that the bridge would be gone now.

She looked at Rosie, and the look that passed between the old woman and the young girl was one that women have shared for eons. An understanding that they must deal with the situation, with no hope of anyone coming to their rescue.

Clementine recalled Granddaddy telling her the MacKinnons were a hardy breed whose ancestors had come from Scotland and were some of the first pioneers to settle in these piney woods of South Georgia and North Florida. She hoped that hardy Celtic blood would step forward now and keep her from behaving in a manner that would have his Gaelic toes turning up in sheer embarrassment.

Rosie gathered her basket, the one that had been passed on from her grandmother to her mother and then to her. A small basket woven from sweetgrass. The art of creating sweetgrass baskets was a skill passed on from her mother, along with many other Gullah arts.

She carried the basket from home to the barn every day. It held her small corncob pipe and her change purse, with what few dollars and cents she had, in case the "rolling store" stopped by the barn. If it did, she would purchase a couple of store-bought items, like the hogshead cheese *Keke* had loved. Of course, he was gone now, but she continued to buy it. Some habits die hard. The rolling store was important to the folk who lived in the backwoods, and they counted on it coming by on Monday mornings.

After she gathered her basket, Rosie took a seat in the small cane bottom chair, her chair, and was quiet. After a few minutes of silence, Clementine stepped over to her.

"Why are we waiting, Rosie? If the water's coming, don't you think we should hurry to the Tea House?"

"We goin' in just a minute. Just one more minute."

Five more minutes passed, and Rosie knew she could wait no longer. The water had to be getting close, and she'd better get herself and the girls to safety. But her heart was breaking as she prepared to leave the barn. She stood, bowed her head and whispered to herself for a couple of minutes.

"We gotta go now. Yeah, we gotta go now," Rosie sighed.

Suddenly the rear door of the barn burst open, and Rosie dropped her basket, rushing to greet the visitor.

"Thank you, Lawd. Thank you!"

Rosie hugged the young man standing in the doorway, his weight supported by a metal crutch on each side of his thin body.

"What's goin' on, Gramma? I heard the bell clanging and then the whistle. I got here as fast as I could."

"The dam at River Junction. It broke and the water is coming this way. We gotta get to the Tea House. To higher ground."

"That might not be so easy, Gramma. Climbing that steep hill with these crutches. It must be close to a quarter-mile up there from this barn."

"I believe it is. But we gotta get there, Dean. No time to waste. Come on now. I'll help you. I'm old, but I still got a lot of strength in these wiry arms. If they can lift t'backy poles, they can give you a lift, too."

Clementine stood quietly, holding Sarah's hand, wondering who this teenage boy was. Rosie's skin was dark as ebony, but this young man's skin was the color of the delicious Tupelo honey she spread on Nana's biscuits.

The boy was tall and thin, with close-cropped, dark hair, and a finely chiseled nose. He was wearing long shorts and a yellow T-shirt that had an artist's paintbrush drawn on it. The words *Jacksonville Arts Festival 1953* were emblazoned across the front. That was two years ago.

But what she couldn't pull her big, blue eyes away from were the heavy metal crutches, one under each arm. He was so thin and the crutches looked so large beneath his long, skinny arms.

As she gave her eyes permission to look elsewhere, they instinctively went downward, to his legs. The left leg appeared to be normal size, but the right one was nothing but skin and bone, the skin somewhat shiny and tight-looking compared to the left leg. And there was a thick brace attached to his right leg, a few inches below the knee.

Was he born with a crippled leg? Or had he broken it somewhere? Perhaps working in the tobacco barn? She had better manners than to ask, but found her mind flitting in several directions wondering what had caused the young man to need crutches.

She wasn't the only one staring and wondering. The young man was checking Clementine out as well. He'd never seen anyone with hair that looked like snow. He'd only seen snow in books but was sure this girl's hair must be the same. Soft and light as air. He wondered what she was doing in the tobacco barn. Maybe she was a cousin or relative of Mr. Sutherland. He, too, had better manners than to ask.

Rosie hadn't missed the exchanging of looks between the two. She pushed Clementine and Sarah toward the door but hung back to be close if Dean needed her assistance.

"You girls go on ahead. Get on up the hill to the Tea House. Me and Dean will be right behind you. Go on now. Hurry."

Dean had been right. Climbing that steep hill took all of his energy and most of Rosie's. They stopped several times for a short rest. Dean never complained, but the sheen on his forehead and his wet palms evidenced how difficult his struggle was.

"We got plenty of time, Dean. Don't rush. That water ain't gonna get here before we get to the Tea House," Rosie stated. She wasn't at all sure that was true, but saying so served her purpose at the moment.

She stepped along beside him, never voicing her concerns that they might get caught in the water before they could navigate the hill. She'd learned long ago that just because a thought entered your head, you didn't necessarily have to let it exit your mouth.

By the time Rosie and Dean reached the Tea House, Clementine and Sarah were sitting on the steps of the porch, and Sarah was crying for the second time that day.

“Mrs. Jefferson said I should take care of my Mary Janes. They're brand new. Look at them now. She'll make me stay in my room. Won't ever let me go outside."

Clementine hurried to the kitchen and found a dishcloth. She returned to the porch and began to wipe at Sarah's shoes. The grass bits and mud came off readily, but the dainty slippers had lost their shine.

"There. That's better. Maybe Mrs. Jefferson won't make you stay inside. That would be an awful punishment."

"Do you ever get punished?" Sarah looked at Clementine, rubbing at her reddened eyes.

"Sometimes. Usually, it's because I sneak a flashlight into my bed and read when I'm supposed to be sleeping."

"Does your mother keep you inside too?"

"No, she takes away my riding privileges."

"What are riding privileges?"

"That means I can't ride my pony, Missy, for a few days. Which is even worse than having to stay inside.”

# 16

# Calling All Men

As they arrived at the mill, Larry slammed on brakes, bringing the old truck to an abrupt stop.

"Good Lord, what's going on?" he asked, glancing over at Andrew. "I swear half the menfolk in the county are gathered here."

He was right. Every man in the community seemed to be present. The only person missing was Sheriff Burke. Like Larry and Andrew, they all feared what catastrophe had caused the whistle to raise its fright-filled voice. The scream of that whistle could spur the community folk to action in a heartbeat. Or, in some cases, paralyze them with fear.

The two men jumped from the flatbed, leaving the doors open in case they needed to take off hurriedly. It was quiet. Deafeningly quiet. No whining of saws that was a constant at the mill, and no one calling across the timber-laden yard greeting a fellow mill worker. But the pleasant, sweet smell of sawdust and pine resin still held sway.

James Hardee, Thomas and Dewey Love, and Wiley Duncan, all from families who had lived here for decades, were huddled on the long porch on the west side of the mill office.

Near the door stood Hoyt Gramley and D. J. Longmire, sipping from their Thermos cups. There must have been at least a dozen more men standing around waiting for someone to tell them something. Anything.

Larry and Andrew joined the men on the porch as Rufus MacKinnon, distant cousin of Andrew, and owner of the sawmill, spoke.

"It's bad boys. The dam at River Junction gave way this morning. 'Bout two hours ago."

Howie Davis, a local cattleman, stepped forward. "Do you mean actually broke, or is the water just flowing freely?"

"I meant what I said, Howie. Stu Johnson, the ranger at Tall Timbers Station, the one near the Junction, called and that's what he reported. He can see a lot from that tower of his. He said the dam completely collapsed and water is flooding out of there like a fellow with a case of dysentery."

The sawmill had been in operation for longer than most could remember. Old Man Harper had passed away eons ago, and there had been several owners during the decades since his passing. But the village had been named for Harper, and the sawmill would continue to be called Harper's regardless of who owned it.

Rufus was a giant of a man with legs the size of the logs he processed through his sawmill. His red hair and full beard—just as red as his hair—was a gift from his Scots-Irish ancestors, and he had passed it on to his son as well. He was a leader in the community and knew how to think before speaking. Larry and Andrew listened, knowing Rufus would have already thought through several scenarios that would be upon them.

Rufus continued, "With all the rain we've had lately, that water will be coming with a lot of force behind it. That means trouble for many folks. Anywhere along that riverbank. And the creeks too. Chances are people living near those places be flooded before they even know the water's coming."

Not a word was uttered. Each man was itching to do something. This small community had been home to most of them for their entire lives. An event of this magnitude, this flood, could wipe out the whole town.

They all lifted their eyes upward as the whap, whap, whap noise of two helicopters flying overhead broke the silence. Rufus recognized the insignia on the choppers.

"That'll be the Corps of Engineers. Already on the case. Let's hope they can get to work on the dam quickly. But repairing that will be quite a job. It'll take some time to get that water stopped. Meanwhile, we gotta do what we can.

"At least most of the main parts of town and this area here at the sawmill are on fairly high ground. But even so, we're likely to have water standing in any low spots.

"I've talked with Mrs. Watson at the school. She'll open the auditorium, so we can bring folks there until we figure out what needs to be done. She'll also organize some women to start preparing food and bringing in water. We don't know what we're facing just yet. We've already lost telephone connection here at the mill. Electricity, too. And that floodwater will push down poles and lines like they're toothpicks.

"Dewey, you and Thomas get to the west end of the county, to Blue Creek, and check on those folks. The Duggar spinsters are out there. And Mr. and Mrs. Black. They're all too old to fend for themselves. Take both your trucks and see what you can do."

The two men nodded and scooted away.

"Me and D. J. will head to Crow Patch Corner," Hoyt hollered. "There's some elderly folks in that area, and the spillway on the east side could lose its footing, too. Might be we can check that out."

Rufus nodded and had to laugh inside. Hoyt and D. J. were the best of friends or the worst of enemies, depending on the day of the week. They often shared a six-pack, played poker together, and had been known to get into fisticuffs over the outcomes of games. Rufus remembered an incident not long ago when Hoyt, being six inches taller and fifty pounds heavier than D. J., laid his friend out cold with one well-placed punch to the jaw. Then he picked him up, stuffed his pockets with his winnings, delivered him to his home and placed him on the front porch. After all, what are friends for?

The remaining men offered to take vehicles to check various other places. That only left Larry and Andrew. Neither had spoken, but their thoughts were rushing as fast as that floodwater. Both had a daughter trapped on the south side of the broken dam, and a huge flooding river separated fathers from daughters. As if Rufus had read their minds, he came closer and let out a sigh.

"I know you got workers at the tobacco barn, Larry, and family too. And I know you're probably thinking you could take a jon boat and get to them. But from what Stu said, the water flowing down the Appahoochee is so swift and turbulent you'd never make it across."

Larry didn't respond for a moment. Rather, he stared down and kicked at the sawdust beneath his feet. When he did speak, he made his case, sounding as if he'd already worked out the problem.

"You're right, Rufus. I've got workers and a daughter on the south side of the Appahoochee. And today, Andrew's girl is there, too. That old bridge across the river was only one more storm from collapsing, so it's sure to have been wiped out. But Rosie, my barn supervisor, she's got a mind that will put most others to shame. She'll take the girls to the Tea House. It's a quarter-mile higher than the barn. They'll be all right. I hope."

Rufus nodded. "Then, what say you two—"

Andrew interrupted then, something he wouldn't have done in normal circumstances.

“We've dispatched men to areas of concern, those along the west end of Blue Creek and Crow Patch Corner, the places nearest the riverbank and streams. But there's another place that could have problems."

"Where's that?" asked Rufus. He thought he'd covered everything.

“As I said, we got the west end of Blue Creek covered. But that creek turns south some five miles down. Then it travels through Smokey Hollow. Where Skidder’s family lives. I was there last week attending his funeral. Those folks are part of this community, too.

“Skidder was my right hand for many years. He was a fine man. His wife and children are still there, as are many other families. They live close to that creek. It's not as big down there as it is on the west side, but the houses are so close to the stream they'll all be flooded when that water comes rushing through. We gotta help them, Rufus."

Rufus nodded, embarrassed he hadn't thought of that. Several men from the Hollow worked at the mill, and like Skidder, they were all dependable and hard working.

"Of course. I should have thought of that. Then you two get on down there. See what’s what.”

Larry drove the flatbed down toward Smokey Hollow. The area was on the south side of town and was one of the oldest parts of the community. The small, slat-pine cabins down there were leftovers from long ago when some of the first timber men, the piney-woods squatters—some of whom were running from the law—had eked out a living and made the place their own. They’d decided to call it Smokey Hollow. It was now home to the black people of the town.

The Hollow was situated on the banks of Blue Creek which, at that point, was just a stream some fifty feet wide and fairly deep. The early squatters had made their home next to it as it provided water for their crops and personal use as well.

Larry appeared to be lost in his thoughts, so Andrew remained quiet for a short while. Finally, he gave voice to his own thoughts, which were not about how Clementine was fairing. He was somewhat relieved when Larry told him about the barn supervisor and how she'd take care of the girls. That didn't mean he wasn't worried, but there was nothing more he could do at the moment.

Larry cleared his throat. "Andrew, you know there's another problem we need to think through."

"What's that?"

"The animals. Our animals. I've got some mules and horses and half a dozen hunting dogs. The tobacco barn is right in the path of Willow Creek. It'll flood right through the stables. The workers will have all fled, trying to get to their places. To safety. I don't expect anyone would have given much thought to the animals. So, no telling what has become of them."

Andrew nodded, "I've got a couple of horses and Clementine's pony, plus a few beef cattle in the back pasture. But I believe that ground is high enough. Believe mine will be all right. God Almighty, but this could turn into a real mess. Glad Norah's in Brunswick. Surely, she'll hear the news and stay there. But then, she's strong-willed when she thinks something may harm her children or me. I pray to God she'll stay put."

# 17

# *Horses and Mules and Dogs, Oh My!*

Clementine fought the urge to rush out and help the young man as he placed his left foot on the bottom step. And she heard the agony-filled groan that accompanied it.

"I got it, Gramma. Let go now," he murmured.

Dean lifted his head, that chiseled nose held high, and with the last ounce of energy he had left, raised himself on those crutches to the second step, his arms quivering with each movement. Clementine looked away, not wanting to witness the pain it had cost the young man.

"Go sit in that wicker rocker, down next to where the girls are sitting," said Rosie.

Rosie was ready for a chair herself and knew she'd better take a couple of minutes to let her body recover before she tried to think through their next move. She had hardly sat down when Clementine sprang from her rocker and flew off the porch, tearing out in a blinding flash.

Rosie stood quickly, unsure what the girl was about. “Chile! Stop! Where you goin’?"

Clementine halted briefly and yelled back, "I've got to let the mules and horses out of the stable. If they're trapped in there, they might drown!"

"No, Clementine. Come back! That water will be heah any second now!"

But Rosie's words didn't make their way to Clementine's ears, or if they did, she chose to ignore them. Clementine's first love was animals, whether they be four-legged, web-footed, or feathered and winged.

"Oh, Lawd. Help us now. We need yo' help," Rosie whispered as she wrung her hands together.

Clementine reached the footbridge, and when she crossed to the other side, made the mistake of looking closely at the stream and saw it was already much wider than it had been when she came down from the Tea House earlier. Debris was floating in the water. She saw several small boards, a page from the newspaper, and what appeared to be an empty cardboard box moving quickly along, pushed by a force from behind.

She turned her eyes skyward and watched as two sandhill cranes lifted their sleek bodies, flapping their huge wings as if their lives depended on them. Which they did. A wild turkey gobbled a loud grappling sound that expressed his fear as he tried to take to the air, which was not an easy task for the old tom.

Clementine stumbled over the edge of the well sweep, but recovered her footing and continued on to the stable. The two large barn doors were standing open, which was a relief. She'd have had trouble opening those. Once inside, she ran down the length of the barn. The left side was where the mules were stabled, and the right side housed the horses.

She didn't even stop to count the animals, just ran down one side and up the other, lifting the latches and throwing the stall gates open. The horses began to trot through the main door as if they understood they'd been given a chance at freedom and perhaps survival. But the mules stood there, seemingly uninterested.

Clementine went inside the first stall, slapped the old mule on the rump, and yelled, "Go on now! Get outta'here!" Following a second slap to his backside, he ambled out, and with Clementine's repeated instruction to move on and her heavy-handed slaps on their rumps, the others followed him.

Satisfied she'd done all she could to free the animals, she started back toward the Tea House. When she reached the footbridge, or where she thought it was, it had disappeared. She stopped. Looked around.

*Oh no! The footbridge is gone. No, not gone. Just underwater. But where? If I step at the wrong place, I'll fall in the stream, which looks kinda deep now.*

She racked her rapidly buzzing brain, trying to remember the exact locations of the trees and plants close to the footbridge.

*There was a loblolly pine on the right side, and the violets were on the left. And, oh yeah, there was a large saw palmetto just beyond the bridge. But I can't remember how far away it was.*

After a couple of minutes, in which she wished Daddy was there, she knew she had to try to find that bridge. The water was coming even faster now. There was no more time to dwell on the situation. No more time to be afraid.

*I can swim. I swam all the way across White Springs last week.*

But saying it to herself didn't remove the fear that swelled in her chest and made her knees tremble like Jell-O. She stood at the water's edge, tried to picture how far the saw palmetto was from it, then took a big leap, closing her eyes as she did so.

The next second she found herself on her knees, the water soaking through her tennis shoes and her rolled-up dungarees. But there was something solid beneath her. She'd chosen the right place to make her leap and had landed on the footbridge, which was now under a foot of rapidly slushing swamp water.

She didn't stay on her knees long, as her body seemed to have a mind of its own and had her sprinting up the hill like a bird dog chasing a covey of quail.

When she got to the steps at the Tea House, Rosie was waiting there, still wringing her hands. Tears were close, but being held in check for the moment.

Rosie sighed, "Oh, chile. Come heah. You are one brave girl. I do believe the Good Lawd watched over you. Come on now. On the porch with you." She put her arms around Clementine's shoulders, and they both felt the first droplets of rain begin to fall.

"No, not more rain. That's the last thing we need." Rosie shook her head and the two climbed the steps together.

# 18

# Mixed Company

Larry parked the flatbed in the open field next to the church. Just as the men in town had gathered at the sawmill, the Smokey Hollow folk had come together at the church. Andrew saw several faces he recognized. A couple of them worked for him, so he veered in their direction. They would have heard rumors by now, but probably didn't know how much to believe. All news travels fast in small towns, but bad news spreads like butter on a hot biscuit. He and Larry walked closer to the group.

He nodded to the men. "Toby, Jesse."

"Mr. Mac."

"Looks like we got a situation on our hands. Guess you men heard about the dam at River Junction?"

"Yessir. Are the rumors true? Did the dam really break?" Toby appeared to be the spokesman for the group. He'd worked for Andrew for a long time and even though he could be prickly, he could be counted on to step forward and lend a hand when needed.

"Yeah, Toby. Afraid so. The water's moving pretty fast and coming this way. The stream that travels through your woods will be overrun, and there's no way to know how high the water will get. It could flood every home that sits close to the stream bank, and if the water's swift enough, it may even destroy the homes."

"You mean we gotta leave our homes? But shouldn't we try to save our property, try to change the direction of the water somehow?"

"It's coming soon, Toby. Moving fast. I believe we should try to get everyone out of here and move them to higher ground. Into town."

Toby stared at his employer for a long moment. He knew Andrew MacKinnon never sugarcoated anything, so if he said it was necessary to get folks to higher ground, then Toby wouldn't question him.

"All right, then. We'll get the old ones, the women and the young ones rounded up. The old folks ain't gonna go without a fuss though, Mr. Mac. I know them. They've seen a lot, and this is bound to upset 'em."

Andrew nodded. "I understand. Just do your best. We don't have a lot of time, Toby. Get your men moving. The school and the churches will be making room to take them in. We'll find somewhere for everyone. But get them moving now."

"Okay. But it might take a while to get everyone transported. Some of the old ones don't have a car or truck. We'll take as many as we can in our vehicles, me and Jesse. A few others have trucks, so we'll make do."

Andrew nodded. "I'll send some men from town. You get the folks ready. We'll find enough cars and trucks to do the transporting."

"What about the old school bus? You know, the one that takes the barn workers to your place, Mr. Sutherland?" Toby asked.

Larry nodded, "Good thinking, Toby. I'll find Bennett and send him down here. That old bus has seen better days, but still sputters along and would take a lot of folks in one trip."

"Mr. Mac?"

"Yeah, Toby?"

Toby scratched the back of his head, took a deep breath, then straightened his shoulders before he spoke. Just yesterday, only a week since Skidder's funeral, the local newspaper printed another article about blacks marching in several cities across the nation, protesting the plight of their people since slavery days.

Once again the young men in the Hollow were itching to start their own protest march here in Harper's Mill. Toby wasn't sure what to do about that issue just yet. So now, he had to ask a question.

"Is there gonna' be a problem with us black folks coming into the white schools and churches?"

In the past, Skidder would have been the spokesman for them, and Andrew would have been looking to him to help in this situation. He recalled his conversation with Skidder the morning of the accident, regarding the growing civil rights movement around the country the past couple of years. A few skirmishes, but only one or two real riots. And to date, there hadn't been any in this small town.

He weighed his words, then spoke with some authority he hoped would ease Toby's anxious mind.

"I can't right the wrongs of the world, Toby. I can only do what I can in my community. And in this community, I'll not stand for anyone being treated poorly. It's my opinion that all people have self-worth and should be treated accordingly. It's just that simple. So, no, I don't expect anyone to cause any problems. But if you do run into any difficulty, come to me or Larry. We'll see to it."

Toby smiled to himself. That phrase, '*I can't right the wrongs of the world,*' was the very phrase Skidder had said Mr. Mac often used in their conversations. And now he was saying the same to Toby.

"Yessir. I'll do that."

"All right, then. Get your people organized." Toby nodded as he walked off.

# 19

# Getting' Deep

Relieved to have Clementine back on the porch, Rosie released the breath she'd been holding. "We'll be all right now. All right now."

Sarah went over to Rosie's chair and, without invitation, crawled onto her lap. The motherless child sensed this was probably the safest place she could be.

"Don't you worry now, Sarah. Yo' daddy will be comin' soon as he's able. Meanwhile, we'll all be fine on this porch. When dark comes, we'll move inside and Rosie'll fix some supper for us."

"Daddy's hunting dogs are still in their pen. Will the flood take them away?"

Clementine stared at Rosie for a second. "What dogs? I didn't see any dogs."

"Daddy calls them his coon dogs," said Sarah

Rosie spoke then, "They're hound dogs and make so much noise Mr. Sutherland keeps them in a kennel out beyond the tobacco fields. Back in that patch that's too low to plant t'backy. That way he don't have to listen to 'em at night. They howl at anything that moves, which is good. What bloodhounds are supposed to do."

"But if they're out beyond the tobacco fields, in a low area, they'll get flooded for sure," said Clementine.

Rosie shook her head, "We can't take care of every animal close to the water, Clementine. Some of 'em will have to make it the best they can."

"But that's just it, Rosie. They can't make it. They're locked in."

Clementine leaped off the porch once again, and before Rosie could say “don't,” was fleeing down the hill toward the tobacco field. By now the water was halfway up the hill to the Tea House, and any sign of the footbridge was long gone. But Clemmie had made a few mental notations when she returned from the barn after her first rescue trip.

*That loblolly pine was about fifty yards—half a football field—to the left of the bridge.*

Jeremy had taught her to use that measurement, a football field, as a way to approximate how far things were. He might be a pain in the neck, but he had taught her a lot.

She stopped at the loblolly pine, where the water was now to the top of her thighs and she had to slog through the water to get to the bridge. Once she got there, it was only a short distance to get across the stream and down to the barn.

She waded down a long, muddy path through the tobacco field, and as soon as she approached the kennel, the hounds were raising so much fuss she was afraid they might come for her. She threw the kennel gate open and the dogs, unlike the mules, didn't need any encouragement to leave. They headed west, away from the barn and the Tea House, splashing through the water that had already gathered in the field. Their howls could be heard even up on the porch at the Tea House.

Satisfied she'd at least given the hounds a chance at survival, Clementine headed back to the Tea House. When she found her loblolly marker, the water was still rising and she felt the first real twinge of fear slither up her spine.

*What if I can't get across? Do I try to ride the water along and not fight it? Will I be swept away? And I know there will be moccasins swimming in that water. Oh, Daddy. Where are you?*

# 20

# Roosters and Hens

In her capacity as school principal, Mrs. Watson had some authority. And she used it now as she began issuing instructions to the volunteers as they arrived.

When she first started teaching at the elementary school, years ago when she was a young woman, she was most attractive and soft spoken, which led some of her students to believe she would be a pushover as a teacher. But it didn't take them long to realize that behind that pretty face was a woman with a steely determination to make her students and her school the best in the district. Even so, the dedication she brought to her position was felt by every student in that small community.

She called out through the emptiness of the auditorium, "Jill, I need your assistance. See if you can find some of the mothers to help you. We need to make a line of tables here on the east side of the room. We'll arrange food on those. And we'll need water."

Jill stepped in and as the women began to arrive, they were given tasks. "Debbie, find some blankets in case we have to stay an extended time. Rita, Barbara, Marilyn, make sure we've got hand soap and paper towels in the bathrooms. Toilet paper too."

Jill was Mrs. Watson's Assistant Principal and would take over when Mrs. Watson retired. But retirement wasn’t anything she was planning on doing any time soon. She was in her element, and it was obvious she was a most industrious person. Perfectly suited to be principal.

Andrew and Larry dispatched several trucks, along with Bennett and his old bus, down to the Hollow. Toby scooted from one house to the other trying to get folks to understand the urgency of the situation. His latest efforts, however, were not proving to be fruitful. At the moment he was trying to get one of the oldsters to come with him. He took a deep breath and started once again.

"I know, Rooster. I know it's not easy to leave your home. But you gotta come with me now."

Rooster Johnson was one of the oldest residents of Smokey Hollow, and also one of the most stubborn men Toby had ever known.

"Ain't going nowhere, Toby. If the water comes, then it comes. Ain't going. Didn't ye hear me?"

Toby had been ready to abandon this effort when Rooster's wife, Elvira, a tiny woman clad in a pair of men's pants and a frilly white blouse, entered the room. She had listened from the rear of the kitchen and kept quiet for a long while. Then, with the aid of her cane, she stomped the floor and came forward.

"Send the bus, Toby. We'll be standing on the porch waitin’ for it."

Then she lifted her chin and looked at Rooster, her husband of more years than she could count. "Come on, you old fool. I ain't put up with your ornery ways to be washed away by some water that can't find its way home. We goin’ with Toby. And we goin’ now!"

She stomped her cane once more, and to Toby's surprise, Rooster nodded and stood, then followed Elvira to the porch. Apparently, sometimes a cocky little hen takes charge when a rooster can't make a good decision.

Toby made his way to the next house, where the residents were more than ready to come with him. Of course, that was because both of them, two elderly sisters, were confined to their beds and depended on someone to help them for everything they needed. The women in the community took turns seeing to their needs, which was customary in their culture. A holdover from their Gullah ancestors, no doubt.

Jesse and Toby were relieved when Bennett rolled in with his bus. Getting the old ones on the bus was an ordeal, but the children thought it was a special field trip of some kind. As it pulled away, headed to town, there was a lot of commotion and noise, and no one noticed the two children at the back of the bus crying out the window, "Mama! Mama!"

"That's everyone, Mr. Mac," Toby reported as Andrew and Larry pulled behind the market in the Hollow.

"I guess all we can do now is wait and see what happens. But I pray that water don't wipe out our homes. Most of us down here can't replace them if that happens."

Andrew nodded, "Let's take one problem at a time. Not much else we can do down here. Larry and I need to check on some downed electric lines. Don't need anyone to trample on those."

"Me and Jesse will help you, Mr. Mac."

Toby called to his brother and they followed Andrew and Larry to the sawmill where the men had agreed to meet to discuss what other issues might need tending to.

# 21

# *Hands Across the Water*

Rosie didn't know what she was more thankful for, seeing those curly white braids dashing through the pines or knowing her grandson was with her and they were all safe. At least for the moment. She shook her head and voiced her thoughts. Something she didn't always do, but today she felt a need to share them.

"You know, Dean, I seen a lot in my time, but this lil' white girl has more courage than most folk I ever seen. And I thought she was a wimpy girl who couldn't do nothing. Well, I got that wrong. She's awful small, but as *Keke* always said, don't judge a book by its cover."

Dean shifted his weight in the rocker and positioned his crutches on the floor. He was not quite so generous in his thoughts regarding this white girl.

"Yeah, but she didn't think about anybody else before she jumped off the porch and ran like a banshee through the woods. If something had happened to her, who did she think was gonna come to help her? Huh? And anyway, when I had two good feet, I'd have run faster than her and woulda been back in less time than it took her."

Rosie nodded. "'Course you would, Dean. 'Course you would."

Comments like that caused Rosie's heart to ache, but she'd learned to let them pass, or at least try. And now, once again, the month of August had brought another tragedy. Perhaps with even worse repercussions than what it had brought two years ago. The polio outbreak that forever changed Dean's life had caused grief for more families than just Rosie's. But a flood could wipe out the entire community.

"Is that Clementine, Rosie?" Sarah called as she saw something white darting in and out of the trees.

Rosie didn't answer.

"What if she doesn't come back? What if she gets lost? If the water is too deep, will she drown? Will she go to heaven like Mama?"

Rosie hugged the girl closer and rocked her in a rhythmic motion as if she were a baby. "Don't worry, Sarah. I just saw some white patches far in the distance. Got to be Clementine's hair. She'll be heah before we know she's been gone." Rosie so hoped that was a true statement.

The sun had stopped trying to penetrate the gray skies and rain was beginning to make another contribution to the already water-logged land. The weather report yesterday had given a small hope that the rain would give way to a more regular weather pattern on Tuesday. That was tomorrow. But this evening, it still fell as if it had no understanding that this "manna from heaven" was anything but.

Rosie's relief at seeing Clementine sprinting through the woods on the way to the Tea House was short-lived. Her pulse raced as she saw Clementine's small body make a wild jump across a floating log. Then she put a hand to her throat as Clemmie's head disappeared beneath the rushing water.

"Oh no! She musta' thought that was where the footbridge lay. But it's on down a ways. She misjudged it. She's a goner for sure!"

She closed her eyes and prayed. “Lawd, don't desert us now. Help this chile. She ain't gonna make it without yo’ help. Please, Lawd."

Clementine had seen the loblolly pine before she made her leap, but something was wrong. This time she miscalculated. Or it wasn't the same pine. Whichever, when she surfaced, she found herself lying on her stomach holding on to a floating log, praying she wouldn’t be the next piece of debris to end up in the Okefenokee Swamp.

"Gimmee one of yo’ crutches, Dean," Rosie called as she stood, placing Sarah in the rocker.

"What you aiming to do, Gramma?" asked Dean.

That look in Gramma Rosie’s eyes was one he’d seen before. One that meant she was determined to do something. Probably something dangerous. And nothing you could say would stop her.

“I gotta help her, Dean. She’s in real trouble.”

“But that’s dangerous, Gramma. You could be in real trouble, too, if you go after her. And she’s a white girl!”

Rosie stood still for a moment. Then she peered over her spectacles and gazed down at her grandson. “Dean, I’m pretty sure the Good Lawd is color blind.”

“But . . .” Dean stammered.

Rosie, too, was aware of the racial issues plaguing the country. And she knew Dean agreed with some of the other black men. About marching, that is. But it never crossed her mind to not do whatever she could to save this child. This white girl.

There was no more conversation coming from Rosie. She grabbed Dean's crutch and was off the porch. The rain was coming down in sheets now, and the ground was slippery. But Rosie ignored anything that might have even thought of getting in her way.

Dean stood then, yelling loudly, "Gramma, you gonna’ git hurt! Get back up here on the porch. That water will take you away just like it's gonna take that stupid white girl!"

Rosie couldn't hear him for the roar that filled her head. *She gotta have some help. And I need some too, Lawd. I gotta help her. Gotta help her. And you gotta help me.*

As she fled down the steep hill, the hem of her dress got caught on the sharp blade of a saw palmetto plant. She slowed her pace enough to jerk the dress away, tearing quite a large hole in it. Then she went on as if she were being pursued by Mr. Sutherland's coon dogs.

She was surprised at how broad the stream had become since they'd climbed the hill to the Tea House earlier. She looked around, trying to decide where she thought the footbridge might lay. She'd made the trip to the Tea House so many times she could do it with her eyes closed.

Unlike Clementine, who used the loblolly pine as a marker, Rosie knew the footbridge lay at a distance of eight long strides of her legs at a diagonal line straight up the hill from the old well. But she was coming down the hill, not up. After surveying the situation, a moment, she took her bearings and hurried on, her feet finding that bridge just where she thought it would be.

Once she was on the other side of the bridge, she breathed easier. But, as with everything else this day, she encountered a problem. The water now completely covered the old well sweep, and Rosie tripped on it, tumbled to the ground and proceeded to roll down the hill several yards, dragging the crutch along as she tumbled. When she came to a stop and caught her breath, she got to her knees, then stood, grumbling under her breath.

"I do wish Mr. Sutherland would remove that sweep. It has tripped more folks than I can count on one hand. And serves no purpose anymore."

Although shaken a bit, all her limbs were still working. The water was now almost waist high, but she still trudged on.

She scanned the pines, hoping to spot a bit of white hair somewhere. It only took a moment to see Clementine hanging on to a log some fifty plus yards down the stream. The log was laying across the stream, lodged into the base of a large stand of bald cypress saplings that grew along the water's edge.

Clementine screamed to her. “Rosie! Help me! If I let go the water will take me downstream. I'm scared, Rosie!"

In the last year, Clementine had taken a spill off Missy, had been chased by a swarm of bees, and had stepped on a huge spider. But she'd never experienced anything as frightening as this. Her mind kept reminding her that she was helpless, and neither Daddy nor Granddaddy was there to help her.

Rosie trudged close along the creek bank taking small steps. So far, so good. Then she moved out father into the water. Towards Clemmie. After taking just a few more steps, she found herself in much deeper water. Then, in a gnat’s eye, she stepped into water that was over her head. She came up coughing, but still uttering her prayer and even more determined to help this girl. She treaded the debris-laden water and reached out her arm, extending Dean's crutch as far as she could.

“Heah, chile, take hold of this crutch. Hold tight now. I'll pull you to this side."

Clementine was trying to decide whether it was better to try and reach out with one hand and take the crutch, or to continue to hold on to the log with two hands.

What if she missed the crutch? Would she be pulled off the log? But then, if she stayed glued to that log, it might eventually be pulled into the stream and be headed down into the raging Appahoochee River.

Either scenario wasn't very comforting. James had once told her that some of those creeks go all the way down to the Okefenokee Swamp.

"And the water moccasins in that swamp are as big as my arm!" he'd said.

The water was continuing to rise, and Clementine had to dig deep for some of that hardy MacKinnon blood she'd heard so much about.

She felt the log begin to shift slightly underneath her body. Her heart was beating so fast she felt short of breath, and her body jerked uncontrollably from head to toe as she let go of the log and reached for the crutch in Rosie's outheld hand. She took a deep breath, stretched her small arm as far as she could, and cried out.

"Rosie!"

As Clementine's hand grabbed hold of the crutch, Rosie was pulled forward, causing her to once again plunge beneath the murky water. Clementine felt herself being pulled under also but refused to let go of that crutch. That lifeline.

The stream was furiously rushing by now, as if by some unseen force. And both Rosie and Clementine thought they might become another piece of floating trash swirling along in the raging waters.

But Rosie never considered giving up. She thrush herself to the surface and struggled to keep hold of the crutch as that was all that kept Clementine from being washed downstream. Her spectacles were askew on her face, and her vision was distorted. But she kept treading water, inching herself toward shallow water where she might stand up. After some desperate efforts, she eventually found her footing. Once she was standing on firmer ground, she pulled Dean's crutch with all her might.

"Hold on, chile. Just hold on now!"

Clementine didn't need any encouragement. She felt as if her hands had been welded to the metal crutch, and she couldn't have let go even if she tried.

When she edged herself away from the log, she felt her body being pulled across the stream, hopefully to safety. And no matter how hard she tried, the tears wouldn't stop flowing.

Rosie stepped back slowly, still pulling on the crutch. Her rimless spectacles, now with bent legs and cockeyed on her face, were so blurred she could barely see. But Clementine's sobs were the most beautiful sounds Rosie had heard today.

"Heah, now. Rosie's got you. Heah, you go."

This was one time Rosie was glad the girl was so small. She took the crutch from Clemmie's hands and pulled her close.

Clementine looked at the old woman and, through her tears, saw Rosie's face smiling down at her. The tear tracks on Rosie's cheeks somehow made it all right that she, Clementine, now cried like a baby.

"Now, we gotta find that footbridge and climb the hill to the Tea House one more time. Heah, take Rosie's hand. With the help of the Good Lawd, we'll make it."

Clementine nodded and gratefully grabbed hold of Rosie's hand, a hand that had reached out and saved her without regard for her own safety.

Even in her present state of mind—still anxious but relieved—Clementine was aware she'd made it possible for the animals to survive and Rosie, someone she barely knew, had done the same for her.

This act of kindness was one she'd remember when she was Rosie's age.

# 22

# Together at Last

Bennett wheeled the bus slowly, not sure whether he should park it close to the auditorium or in the pine straw lot.

A minute later Mrs. Watson came out of the auditorium and began issuing instructions. "This way, Bennett. Bring the bus close to the rear door. Some of these people have difficulty walking, so get as close as you can."

Bennett nodded and pulled the bus within a couple of feet of the door. He and the principal had a bit of history, and he knew her well enough to know she wouldn't tolerate anything less than what she demanded.

Mrs. Watson had been his teacher when he was in sixth grade. She was a new college graduate and Harper's Mill Elementary School was her first assignment as a teacher. It didn't take long for her to build a reputation as an excellent teacher, and one who wouldn't entertain nonsense from her students. Particularly ones like Bennett who delighted in playing tricks on friends, picking at the girls, and reporting "the dog ate my homework" on a regular basis. He had one memorable experience with Mrs. Watson and how she dealt with students such as he.

One afternoon during recess, Bennett and a couple of other boys were kicking a ball around on the ballfield. Bennett was struck in the head when the ball came his way and he hollered, "Tony, you piece of shit! I'll get you for that!"

Mrs. Watson was standing at the edge of the ballfield and heard Bennett's exclamation. There was no way she could let this opportunity to teach that young man a lesson pass. So, she called to him.

"Bennett! Come here. Now."

She waited for him as he sauntered over, his face revealing his irritation at being summoned. Then she escorted him to the boy's bathroom and led him to the lavatory.

"Here. Take this," she said, handing him a bar of soap.

"I already had a bath, Mrs. Watson," retorted Bennett.

"Well, I believe you forgot to wash your mouth. So, let's see you lick that soap a couple of times, then rinse."

"But . . . that's . . . that'll taste awful!"

"Yes. I expect it will." Bennett licked the soap, coughed several times, then rinsed.

"Again," Mrs. Watson scowled at him. He licked and rinsed once more.

"I hope you learned a lesson from this episode, Bennett."

He nodded, "Yes, ma'am. I did. I learned not to say shit when I shouldn't!"

~ ~ ~

Toby and Jesse were on hand to help the old ones down from the bus.

"I hope to hell Mr. Mac was correct about the white folks being all right with us coming here, Jesse. If they ain't, we'll load everybody in the bus and head to the Hollow and take our chances I guess," said Toby.

As he followed behind Elvira and Rooster, Toby opened the door for them to enter the building.

“Well, at least no one is makin’ a fuss. Yet,” he said as they entered the room. There were several black women with their children gathered in the front corner of the auditorium, away from the white women and their children, who were in the back of the room.

“So then, we'll keep ourselves separated. That's good. Maybe there won't be any problems if we stay apart.”

As soon as he made that statement, two white ladies, neither of whom he was acquainted with, moved a few steps in his direction, then stopped.

Toby looked behind himself. Jesse was ushering in the rest of the group. He saw Skidder and Corina's two children, a boy and a girl. Then there were the two daughters of Marlee and Theo, his sister and brother-in-law, and several other ladies, who had brought food from their pantries.

The two white women moved another few steps forward, looking as if they might approach Elvira and Rooster.

“Oh, good Lord, I hope Elvira don’t stomp her cane at those women,” whispered Toby. That had Jesse laughing under his breath. But he kept his fingers crossed, just in case.

For a long moment, no one said a word. Then a small white boy, about six years old, skipped across the large room, ran to Corina's son, Luke, and took him by the hand.

"Come on. I've got some toy soldiers in the kitchen. Let's make a trench along the wall. We can use Mama's Tupperware and make a hill for the soldiers to hide behind.”

The two small boys took off across the floor and left the adults staring. It appeared the children didn’t see skin color as an issue. Only the adults had that problem.

One of the women introduced herself as she reached Elvira and Rooster. "Hey, I'm Charlotte. Let me help you find a comfortable seat. Then we'll find something to drink."

Elvira nodded and pulled Rooster along as if he were a child, which he sometimes appeared to be.

Within minutes, Bennett was about to pull the bus away. Mrs. Watson took a moment to come out and wave him off.

"You're a tremendous help, Bennett. Thanks for getting everyone where they need to be."

She hurried inside then, and Bennett headed to the sawmill to see if there were any new instructions for him. He was pleased he and Mrs. Watson had buried the hatchet many years ago. But he was always careful to keep his colorful language in check in her presence.

Toby was relieved the influx of his people had not created more difficulty in the community. The flood itself was enough. When he felt everyone was fairly well settled, he started to leave the auditorium. Then he looked around. A child was crying—no, screaming—in the far corner. His sister, Marlee, was trying to soothe her. He could only hear bits and pieces of the conversation, but enough to know he'd better go see what was happening. He knew that's what Skidder would have done.

"Hey, no need to cry, Gracie. We're all safe now. We'll find some sandwiches and cookies. Come on. Come with me," crooned Marlee. But the child refused to budge and continued to scream. "Mama! Mama!"

Toby looked closer. "That's Skidder and Corina's daughter, Gracie," he commented.

Jesse watched as Marlee continued to try and appease the child. "I thought he had a boy, too," said Jesse.

"Yeah. That's him in the corner with that white boy. I know everyone's stepping in to help Corina since Skidder's accident. Handling two children by herself can't be easy."

He strolled to Marlee's side. "What's wrong. Is the child sick?" Being single, Toby had no experience with children, but even he could see this one was distraught.

"Corina's missing, Toby. We thought she was on the bus with us, but we can't find her anywhere. Gracie here is not going to stop crying until her mama comes. You can bet on that."

"What? Whadda you mean, missing?"

"I mean she must not have gotten on the bus. You gotta know she's not been herself lately, Toby. Skidder's death has left her in a terrible state. That's to be expected, I guess, but I'm not sure she's even thinking straight right now."

"All right. Me and Jesse will go to the Hollow and search for her. Do the best you can, Marlee."

He inclined his head to Theo, "I think you better stay here. The situation seems all right at the moment, but some of us menfolk need to be here with our people."

Theo nodded. He was not nearly as outgoing as Toby and was happy to stay at the auditorium. He was also a good cook, so he might offer his assistance to the ladies in the kitchen.

Jesse stopped to see that his wife, Wanda, and his infant son were settled in a corner with plenty of food and water within easy reach. "We gotta go now. Corina's missing," he told her. She practically pushed him away, telling him, "Go be useful somewhere. Me and Rudy are fine. Go."

Toby decided finding Corina was more important than helping Mr. Mac with utility lines, so he and Jesse headed to the Hollow.

# 23

# What's So Funny?

Rosie's thin dress clung to her body, but even the late August heat couldn't stop the shiver of the chill she felt. But Rosie was a survivor. Came from a family of survivors from her earliest Sierra Leone ancestors to her own *Keke*. And she would survive this ordeal as well. She just wasn't quite sure how at the moment. She and Clementine were out of the deep water, but they still had to find that footbridge, and Rosie wasn't sure she could locate it now with the water considerably higher than just a few minutes ago.

"Clementine, you keep hold on to the other end of this crutch now. This water may be over yo' head any minute now. And if you fall, I don't know if I can lift you again."

"I won't fall, Rosie. I'm stronger than I look."

Clementine trembled and her eyes kept betraying her. Whether she wanted them to or not, tears continued to travel down her face. At least the rain provided some cover for her.

“Rosie? Will I ever see Daddy again?” Clementine asked. She’d tried to keep her worst fears inside, but somehow, they came forward of their own volition.

“What? Of course you will. And I’ll live to see my sister, Tonja, too. You just stay close with Rosie. My Gullah ancestors lived through worse times than this, girl. And we will too. The Good Lawd won't let us down. You watch."

Clementine would have given anything to see James or Jeremy right now. Both of them were strong, tall and muscular. One of them would have insisted she ride on his shoulders as she had done when she was younger. But even more than wishing for her brothers, she longed for Daddy or Granddaddy to appear out of the blue. Nothing was too difficult for them. She believed that with all her heart.

Ironically, the rescue team arrived just a few seconds later. And this team was rather small. When Clementine looked far to the top of the hill, she could see the Tea House. Then she smiled.

"Rosie. Look."

Rosie lifted her head and looked towards the Tea House. She wasn't sure whether to feel gratitude or to be scared. Either way, her heart swelled with pride.

There was Dean, hobbling along on one crutch, coming down the hill to meet them. If Clementine could have seen his face, she would have witnessed that he was struck with the same condition that had accosted her. Tears streaming without pause.

Rosie pulled the crutch closer and they stopped their struggling feet for a moment. "That's my Dean. My grandson. He's comin' to help us." Rosie lowered her head and mumbled words too soft for Clementine's ears to hear.

"Nana MacKinnon told me that God expects you to use your own talents when in trouble, and when you've exhausted them, then you turn to prayer. I guess maybe I should try that, too," said Clementine.

They moved on slowly as they were past exhaustion. And the rain still poured. Could Dean truly help them?

With his one crutch, he was making his way down the steep incline. He'd watched carefully as Rosie found the footbridge earlier, and he knew exactly where he should go.

Whether he could help them was debatable, but the fact he was making an effort gave Rosie a burst of energy she'd been unable to find on her own.

Clementine was shocked. She would have thought he couldn't do anything to help anyone. But she, too, found herself hopeful, and the two plodded on.

When Dean reached the footbridge, he was standing in chest-high water, and he held on to his crutch with both hands. He yelled in order for them to hear him.

"Come on now, Gramma. Get on back here. Make a straight line to where I'm standin'. That footbridge lays under the water right in front of my crutch. Just keep your eyes on that crutch. Come on. This water's movin' fast. We gotta get to the Tea House. Hurry now."

Once again Rosie struggled to trudge through the churning water, holding onto the crutch that was Clementine's lifeline as the water was now up to her neck. But holding on to the crutch with Clementine on the other end kept Rosie off balance. When her knees buckled and she went down, she thought she might not be able to get up again. But Clementine lifted her arm and Rosie bobbed to the surface.

A few moments later when her foot planted itself on the footbridge, Rosie breathed a sigh of relief and sent one more prayer. She pulled hard on the crutch and brought Clementine closer. The two had conquered their biggest obstacle. Finding the footbridge. As soon as they got across, Rosie grabbed Dean and hugged him.

"Dean, I don't think I could have found that bridge again. Not from that side of the creek."

As is the case with most teenagers, Dean didn't like to show such emotion. Especially in front of that white girl.

"Aw, come on, Gramma. Stop that blubberin'. We gotta make it up that hill again. Keep moving. Both of you."

What a strange lot they were. An old black woman, a small cotton-haired white girl, and a tall lanky cripple. When they finally arrived at the steps to the Tea House, the three of them plopped down, their muscles quivering from exhaustion, their soggy clothes clinging to their tired bodies.

As they sat down, the most unexpected thing happened. No one seemed to know who started it, but suddenly they all started laughing. Uncontrollably.

Dean tried to choke his laughter inside. When that failed, he laughed even harder. And that was followed by several loud snorts. Clementine had a giggle fit that sounded like birds twittering all around. Then when Rosie joined those two—her older voice cackling like a witch–she totally lost control and bent double in riotous guffaws.

Finally, Dean, being the male in the group, decided enough was enough.

"Okay. Let's stop this ridiculous . . ."

But when he tried to stop, the laughter bubbled up inside and he had to lean on his crutch to keep from falling over. Then they all started again. Clementine couldn't stop the giggles that exploded within, but then, that was not unusual for her. Granddaddy often chided her when she had one of her giggle fits.

Sarah sat at the far end of the porch and for several minutes watched in silence the spectacle unfolding on the steps. Slowly she crept from her rocking chair, walked over and stared as the three bedraggled, soaked, smelly survivors continued their outrageous behavior.

She looked from Rosie to Clementine, then to Dean, then back to Rosie. She took a deep breath, put her tiny hands on her hips and stomped her foot, still clad in her now-ruined Mary Janes.

"Stop that! Mrs. Jefferson says laughing too much is the work of Satan! You had better stop right now or I'll tell her all about it!"

That brought even more laughter. It continued a few more moments, then Dean offered his hand to Rosie and pulled her up. Clementine stood on her own, stifled one last giggle, and they made their way to the chairs, where they struggled to regain some measure of composure. But it was difficult.

# 24

# Ante Up

If Andrew MacKinnon had tried to imagine a worse scenario for the community, he couldn't have. And certainly, a flood wasn't anything he would have dreamed of. He vaguely recalled his father telling him a flood had occurred when he was a young boy, but somehow that seemed to be a tale. Couldn't have been real. Well, this flood was real and causing problems for everyone.

He and Larry dispatched several men to comb the roadways looking for downed utility lines. So far, no one had reported any casualties, but Andrew knew only too well that electricity could kill a man in a few seconds.

He'd removed some electric fencing from his property recently when a coyote had been caught in it and perished. Yes, it had been put there to stop the coyotes, but Clemmie had been with him that morning, riding alongside on Missy, and she'd cried at how cruel an electric fence was. And, if he was honest with himself, finding that carcass was disturbing to him too, so he'd removed the electric wire.

As they moved along, Larry's ancient truck was getting more of a workout than she particularly enjoyed. “I hope she holds together a little longer, Andrew. Her tires are as slick as a hot cow paddy in August, and I pray we don't have a flat."

This was not a good time for such. Every second counted as he and Andrew scurried along the roadways looking for downed lines, fires that may have started as a result of them, or any other of a hundred possible dangers that might arise during this ordeal.

Larry slammed the brakes to avoid a raccoon as it flitted across the highway, and Andrew found himself flung forward.

"Dammit, Larry. A little notice might have been in order," Andrew said, and immediately regretted his tone.

"Sorry. My nerves are on edge. No matter how hard I try, I can't keep my mind from wondering if Clemmie's all right."

"Yeah. I know. Me too. But I promise you, Rosie will find a way to take care of our girls. She's highly intelligent, quite resourceful, and has weathered some disasters in her time. Some folks seem to have a well of strength that sees them through. Rosie's one of those. She'll tell you her ancestors from Sierra Leone survived when many others didn't. She believes her strength in times of peril comes from them."

"This Rosie's been with you awhile I guess?"

"Yeah. And her daddy before her. He and my father worked side by side in the tobacco fields in the early days. Daddy always told me he learned more from Rosie's dad than he had from his own.

"Rosie's father came to this part of the country from one of the Sea Islands where he worked rice, tobacco, and cotton. He and his family are part of the Gullah/Geechee folks that still live in those islands. His ancestors were some of the first people to have been caught in the dreadful slave trade of the sixteenth—or maybe it was the seventeenth—century. Don't know the exact dates, but he could tell you more than you might want to hear. Heartbreaking stuff. He was a walking history book."

"Then I guess I'll trust this Rosie to take care of Clemmie. We've got enough to keep ourselves busy."

He looked out the window, still amazed at the amount of water he saw alongside the roadway. He looked over to Larry.

"I didn't see Toby at the mill. Said he'd be there. Unlike him to not show when he said he would. Guess something must have happened. And I wonder why one of those women in Smokey Hollow hasn't harnessed him yet. You'd think he would be a real catch for some lady."

Larry smiled. "Maybe he's like I was. Looking for just the right girl." Larry turned his face away, and Andrew didn't comment further. What was left unsaid was that there would never be another "right girl" for Larry.

Andrew continued, "Yeah, well, he's got a bit of a temper, but that's not necessarily bad. Comes in handy at times. According to Skidder, Toby's all for pushing for civil rights. Believes in following Martin Luther King's call for marching to bring about change. From what I've seen, he's got a good head on his shoulders, and Skidder thought a lot of him. That counts in my book."

"Toby wants to march, you say?"

"That's what Skidder was telling me. Toby and some other men in the Hollow are upset about the young black man who was killed in Mississippi. That's a tragic event. One that will have ramifications we don't even know about yet."

"Yeah. I'm afraid so. I overheard some of the men in the barn talking about that incident just yesterday. Of course, as soon as I came in, they clammed up. But I agree with you. That incident, that death, may be the first of more disturbing situations to come," Larry said.

"Skidder and I discussed it a bit. There's bound to be more problems. If you read much history, you learn just how dreadful slavery was. And slavery left a deep scar on America. One that we may never be able to erase. No matter how hard we try."

Andrew continued to scour the roadside as they drove on. He supposed this flat land, with its propensity to become boggy in some places, and the haven it provided for some less-than-desirable species such as rattlesnakes, bobcats, bears, and alligators, was not a place some folk would want to be. But Andrew saw beauty in the tall, elegant pines with sun streaking through their boughs and the straggly, spongy wiregrass that sought shelter beneath them. To him, even the scrappy blackjack saplings, the gallberry shrubs, and tyty bushes were sights he relished.

This was the only place he'd ever want to be. But with the political, social, and racial tones that were prevalent today, he feared his world was changing. Even so, this was home. And today he would do his part to preserve it and keep it from disintegrating in this natural disaster that had seen fit to visit. The other issues would have to be tackled one at a time.

Larry shifted down a gear as they veered off Highway 12 and headed into a deep ravine known to locals as the clay pit. A place the men often gathered to play poker. Many of the wives didn't particularly approve of their men playing poker in the carved-out gully, but most times the games were harmless enough.

Shortly they had to traverse a bridge, an ancient one created by using long, stretched-out timbers laid across it. Larry shifted down another gear and crept along the bridge, which thankfully was not flooded.

"Huh. This bridge isn't under water. What do you make of that, Andrew?"

"Well, it lies west of the dam, but also a bit south. Maybe the water's beginnin' to slow. That tells me the Corp's managed to slow down the floodwater somehow. Maybe they've used those flatbed tugs that are tied to the dock down at Shuler's port. They were used to transport tobacco and cotton years ago, but they've been tied there as long as I can remember. Perhaps they've positioned them to divert the water, or at least slow it down."

"Let's hope so."

They left the truck and walked around the area. The clay pit was just that—a pit that had been dug out of the clay and now was used as a place to dump refuse and discarded pieces of household furniture.

Down in the far corner, next to a stack of empty beer cans, was an old, discarded dining table, with half a dozen weathered beer kegs pulled close around it. Seats for the poker players.

Andrew looked down at his feet as he ambled along. "Hey. Take a look. Buried treasure." He smiled as he saw several coins lying underneath the table. Some quarters, a couple of nickels, a few dimes, and a handful of pennies. But no paper money. He stooped to collect one of the coins. He held it in his hand and grinned at Larry.

"Looks like they were playin' for some pretty high stakes." He laughed, and it felt good, if even for a moment, to let go of his worry for Clemmie and the unbearable situation they found themselves in. He hoped the poker players would return to their games, so he replaced the coin back under the table.

Larry raised his eyebrows. "Who knows, might be enough to ante up for another game."

## 25

# Playing Dress-up

Rosie, Clementine, and Dean were a sight even to themselves. Rosie's dress, ripped by a saw palmetto and torn again by some briers as she tumbled down the hill, was beyond redemption.

She looked down at her dress, then to Clemmie and Dean. "I think the first thing we need to do now is to get ourselves cleaned up somewhat. Then we'll tackle whatever comes next."

Clementine's dungarees and tee shirt were past washing, and she knew Mama would make them into cleaning rags. Dean's long shorts were wet but otherwise wearable. But his tee shirt, the one with the artist brush, was beyond dirty. He hoped Rosie could clean it up for him. It was his favorite.

The rain was still falling, if somewhat less, and evening was creeping in on them. Shortly, it would be dark, which was a good thing. Or maybe not.

Rosie was afraid some critters in the woods would come to the Tea House and poke around. Searching for food. She wasn't one to let her imagination run wild, but she did give a moment's thought to the black bear she'd seen prowling near the edge of the woods a few weeks ago.

Clemmie's thoughts ran along the same line as Rosie's, but she wasn't as reserved in her comments, however, and voiced her concerns.

"I'm not worried about bears or bobcats or wild hogs. But I am afraid of snakes. I don't care if it's a harmless tree snake, a black racer, or the worst, a rattlesnake. They're all the same to me."

When she was hanging on to the log for dear life, she was more afraid of a moccasin swimming by than she was of being swept away by the water.

As for Dean, as long as it wasn't another bout with polio, then he didn't fear much of anything. *Keke* had told Rosie more than once that a near-death experience often gives one a new appreciation for life and erases many fears that may have been harbored for a lifetime. And she'd witnessed that with her grandson.

Rosie stood, taking charge of the bedraggled bunch. "It's getting dark now. Let's go inside and get on 'bout cleaning ourselves up and finding some dry clothes. Then Rosie will find some vittles for us. Y'all take yo' shoes off now. Don't want to track mud into the Tea House. Jeremiah would have my head."

Sarah took her Mary Janes off also, as that seemed to be the thing to do. Besides, they would never be the same again. She led the way, this being her home. It was dark inside, and they were barely able to see. Rosie was sure Mr. Sutherland would have a stash of candles or kerosene lamps somewhere. She called to Dean and Clemmie.

"Dean, you and Clementine make your way to the kitchen and see if you can find some candles or kerosene lamps. And some matches. We liable to break something if we not careful."

"Daddy keeps candles and lamps in the bottom cabinet in the kitchen, next to the stove. Mama would sometimes read to me by lamplight if the electricity wasn't working," said Sarah.

Dean and Clemmie found the candles, along with a couple of lamps and a box of long-stemmed matches.

"I'll take the lamps, Dean. You carry the candles," offered Clementine.

"Take the candles yourself, girl. Think I can't tote something heavy because I'm a cripple? Huh?"

"No, I just . . ."

Not knowing how to respond, Clemmie gathered the candles and took them to the parlor, where Rosie and Sarah were waiting. A few moments later, Dean appeared in the doorway with a lamp under one arm and both crutches under the other. Clementine took note of this as she watched him.

She'd once seen a dog with only three legs and he ran nearly as fast as he would have with all four. Maybe that was what Nana meant when she told her "We can all do more than we think we can. But we have to be tried first." It seemed that Dean had been tried.

The parlor was a large room where several hand knotted Tabriz rugs hugged the hardwood floors, and a colorful runner traveled down a long hall with rooms off either side. Rosie lit the lamps, placed one on the sideboard in the dining room across the way and the other on a table close to a window at the front of the house. If Mr. Sutherland happened to come, she wanted him to see that light. To know they were all safe.

Rosie had been inside the Tea House many times in her life, but only on this floor, never upstairs to the family's quarters.

"Sarah, can you take me to yo' mama's closet?"

"Yes, Rosie, it's upstairs. Follow me."

Rosie lit three candles, handed one to Dean and Clementine and held one herself. She thought Sarah might not be able to handle one at her young age. They followed the child along the steep staircase where the walls were lined with large, oil paintings of people.

"Gramma, you ever seen pictures such as these?" Dean asked as they moved up the stairway.

"No. Never been in any big house 'cept the Tea House. And I believe those folks would be Mr. Sutherland's ancestors. Like his grandma and grandpa. Maybe aunties and uncles."

Dean was taking in the various aspects of the paintings. "Just look at the details. See the brush strokes? Drawing is a lot different than painting. That much I can see," said Dean.

Sarah stepped into the first room on the right. "In here. All Mama's clothes are in this closet. And her shoes."

Rosie opened the closet door and stared for a moment. The closet was larger than her kitchen and full of clothes. Dresses, slacks, blouses. And so many shoes Rosie shook her head in disbelief.

"My, oh my. I never did see so many shoes."

She picked up a brown leather flat and nodded. "Well now, ain't that something. Size seven and a half. I might be able to squeeze my size eights into a pair of them. Might be tight, but I'll manage." She was about to slip her foot into one of the shoes when she felt a hand on her arm. Sarah was staring up at her.

"Those are my mama's shoes. They don't belong to you." Sarah's voice quivered, and she was one step away from bursting into tears. Rosie chided herself for not thinking of this before she acted. She nodded to Sarah.

"Yes, Sarah. They do belong to yo' mama. If she was here, I would ask her permission to borrow a pair. Just 'til mine dry out. But she's not, so maybe I should ask you. Do you think she would mind if I wore a pair for a short while?"

Sarah chewed on her index finger for a moment, then nodded. "No, she wouldn't mind. She'd say yes. She always let me wear them. Any time I wanted. I like the red ones with the tall heels. But I can't walk very well in them."

"Thank you, Sarah. I'll return them as soon as mine are dry." Rosie chose a pair of soft, leather ankle boots. She smiled when she slipped one on without it pinching her foot.

"Well, I'll be," she said with a smile.

"Mama wore those when she worked in her rose garden. They were her favorites." Rosie pulled the other boot on and then asked again before she looked through the clothing.

"And I need somethin' to wear. My dress is wet and ripped to shreds; I think I'm gonna have to put it in my rag box."

This time, Sarah knew her role and her lines. "Mama has lots of dresses and pants. She calls them slacks. And she was skinny. Like you, Rosie."

Rosie chose a pair of navy slacks and a sleeveless white top with a Peter Pan collar. Finer clothes than Rosie had ever worn. The slacks were a bit short, but otherwise fit well.

"Now, we gotta find something for Clementine and Dean. Let's think 'bout this for a minute. Sarah, which closet is yo' daddy's?"

"That one. There." Sarah pointed to a door on the opposite side of the room. Rosie opened the door and was again greeted with more clothes than she'd ever thought one person could wear. This closet had just what she needed, and she spotted it quickly.

"Clementine, come here," called Rosie as she held out a short-sleeve, light-blue chambray shirt. One she'd seen Mr. Sutherland wear on occasion.

"Let's have you try this on. See what we got."

Clementine changed in the closet and emerged wearing Mr. Sutherland's shirt. On him, it was a shirt. On Clemmie the hem reached below her knees and the sleeves hung past her elbows. But it smelled of lemons and something fresh and green, and it felt so much better than her soggy, dirty dungarees and tee shirt.

"Just what I thought. That'll do." She nodded to Sarah. "Now we need somethin' for Dean."

By now, Sarah was an eager participant in this project. She went into the closet and brought out a short-sleeve shirt, one with a quail embroidered above the pocket.

"Here. Put this one on. Daddy likes this shirt. You will too." She held the shirt towards Dean.

He grabbed it in one hand and disappeared into the closet. He didn't like the idea of wearing someone else's clothes, but his tee shirt was wet, caked with mud, and smelled to high heaven. His knee-length shorts were still in fair condition, so he kept those on.

Rosie had only had one child, a daughter, and she didn't dwell on thoughts of her often. Even so, she knew a bit about little girls. And, like Sarah, she now knew her role and lines.

"Good. That's good. Well, now we all got dry clothes. Next thing we gotta do is find something for our supper. We all could use a little food 'bout now."

Rosie searched the refrigerator and came up with some cheese slices. Then she found saltine crackers and cut up a couple of apples from the cupboard. They all sat at the small kitchen table, where Rosie bowed her head and asked her charges to do the same.

"Lawd, we thank you for yo' blessings and kindness to us. Keep us safe now and save us from our sins. Amen."

Dean opened his eyes the slightest bit. Just enough to see Clementine had done the same and was staring at him. Neither said a word.

## 26

# Looking in All the Wrong Places

Toby wheeled his 1950 Ford F-3 pickup—the love of his life—into the empty lot next to Skidder's house. He'd bought the truck recently, and even though it was five years old, to him it was a beauty.

He'd skim his hands down the sides of the fenders anytime he walked by. Jesse often chided him, "Toby, if you'd give some woman as much attention as you do this truck, you might not be sleeping alone every night." Toby would always grin.

As he approached the porch at Skidder's house, it occurred to him that the place would now be Corina's, but thinking of it that way might take some time as Skidder had been a crucial part of the fabric of Smokey Hollow.

He hurried up the steps to the porch. Skidder's work boots were placed by the door. As if waiting to be worn again the next day. Toby stood at the door, knocked, then turned the knob and pushed. Most folks in the Hollow never locked their doors. No need. First of all, none of them had much worth stealing, and secondly, no one in this community would steal from another.

As he expected, the place was empty. In more ways than one. An unsettling feeling clung to the place as he strolled through the rooms, and a quick shiver coursed through his body. Skidder's denim jacket was hanging on the coat tree inside the front door. He moved farther in, then on toward the kitchen and the bedrooms.

The place was spotless, which didn't surprise him. Corina would keep it that way. When you saw her, every hair was in place and her apron would be fresh every day.

Skidder had always laughed and accused her of being obsessed with keeping things clean and orderly. “Woman, even if it was dark as Hades, I do believe you could find your hairpins with your eyes closed. They’d be standin’ like soldiers, waiting for you to put them in place.”

Of course, since Skidder had come from a home with no mother and had to fend for himself much of his life, Corina's penchant for orderliness was much to his liking.

When Toby entered the kitchen, he halted and caught his breath.

"Oh, Holy Jesus." He sat down in the nearest chair.

The table was set for four. Four plates, four glasses, four place settings of silverware. As if Skidder were still here. That scene had Toby’s brain twirling in circles. What did that mean? Was Corina truly off in a world of her own? Was she pretending Skidder was still here? What?

He pulled the door closed behind him as he exited, then hiked around to the back yard. Nothing gave a clue as to where to find Corina. Maybe they'd been wrong. Maybe she was in the ladies' room at the auditorium. Or maybe she was helping in the kitchen. Even as his mind offered these suggestions, he knew he was whistling Dixie.

If Corina had been in that auditorium, she'd have come running when her child screamed. Toby had learned that much about mothers from watching his own. You don't mess with a mother's children. It was his opinion that a scared mother is more dangerous than a cornered rattlesnake.

She couldn't be hiding, could she? He stared down at his feet for a moment and shook his head. His mind wouldn't let go of the picture of the table set for four.

The sawmill was the gathering place so Toby headed there. As he pulled his truck next to a large chinaberry tree, he saw several men from the Hollow standing on the far end of the porch, awaiting their next assignment.

He saw Mr. Mac at the door talking to Rufus. He was too far away to hear their words, but he could see their expressions and that told him a lot. Mr. Mac wasn't given to wearing his troubles on his face, but that was what Toby saw. He was almost afraid to ask if something more disturbing had happened.

Andrew saw Toby and waved him over. When he got closer, Andrew called, "Glad you're here, Toby. Larry and I have secured some of the downed electric lines, but I know there are more to be found. If you and Jesse would help us, the four of us working together can make twice as much progress."

Toby nodded his understanding. "I agree, but we got another problem I believe we need to tackle first."

"What's that, Toby? Couldn't be much worse than the ones we're already dealing with."

"No, sir. I mean yessir. I believe it is."

Andrew's thoughts ran so quickly to Clementine and the tobacco barn that he stood rigid and had difficulty speaking.

"Is it something about Clemmie? Or Larry's girl?"

"Oh, no, sir. Nothin' like that. It's Corina. You know, Skidder's wife? She's missing. She didn't get on the bus going to the auditorium. She put her two children on there, but she's not to be found. I been to the Hollow and checked her place. She's not there. And, Mr. Mac? Marlee told me Corina's been acting strange lately. Appears she's taking Skidder's death pretty hard. Maybe not thinking so well."

Andrew's relief over worry about Clementine was short-lived. Corina's disappearance would indeed need to take top priority.

Rufus sighed, "Seems like this day is gonna be a difficult one. All right, Andrew. You and Larry go on to the Hollow with Toby. That woman's got to be somewhere close by. Where else would she be? That's her home. That's where you'll find her."

Toby and Jesse sped off with Andrew and Larry close on their bumper.

27

# *Oh, What a Night!*

There was something comforting about sitting around a small kitchen table with soft, drizzling rain falling, a breeze blowing through open windows, and a kerosene lamp providing a warm yellow glow throughout the room.

For a few moments, Rosie's mind wandered to long-ago days. Days when both her parents were alive. Sweet memories she hoped would never fade away.

She'd called her father *Keke*, as he had wanted. Her mother she called Vannah, which was what *Keke* called her.

The story *Keke* told was that he'd seen a most beautiful woman when he traveled with his employer taking rice to a port in Savannah, Georgia. He would grin as he started to tell his tale.

"There she was. That long, dark hair tied back with a red ribbon. Sashayin' along that riverfront lookin' like she didn't have a care in the world. But when she saw me, she stopped, looked again, and a smile spread on her face. I knew then she was meant for me.

"I tried to talk to her, but she wouldn't tell me her name. Then later, when I went to that same port with another load of rice, I seen her again. This time, I was determined to know who she was. So, I was bold enough to approach her.

"I'm Barrie. What are you called?" I asked. She still didn't answer, so I decided to give her a name. "I'll call you Savannah. A beautiful city and a lovely name for a lovely lady.

"We eventually talked a while. Her ancestors had come from Sierra Leone, as had mine, and her given name was a real tongue twister. So, I just continued to call her Savannah." Of course, Savannah became Vanna, and Rosie had called her Vanna as *Keke* had.

Rosie managed to put together some vittles—as she called them—and after supper was over, she sent Clementine off to help Sarah find her pajamas and get her ready for bed.

Rosie was trying to keep the day's events as normal as possible, which was a real struggle. She cleared the dinner table and dishes, and Dean hobbled off to check out the library he'd spied when they first came in.

He was amazed to see so many books in someone's home. He walked slowly along the tall shelves of books, dragging his fingers across some of them. There was a rolling ladder that would be used to reach books on the upper shelves, but Dean knew he'd never be able to manage that.

Books had a smell. To Dean, it was a comforting smell. As if they were cared for. Had a place in someone's life.

*I wonder if Mr. Sutherland's read all these books? I bet not. Nobody can read that much. But I sure would try if I had these at my house.*

It only took a couple of minutes for Dean to discover a whole shelf devoted to art. Books about famous artists, such as Monet, who painted glorious canvases of flowers of all kinds. He found a large, leather-bound book full of unusual paintings. These were by a fellow named Picasso, and Dean wasn't sure he liked those. He studied the pictures, turning them one way, then another.

*I guess if these paintings are in this artbook, then they must be considered art, but I don't think I'd hang one of 'em in my house. Too strange for me.*

Then he came upon a book that grabbed his attention. A book about a famous person he remembered studying at school.

*The Works of Leonardo da Vinci! Now, this here is what I call art. He's got black and white drawings and oil paintings, and I know he was a genius in some other areas, too. I remember studying him. Can't remember everything I learned though. I wonder if Mr. Sutherland would allow me to borrow a couple of his books?*

He knew Mr. Sutherland, of course, but wasn't sure he should make such a request. What if he got Gramma Rosie in trouble by asking? No. He'd better not ask. But one day he'd find a way to learn about these artists. One day.

Polio had brought many changes in his young life, school being one of them. He'd not returned to the classroom since having contracted polio. A wicked disease that left him crippled. He didn't think he could bear the stares the other students would have given him. Him hobbling along on his crutches and that hideous brace. No. He'd decided he was done with school.

That had been two years ago, and Rosie had given up on trying to get him to return. Some things she knew he'd have to figure out on his own.

Rosie came back to the parlor where Clementine and Sarah were sitting on the floor near the lamp in the window. Clementine was reading from a thick book, and Sarah was listening to every word. When she saw Rosie, she spoke up.

"Listen, Rosie. Mowgli has a lot of friends in the jungle. And he talks to them. And they're all animals."

Rosie sat in a damask-covered rocking chair, one with a lace doily hugging the top of it. The chair was a small one, obviously meant for the lady of the house. Then she began to listen. Clementine's voice was clear, and Rosie was surprised that she also found the book interesting.

*"We be of one blood, ye and I," said Mowgli, giving the words the Bear accent which all the Hunting People of the Jungle use.*

*"Good! Now for the Birds," Mowgli repeated, with the Kite's whistle at the end of the sentence. "Now for the Snake People," said Bagheera.*

This was the part of *The Jungle Book* Clementine liked least of all. She didn't even like to read about snakes. She stopped reading.

"Go on, Clemmie. Read some more," begged Sarah.

Just then, Dean strolled in with a heavy, art history book tucked under his arm.

"That's a stupid book. For children. I don't want to hear any more of that dribble," he said.

Rosie was taken aback at such an attitude from Dean. She decided he was exhausted from the day's climbs and was not himself. But still, she needed to let him know she'd not missed his less than appropriate comment.

"You may not 'preciate the book, Dean, but it sounded pretty interesting to me. And you mind yo' manners. You been taught how to behave. You heah me?"

Clementine closed the book and set it aside on the floor. "It's all right, Rosie. I'm kinda tired of reading anyway. Maybe I'll read more to Sarah tomorrow."

Sarah started to whine. Then, being a child, asked the obvious question. "Rosie, are you staying here with me tonight? What if Daddy doesn't come? I'm scared."

"Come heah, Sarah. Come sit with Rosie." The little girl did as Rosie said and walked closer. Rosie continued, "Yo' daddy will be breaking the speed limit trying to get to you. And before you even know it, he'll be coming in that door calling out, "Sarah? Sarah? Where are you?" Then she pulled Sarah into her lap and held her close.

Dean sat on the floor a short distance from Clementine, but close enough he could see her expressions. He tried to keep his own expressions to himself. Didn't want anyone to know what he felt or thought. But this girl was unique. Every thought that ran through her mind was written on her face.

He wanted to sketch those expressions. Wanted to capture that forlorn, vulnerable look he'd caught a glimpse of earlier when she came out of the closet wearing Mr. Sutherland's shirt that fell below her knees and made her appear to be even smaller than she was.

Rosie rocked and hummed a song Vanna had sung to her when she was a child. The words wouldn't mean anything to this child. They'd been sung in the Gullah language, so Rosie hummed softly and, as expected, Sarah drifted off in minutes and was sound asleep in her arms.

"Dean, go find a pillow and blanket. I'll make Sarah a bed down heah. She might wake in the middle of the night and be scared if we put her upstairs in her room."

"I'll get them," Clementine called. She jumped up, scampered up the stairs and came down with a blanket and pillow in less time than it would have taken Dean to gather his crutches.

"Here you go, Rosie," she said as she returned to the parlor. Dean was leaning against the wall and sent her a look that would curl her hair if it wasn't curly already. He said nothing, but the expression on his face told Clementine she had once again acted without thinking first. He sat down, his crutches making a loud thud as they fell to the floor.

"I was only trying to help," Clementine said softly, then sat down and tried to shrink closer to the wall. She'd never had words with anyone other than her brothers, and that didn't count she guessed. They'd never hurt her. But she wasn't so sure when it came to this boy. She guessed Dean had been fearful for his grandmother earlier and was now allowing that fear to express itself.

"Yeah, and your 'only trying to help' almost got Gramma killed today. If you hadn't taken off tearing through the woods like a wild hog, she wouldn't have had to come after you. You're too impatient and thoughtless for your own good. You need to learn to think of other people, too."

Rosie stood, walked across the room and placed Sarah on the bed of blankets near the sideboard where one of the kerosene lamps was placed. With the child this close, Rosie could keep an eye on her.

She ambled over to her rocker again and sat down. She was appalled at Dean's outspoken comments. His attitude toward Clementine. She'd never seen him act in this manner. Was it because he was afraid? Afraid he might not be able to move quickly if the moment called for it?

She called to him, "Dean, that'll be enough. I won't stand for any more of yo' rude, disrespectful comments. If you want to be helpful, then go to the kitchen and see if there's a Sterno stove anywhere. Old Miz Sutherland had tea every day no matter what. So, I 'spect she made sure there was a Sterno stove. At least a one-burner one, for when the 'lectricity was out. A cup of tea would be good 'bout now."

If Clementine was tired, you'd never know it. Having rescued the animals, and been rescued herself, it would be reasonable to think she'd be falling asleep on her feet. But no. She was so wired with anxiety she could barely contain her twitching legs that wanted to flee. To escape. Escape what?

She was too young to understand that the body sends out chemicals, hormones, to give one strength to perform unthinkable tasks. To survive. And that's what she had done. She'd survived. The only problem was that those fight or flight hormones had not yet spun themselves out, and she was left with a feeling of ants crawling from her head to her toes.

She almost wished Rosie would rock her and put her to sleep. She pulled her knees to her chest and wrapped her arms about them, the long shirt covering her like a burial shroud.

"Rosie, do you think my daddy or Mr. Sutherland will come? It's getting awful late. Maybe they were caught in the floodwaters."

"Don't you worry 'bout yo' daddy or Mr. Sutherland. Those men are smart, and I know they out right now helping someone else. They likely can't get across the Appahoochee, so it could be a day or two before they get here. But we all safe here. No need to worry now."

As Rosie had suspected, Dean found a Sterno stove in a kitchen cabinet and proceeded to heat a kettle of water for tea. He'd made enough tea that he needed no instruction, and after rummaging through the walk-in pantry, he found several tins of tea, though not any he'd ever had. He selected one labeled Earl Grey. He knew Gramma liked her tea very hot. With sugar and cream. He decided to leave off the cream as the Frigidaire had been off for hours and the cream may have spoiled.

Once the tea was ready, he laid out a tray, poured three cups and placed the sugar dish on the tray. Then he called out in a harsh voice, "Hey, girl. If you want to do something, come fetch this tray for Gramma."

Clementine stared at Rosie and the old woman could read her face. "You go on. Bring Rosie some tea. Dean just in a snit some days. He hates having to ask for any help. Don't pay him no mind. Tomorrow he'll be all right again. Go on now."

Clementine made her way to the kitchen and stood in the doorway. Wondering what she should say. Dean glared at her. "Here. Take this tray. And don't spill it. Gramma likes her tea hot so be careful."

Clementine nodded, lifted the tray and headed to the parlor with Dean following behind her. She could hear his crutches stomping the floor with every step he made. She felt him getting closer and the slightest quiver of fear skittered through her.

*Maybe if I keep quiet, he'll not notice me. And Daddy's coming. Any minute now.*

# 28

# Tell Me a Story

Rosie smiled when Clementine appeared with the tea. "Good. That's good. Old Miz Sutherland thought a cup of tea cured just 'bout anything under the sun. I remember Vannah bringing me to the Tea House when I was 'bout seven or eight maybe. Seems I was coughing and coughing, and Vannah tried everything she knew to stop it.

"Well, Miz Sutherland fixed me a cup of her tea. This was tea that came from across the ocean according to her. From a place called London. Told me to sip it 'til it was all gone. Well, I did. But it didn't taste like any tea I'd ever had before. It was just awful.

"Only later, when I was a bit older, did Vanna tell me Miz Sutherland had laced that tea with a touch of Mister Sutherland's Jack Dan'l whiskey!" she laughed.

"I laugh now, but as I remember, it was truly awful. But it did stop that fit of coughing."

Dean deposited his long-legged, lean frame down on the floor, positioning his crutches beside his body. He then flung the brace open, as if his leg needed a respite from being so confined.

Clementine was careful to keep her distance and snuggled close to the wall, wishing she'd thought to bring a blanket and pillow for herself. What were they going to do now? She had no idea what time it was, but certainly it was late.

It began to dawn on her that maybe what Rosie said was true. It might be several days before Daddy came. Or maybe she was right. Maybe he had been swept away in the water. She couldn't erase the picture of the Appahoochee from her mind, the one from early this morning when the bus inched over the bridge with the water crawling so close it was nearly touching it. She was sure that bridge no longer existed. So how was Daddy going to come for her?

Dean swiveled his head in Clementine's direction, looking at the white girl, her long, braided hair now full of leaves and bits of grass, with wispy curls sneaking out at various places. Again, he wanted to sketch her. She had so many interesting angles to her face, and he remembered when she took off to the barn to release the horses, he'd seen something in her face, some strength, some determination that seemed incongruous in such a young person. Could he capture that in a sketch?

For a few minutes, they all sipped their tea quietly. Perhaps old Mrs. Sutherland was right that a cup of tea did help, as the three parlor dwellers relaxed for the first time that day.

A bit of time passed and the teacups were now empty. Clementine was usually in bed by now, though sometimes she would sneak her flashlight under the covers and read her latest library book, hoping Mama wouldn't catch her.

"Do you like to read, Rosie?" asked Clementine. She'd seen the book Dean had brought from the library and wondered if perhaps she should find one as well.

"Sometimes. But my eyes ain't what they use to be, and it's sometimes hard for me to read, 'specially at night. And after my spill today, the legs of my spectacles are bent and don't want to stay straight on my face."

Clementine nodded but didn't ask any more questions when she saw the arrows shooting from Dean's eyes. Arrows directed at her.

"Gramma reads very well," Dean retorted. He didn't like this slip of a girl questioning his gramma. She'd not had a lot of education, but Rosie was quite intelligent and he was aware of that. "She probably reads better than you. And she does something else. She's a storyteller. And a good one, too."

But he softened his voice as he spoke now. He knew Rosie would not allow him to continue to berate the girl, even if she deserved it. She was white, after all. But even he was aware that had she been just a wee bit older, he'd not have been so open with his hostility toward her as she'd shown she had some feisty characteristics already.

Clementine sent Rosie a small smile. She was unsure how to react now that Dean was becoming so vocal and appeared to not care much for her.

"Can you tell us a story?" asked Clementine.

"Oh, chile, you don't want to hear Rosie's stories. They be so old nobody even knows what I'm talking 'bout."

Dean lifted his chin to Rosie. "C'mon, Gramma. You got more stories than Mr. Sutherland's got library books. Looks like we stuck here, so it would be a good way to pass the time."

Rosie stared at Dean for a moment. He was right. It was going to be a long night. "Well then, if you think that would help. Let me think a minute. What story should I tell y'all?"

"Tell this girl the story of our people. The ones that were kidnapped and brought over as slaves. She don't know nothing about that time except what she might have learned in school. And they don't teach you much there."

Rosie nodded. "Uhmmm. Well, that is quite a story. But not everybody wants to know about that time and what our folk went through."

Clementine sat straighter and leaned in Rosie's direction. "I would like to hear that story. Dean's right. We didn't learn much in school about slavery. Sometimes I think people believe if you don't talk about bad things that have happened then they just go away. But Granddaddy says we should learn more about history so that maybe then we won't make the same mistakes."

Dean looked at Clementine. "How old are you, girl? Eight or nine?" he asked.

"I'm eleven. I'll be twelve in January."

"What? You can't be eleven. I'm fourteen, and I'm twice as tall as you."

"James and Jeremy, my brothers, are tall like you. But my Nana MacKinnon was a small woman. Mama says I might be like her."

"Is that why you pulled that stunt today? Dashing off to let the animals go free and making my gramma have to save you? What? You trying to prove you as big as everybody else?"

Clementine didn't quite know how to answer that question. Was that what she was doing? Trying to be like her brothers? She stared at her feet and kept her thoughts to herself, as she figured that would be the best way to respond. She was glad Rosie was here as she was beginning to feel anxious and fearful where Dean was concerned.

Rosie bristled, but keep her voice calm. "Dean, you hush now. This girl saved the horses and mules. And the dogs, too. She's got courage that some folks don't. You keep quiet now. I'll not tolerate another disrespectful word out of you. Now, if y'all will listen, I'll tell my story."

She held her empty cup out and Clementine poured her another cup of tea. Rosie peered down into her cup at a few floating tea leaves. Swirling around as if they might tell a story of their own.

"I'll tell the story like *Keke* told it to me as he knew it word for word. So, don't interrupt me with questions. Just hold 'em 'til I'm finished. And the story was told to him by his grandmother who heard it from her mother and so forth.

"The story wasn't written down, so my tellin' it is the way it's been done for ages now. Maybe one day you'll write it down, Dean, for when I'm gone. You the one who can do that."

She leaned her head back, resting it on the lace doily on the top of the chair. She took a deep breath and for a second closed her eyes as if she needed to get the scene in her head before proceeding.

"This be the story of Kadie, *Keke's* great-great-grandmother. Or maybe great-great-great. I'm not sure. But the story is the same. And Kadie was from another place and time."

And so, she began . . .

# 29

# Need a Nurse

Mrs. Watson made a swift headcount in the auditorium. She'd tried to keep everyone corralled in this one room, but it was beginning to feel a bit crowded. And there hadn't been any arguments or harsh words. Until now.

Like Andrew, she'd followed the newspaper items relating to social unrest and the death of the young black man in Mississippi. She had hoped this community would be spared such incidents. And, so far, no problems had arisen. But today she was afraid there could be trouble with blacks and whites sharing this enclosed space. And she wasn't sure what might happen.

But when she listened closer, she realized it wasn't a black-white argument going on. It was simply two white women going after each other. Both of whom were her former students.

Alex's voice rang out, "If you boys don't stop with that noise, I'm going to lock you both in a closet. You hear me!"

Her two boys were zipping around the room pretending to be World War II kamikaze pilots and providing all the necessary noises that went along with that scenario.

Seeing the ruckus was between two white women, Mrs. Watson's anxiety was relieved. But perhaps she'd better send for Andrew MacKinnon. He appeared to be ramrodding the townsfolk and trying to keep order. Her responsibility was to keep the auditorium safe and make sure they had food and water. But they were filled to capacity now, so she would ask Andrew to find another place for any new arrivals.

Ann Barber, Room Mother for the second grade and one of Mrs. Watson's favorite people, approached her. "Mrs. Watson, I don't mean to add more problems to what we have already, but my Timothy feels awfully warm. I believe he's running a fever."

"I see. I'll come by in a minute. Right now, I see Bennett has arrived with more folks from the surrounding area. I need to speak with him."

Bennett had been waiting patiently by his bus, then hurried to meet her as she walked his way. "Mrs. Watson, this is the last load from Blue Creek. Most of 'em need enough space to park a wheelchair or lay on a cot."

Mrs. Watson put a hand to her forehead, then shook her head, as if that motion would bring a fresh idea. She was all out of ideas to accommodate another influx of needy ones.

"Bennett, don't unload your bus yet. We're bursting at the seams here in the auditorium. I think maybe you should take them to the Corinth Baptist Church. You know, just a few blocks north of here. You know the one."

"Yes, ma'am. Jennie hauls me there every Sunday morning come rain or shine."

He grinned, recalling that before Jennie had agreed to marry him, he'd had to make a few difficult promises. He had asked the big question and waited. And waited. Finally, she responded.

"I'll marry you on three conditions: You got to lay off that Schlitz beer, you got to attend church with me every

Sunday, and you've got to train that tongue of yours to refrain from using such foul language."

"What? No Schlitz? Ah, come on, Jennie."

"You heard me."

"All right. All right. I can leave off the beer. And going to church I can handle . . . I think. But, Jennie, you gotta understand something about my 'foul' language as you call it. I don't mean to say shit so often, but sometimes it just comes out before I know it. But that's about the only cuss word I use. And I say dammit once in a great while."

"Well, two out of three isn't too bad, I guess," she said with a smile.

That had sealed the deal and they'd been together three years now. And Bennett didn't miss the beer, and church was all right, too. But even with Mrs. Watson's soapy intervention and Jennie's request, damned if his vocabulary didn't still contain the word shit!

Mrs. Watson continued, "I'd thought to get Andrew MacKinnon's ideas before making my decision, but I have no choice. We're unable to take any more. Make your way to Corinth, and get the older folk settled the best you can. If I know Andrew, he'll already have the place opened and ready. But wait a minute. I'll get Roger from the kitchen. We're pretty settled here, so we can spare him to help you."

She hurried to the kitchen. "Roger, would you please go with Bennett and help him get those people on his bus settled at Corinth Baptist?"

The two men had lived in Harper's Mill all their lives, and Mrs. Watson knew they were good friends from early on. That was one of the pluses of living in a small community. Friends remained friends for a lifetime. Of course, sometimes enemies also remained enemies.

Bennett started the bus, let the engine spit and sputter before giving it gas, then crept away from the school and headed to Corinth Baptist Church. When he got there, he wasn't surprised to see his wife, Jennie, standing at the door directing traffic.

"Hold on to that banister now, Mrs. Faircloth. Don't need any injuries getting into the church."

Jennie was a good one in a desperate situation. She'd not had the education Mrs. Watson had, but she could run a good show herself. Bennett smiled when she waved to him before moving on to assist Mrs. Faircloth. Then she returned to the door and resumed her duty.

"We'll put the wheelchair folk along the west side of the sanctuary, Bennett. We've opened the Gathering Hall, and those that need cots will be stationed there, where there's more space."

Bennett nodded and he and Roger began to help maneuver their charges to the proper places.

"Is that everybody, Bennett?" asked Jennie.

"Yep. That's everybody from Blue Creek. Don't think we missed anyone."

"Bennett, I need you to go to the auditorium. See if Mrs. Watson has any water to spare. We got plenty of food, but we're short of water."

"Ok. Gimme a few minutes. If she's got any, I'll be right back. If not, I'll find some and bring it to you."

He rolled the bus up at the rear entrance of the auditorium, where it would be easier to load the five-gallon bottles of water. However, once inside, he halted abruptly.

"Holy shit! What's goin' on?" he said as his ears retreated from the din of noise flooding them.

He heard a couple of women screeching at each other. "I don't need you making my decisions, Phyllis. I know how to handle my own children!" yelled Annice as she pulled her youngest to her side.

Several more women were yelling across the room, children were crying, and it appeared Mrs. Watson was unable to bring any order to the chaos. That fact alone gave Bennett pause. That woman could bring order to an army battalion, but not to this unruly, screaming bunch of women.

He looked around, hoping to find someone, anyone, who could let him in on what had happened in the few minutes he'd been gone. He felt a tug at his elbow. Eddie, the janitor at the school, was standing there.

"Bennett, best you stop here. Them women's been at it a few minutes. Don't think we better interfere."

"What the hell's happenin', Eddie?"

"Danged if I know. Seems Ann Barber's little one's been running a fever. For several days, she reports. Now it looks like a few other children have fevers as well, and their mothers are accusing Ann of bringing some kind of disease into the auditorium.

"Sarah Sue is scurrying about trying to help calm the waters. And you know Lou Ann. She's smart as a whip and she's also trying to help Mrs. Watson get things under control. But then Clara Bartram opened her mouth, and she's got a tongue on her that'll slice a watermelon. She's hot under the collar all right."

Bennett thought for a moment. Sounded to him like they needed the sheriff or someone to police the place! Well maybe not that, but certainly a doctor. But the nearest physician would be in Brunswick and that was too far.

"Maybe I better be trying to find Nurse Gould. She might be able to help."

Nurse Gould was the public health nurse who made rounds to the schools in the tri-county area, dispensing immunizations as required by the state government authorities. She knew every school-aged child and most of their mothers. But many of these children were under the age of five, so she may not know them yet. Still, she was the only medical person close by. Anyone with a serious ailment had to go to Brunswick or Jacksonville. Or maybe on to Savannah.

"Eddie, y'all have any water to spare? Jennie's at Corinth and they need some. If you could take it to her, I'd appreciate it. I'll get on down to Sumatra Springs and try to find Nurse Gould. We didn't need this!"

As he left, he could hear Mrs. Watson using her best "principal in charge" voice.

"Now, ladies. Calm down. We're not getting anywhere with your screaming at each other."

Just then Sandra walked over. She was friends with all the women and attempted to calm the waters. But the women didn't care to be calmed, and the screeching returned with a vengeance.

Bennett was glad to make his escape.

# 30

# Kadie Holds Court

The patter of the rain on the windowpanes echoed in the silence. The glow from the kerosene lamps swaddled the room in a cascade of mellow shadows that danced across the floor, making for a most inviting site to listen to a heartbreaking story that would never be forgotten.

"Dean already heard this story many times, Clementine, but the first thing I need to tell you is that Kadie, our ancestor, lived in Africa. In a place called Sierra Leone, according to *Keke*. That's where my name, Sierra Rose, comes from."

As Rosie said, Dean had heard the story many times, but never seemed to tire of it. Perhaps that was because the story was the only connection he had to his people, the Gullah/Geechee, since he and Rosie were the only ones left in his family. Except for Tonja, Rosie's sister. But Dean had never seen her. She may even be dead for all he knew.

"Now at the time Kadie, our ancestor, was kidnapped she was just a young girl, you see. She was 'bout yo' age, Clementine. Maybe ten or eleven. But she was a grown woman when she first started telling her people the story. And even though years had passed since that time, the memories were as clear to Kadie as if they had happened yesterday. I suppose some things just leave lasting marks."

Rosie shifted in her chair and leaned forward with her arms resting on her lap, her hands wrapped around her teacup. She looked from Dean to Clementine and nodded.

"*Keke* told me the story in the Gullah language 'cause I know that myself, but I need to tell it in English so's you two can understand it. Dean, you know a bit of the language, but Clementine don't. Now, listen as I begin my story."

She took a deep breath as if telling the story was going to be difficult. "So, this is Kadie's story. In her words . . ."

*That day was like any other. Me and Jenneh, my best friend, were outside under a kapok tree pounding the cassava. When we finished pounding, we would mix a bit of ginger beer in it to make it sweet and then take it to my mother so she could make it into fufu. She served that along with rice, our main meal every day. She always said, "If I haven't eaten rice today, then I haven't eaten!"*

*We pounded the cassava a few minutes, then got distracted and fell into giggles watching two small piglets running about our feet. We knew they would be served as dinner one day, but when they were this small, we made pets of them.*

*Somewhere far off, down in the swamp, we heard loud shouting. Then high-pitched screams. And Mama came flying out of our house and grabbed me and Jenneh.*

*"Get inside girls. Inside."*

*She ushered us through the open doorway, and we hunkered down in a corner of the front room. Our house was like all the others, made of dried mud bricks, some palm fronds and coated with clay. The roof was made of the bamboo from the forest as we lived near the coastal swamp where bamboo was plentiful.*

*A few minutes later, when I was brave enough to peek out the door, I saw smoke coming from the house across the road. Where Jenneh's family lived. I then saw Jenneh's mother and sister rushing down the lane, with several men chasing after them. Little did I know we'd never see them again.*

*My mother pushed me and Jenneh into the far corner of the cooking room, behind a tall bamboo screen where we bathed at night. She put her fingers to her lips. "Shh. Shh. Don't make a sound," she whispered.*

*Me and Jenneh squatted down and held on to each other. We were as quiet as two little church mice. But that didn't stop that mob of men from bursting through our front door.*

*"You get away, now! Leave us be!" screamed Mama as the men grabbed her. She kicked at them and they slapped her to the floor, bound her hands, then pulled her up and pushed her along.*

*When the men spotted me and Jenneh in the corner, they laughed and lifted us by our hair 'til we stood on tiptoes. Then they tied our hands together, and we knew there was no escape. We were hustled along through the village with several other women and young girls. We couldn't see Jenneh's mama and sister, but some of the other girls were friends we played with.*

*My mind was racing about wildly, and I was praying my father and uncles would come to help us. They were fishing down in the river, as fish and rice were what we survived on. But they didn't come. The screaming of the women and girls got louder and louder. Mama fell when she tried to get to me and Jenneh, and the men only laughed, kicked her in the head, and pulled her up again.*

*We'd heard stories of strangers coming into neighboring villages, kidnapping women and girls and selling them to the slave traders from across the ocean. But we never expected anyone to come to our home, Bunce Island, and go deep into the swamp where we lived. But we were wrong. These men were searching for slaves to sell, and capturing women and girls was easy.*

*The most disturbing thing—something I didn't think of until much later when I was able to process that day in my mind—was that some of these men were not foreigners. A couple of them were men from our own country, men from Sierra Leone, and they were gathering their own people and selling them to the traders. That fact is something I still have difficulty understanding. Later, Jenneh told me she recognized one of them as the man who brought fish to the market in our village. I guess kidnapping was more prosperous than fishing.*

*Course now that I'm older, I know there's bad people in all cultures. But my father and uncles, and most of the men in our village took care of their families and any others that needed help. Mama says that's just what our people do. Care for others as we do our own.*

Clementine's attention was riveted on Rosie's face as every emotion the woman described danced across it. And this story of Kadie, the long-ago ancestor, was the most moving story Clemmie had ever read or heard. She was not even sure Mama would have allowed her to read it, as it was filled with such heartache that she found herself choking back tears as she listened.

She was so engrossed she temporarily forgot the terrifying flood, her trips to rescue the animals, and even the desperate minutes of trying to hold on to the floating log until Rosie pulled her to safety.

# 31

# Keep Searching

Larry and Andrew pulled their truck close to Toby's at the small marketplace in Smokey Hollow. All was quiet and the place was deserted, except for a young Bantam rooster strutting around and a few hens pecking the dirt hoping to catch a slow-moving worm. Larry checked inside the marketplace and Andrew went through Corina's house as Toby had done.

"She ain't here, Mr. Mac. I done checked. Ain't like her to leave her children and go off somewhere by herself," Toby stated.

"Yeah, I agree. Then we'll keep searching. Why don't you and Jesse head to the auditorium one more time. Maybe she's been found there after all. Me and Larry will go down to the post office and check with Edna. She sees everything that passes by her front window. She may have caught a glimpse of Corina. We'll see you at the sawmill. Rufus is hoping someone from the Corps of Engineers will come let us know something about the conditions at the dam. The helicopters have been whirling around all morning. Let's hope they've made headway with repairs."

"We'll do that. Catch you later."

Toby and Jesse were itching to have a task. Not finding Corina was disturbing to both of them, even though they never said as much to each other.

All four men pulled away, leaving the Hollow behind. After traveling for a couple of minutes, Larry began to laugh aloud and Andrew raised his eyebrows.

"Don't know what you find entertaining, but please share it. Can't think of anything funny myself."

Larry glanced at Andrew. They'd known each other for many years, but Andrew worked in timber and Larry in tobacco, so their work took them in different circles.

"I was thinking about my old truck here. She must have heard me discussing trading her in for a newer model the other day. Because today she's running better than she's done in years."

Andrew smiled. Like Toby and Jesse, these two men didn't discuss what was actually on their minds. Their daughters. But the look that passed between them spoke volumes. Some things didn't need to be said. They were simply understood between friends.

~ ~ ~

The sawmill looked like an anthill that had sprung up overnight. Men were scurrying in and out the door, yelling across the lumber yard, getting instructions from Rufus and reporting anything they may have seen along the roadways and fields. Larry and Andrew left the truck and moved closer to listen as Rufus was motioning everyone to gather around.

"Hold on a minute, fellas. This young lad here is Bud Black. He works for Stu at Tall Timbers Station. Stu sent him down to give us an update on what they can see from the tower."

Bud stepped forward, jerked his ball cap off, cleared his throat, and took a deep breath. He knew all of these men. His father had been friends with them, but he'd passed away a couple of years ago, so Bud was now expected to be the man of the house. But he didn't feel so manly at this moment, looking out at the men of the community staring at him as if they expected him to know what to do next.

"Evening, men. As Mr. MacKinnon said, I work at Tall Timbers Station with Mr. Johnson. He sent me down here to tell you what he can see from his place. And you can see a lot from that tower. It's something, I can tell you. But you know that already."

Bud never expected to have to speak to a group such as this. He was young and had only worked at the Station for a short time, but every day he proved his worth. He swallowed hard and shuffled his feet, all the while twisting his ball cap in his hands.

"Anyway, he says to tell you the Corps has made progress at the dam. They've erected some temporary barriers. Brought ‘em in by them helicopters you been seeing fly overhead. There's two dozen or more men there. Some of 'em are tied around their middles with ropes to keep from getting pulled into the water and being swept away. And they all wearing life jackets.

“The helicopters are dropping sandbags all along the edge of the river, and Stu says that appears to be slowing the water, too. The men from the Corps talked about things like putting in more bulkheads, upstream bar-rock anchors, and a lot of engineering stuff I never heard of.

“And one more thing he says is important to tell you. He's been on his radio, which still works 'cause it's got a battery, and the weather report for the area is looking good. The rain will be over shortly this evening, and tomorrow the sun should be out. So, if them barriers hold tonight, we should all be able to get on with our business. Thank you."

Bud put his ball cap on and stepped down from the porch. Public speaking wasn't tops on his list of favorite things to do.

"Thanks be to God," mumbled someone in the crowd. And that summed up the feelings of every man there. Rufus took the floor again.

"I know you all have families and properties to look after. As do I. Right now, I think the biggest problem we have, assuming that water has been slowed a bit, is downed lines. And there have been reports of stray animals on the highway. Guess maybe they were being held in electrified fencing, and since that's not working, they're wandering the roadways and may be a nuisance. So, I'll ask all of you to check your place first, then see if you can help someone else who may need a hand.

"It'll be dark in another couple of hours, so get your lanterns, kerosene lamps, whatever you need to make your way about. And be careful with the lamps. We don't need a fire on top of all this.

"The auditorium, the Corinth Baptist Church, the First Methodist, and the Garden Center are open. They have food, water, and cots. Make use of those resources. Maybe tomorrow will be a brighter day for all of us. I'll stay here at the mill all night, so if anyone needs to get a message, or needs help, this will be the place to come. And, most important of all, keep your eyes peeled for anything that looks unusual or out of place. We still haven't found Skidder's wife. She's still out there somewhere."

Heads nodded and the relief they felt with Bud's news was palpable. Shortly, each man took off to check his own place. That is, except for Larry and Andrew. They had a unique problem still. How to get across the Appahoochee? As they walked to the truck, Andrew shared his thoughts.

"Larry, I know you're itching to find a jon boat and try to get across the river. And so am I. Right now my ridiculously logical mind, as Norah calls it, tells me we got to wait 'til morning. But I will tell you that another part of my mind, the part that's not so ridiculously logical, wants to grab a boat and head to your place."

Larry rubbed the back of his neck and looked at Andrew. "I believe you're reading my mind. I would like nothing better than doing just that—heading for the Tea House. But you're right. It's too dangerous. We gotta take care of ourselves so we can take care of our girls. That means we wait."

"I agree."

"Andrew, Rosie will take care of them. Our girls. And that grandson of hers. But he's crippled and climbing that steep hill to the Tea House would be difficult for him."

"Crippled you say?"

"Yeah. He was stricken with polio about two years or so ago. Left him with one leg that's unable to bear any weight, so he gets around on crutches. And that's too bad. He was a good student, but he dropped out of school and that worries Rosie. She and her daddy believed in getting as much education as possible."

"Polio. God-awful disease. Can't think of anything worse for a child to deal with," said Andrew. His greatest fear for Clementine was that she'd fall off Missy one time too many and end up with a broken arm or something of that nature. His mind wouldn't let him entertain a thought as awful as her having polio.

They sat in the truck for a few moments, trying to decide their next move.

"We can't go to the Tea House, but we can go check on your place, Andrew. And what about your daddy, old Mr. Mac? Where is he?"

"I don't know exactly, but chances are we won't find him in one of the shelters. He's still able-bodied, and his mind works better than mine most of the time. He still lives out on Lirey Road. Doesn't keep cattle or farm anymore, but when

Mother died recently, he refused to come live with us. Guess as long as he's able, it's all right."

"And your place? Want to go check on it?" Larry asked.

"No. I'm on fairly high ground. Don't have any electric fences, so no issue there. I'm just glad Norah's not here. She'd be so worried about Clemmie I couldn't bear it.

"No, my place can wait. Right now, we gotta search for Corina. When it's dark, it'll be even more difficult to find her. If Skidder were alive, he would be here doing whatever he could to help anyone. No. We're gonna keep searching."

"All right. Then let's make a plan as to where to go first, second, etc. I think we ought to go by the auditorium and see if Toby and Jesse learned anything. Maybe they can take the north end of the town and we'll take the south. Make more time that way."

# 32

# Don't Ask

Dean was correct. Rosie was a great storyteller. But then, it was what her Gullah people did. Tell the stories of their ancestors. How they survived the horrors of the Transatlantic Slave Trade and the infamous Middle Passage which would often take as long as several months, depending on the weather and how angry the Atlantic might be at any given time.

Clemmie watched as Rosie put her teacup down on the oak table next to the rocker. She desperately wanted to know what had become of Kadie and so hoped Rosie wasn't going to stop now.

Rosie removed her spectacles and rubbed her eyes. "We gonna' stop here for a few minutes. I need to stretch my legs. Dean, go to the kitchen and see if you can find something in the way of a snack. Some more fruit or whatever you can find. It's getting on to midnight now, and my stomach feels like my throat's been cut.

"Ain't usually awake this late, but now that I am, a little something to tide me over 'til morning would be good. Then I'll finish my story, and we'll all try to get a few hours' sleep. No telling what we might be faced with tomorrow. But whatever it is, it can't be bad as today. The rain's barely drizzling now, so I pray tomorrow we'll see some sunshine."

She stood tall, stretched her arms above her head and strolled out to the front porch, relishing the feel of the soft boots. Her tired feet could get use to such.

It took Dean a couple of minutes to reattach his brace and stand, but he was accustomed to that now; then he gathered his crutches. He looked at Clementine who still sat close to the wall, madly scribbling on a writing pad she'd found on the desk in the library.

"What you writing?" Those were the kindest words he'd said to her all day.

"Thoughts about Kadie's journey. I'm gonna tell Mama and Daddy what I can remember about the story."

"Huh. Well, why don't you come help me in the kitchen? I'll find some food and you can bring it to the parlor."

Clementine nodded and stood, then followed behind him. He was certainly right about one thing. He was much taller than she.

"Are you sure you're eleven years old?" Dean asked.

Clemmie nodded, then decided to brave a conversation with him. "Why do you need crutches?"

She wished she hadn't been so brave when she saw the look that flitted across his face. Like he'd been asked to dance the waltz on one foot.

"Because I can't put any weight on my right leg. It's too weak."

"Did you fall from a tree or something?"

"No, I'm not that stupid. I had polio. You probably don't even know what that is, do you?"

"I heard Mama and Nana talking. Mama says Nurse Gould will be coming in September to vaccinate everyone for that disease."

"Well, that's just a bit late for me, I guess."

Dean moved on toward the kitchen, and Clemmie again followed a few feet behind him, observing how he placed his left foot firmly on the floor before moving forward.

"Will you ever be able to use your leg again?" Clementine continued.

"No. The doctors in Savannah said most polio patients get along all right with a brace, and some of 'em don't even need that. Then some people need crutches. But I'll always need both the brace and crutches."

"So, are you used to the brace and crutches now?"

"Might as well be. The doctor said the nerves in my foot were badly damaged, and the only way I can ever walk on that leg again would be to have the foot amputated and a prosthesis put in place. But that costs lots of money. So, no. I'll never use it again."

"What's a prosthesis?"

"You don't know much, do you? A prosthesis is a plastic limb. Takes the place of the bad limb. A foot in my case."

Clementine had no words now. She'd only had the mumps and an occasional bout with croup. She couldn't imagine only one good foot. She could just picture herself trying to climb on Missy or dash through the pasture chasing the goats. With only one good foot, it was unthinkable.

Dean opened the Frigidaire which had now been without electricity for hours. He checked each shelf. Gramma Rosie would skin him alive if he brought her something that had spoiled already.

He closed the door and glanced about. On the small pie safe against the far kitchen wall was a metal cake plate with a glass cover. He lifted the cover and gave a half-smile when he realized what a great find he'd made. Coconut cake.

"Now this is what I call dessert." He grinned, and Clemmie found herself returning the smile whether she intended to or not.

"Let's find some plates."

"They're above the stove. At least the fancy ones are. I used two earlier when Sarah and I had our lunch. But it's real china."

"Real china is what we'll use then. Coconut cake is my favorite, and Gramma makes the best one you ever tasted."

Clementine placed the plates, forks, and cake on the tray. Then she scrounged around opening drawers, searching for a knife.

"Here. I got it already," Dean said, removing the large, serrated-edge knife from under his arm where he had stuck it a few moments earlier.

"You take that tray. So, what kind of name is Clementine anyway? I never heard anybody called that before."

"Do you know what a clementine is?" she asked, knowing he probably wouldn't.

Dean snorted, "Sounds like some kind of vine that grows in the forest."

"Well, I don't think I've heard of that kind of vine, but a clementine is a citrus fruit that grows in Florida where Mama grew up. They're kind of a cross between regular oranges and mandarin oranges. Very sweet. Mama likes them. So, she and Daddy decided to name me Catriona Clementine MacKinnon. Catriona was my Nana's first name."

Dean didn't comment but motioned with his head for her to go on. Clementine turned to look at him as he followed behind.

"Does Rosie's story have a happy ending?"

"What? You don't know much history, do you? Ain't nothing happy about that story, but it's about my people, and it's all I know about them. I never get tired of it."

"Your people?" Clemmie asked.

"Yeah, the Gullah/Geechee folk. Gramma Rosie says some of 'em still live along the coast in those places they call the Sea Islands. In Virginia, South Carolina, here in Georgia and even down in north Florida. Gramma was born on one of them islands. She and her sister, Tonja. But Tonja left here a long time ago."

Clemmie chimed in, "When we were out in that water, I didn't think I'd ever see my family again. But Rosie said I would. And she said she would see her sister again. Does she live close by?"

Dean shook his head, "No. I ain't never seen her. She was gone from here long before I was born. Rosie says she went to South Carolina. To a place called St. Helena Island."

"And what about your mama? Does she live with you and Rosie?"

"I don't have a mama. She's long gone, too. Gramma Rosie's the only mama I ever had."

Clementine opened her mouth, then closed it. Something told her she might be asking too many questions. A fault her brothers always reminded her of.

"And you? You got a mama?" Dean asked.

"Uh-huh. And a daddy. And a granddaddy. But Nana died a few weeks ago. And I have a great-aunt, too. She's Granddaddy's sister. And she's even older than he is. We call her Aunt Maori. I also have two brothers, who irritate me all the time. They think they know more than anyone and keep telling me I'm too young and too little to do anything."

Dean raised his eyebrows.

*They might not think that if they'd seen you today. Even though you were stupid and put Gramma Rosie's life in danger, you showed some backbone when you ran like a banshee to let all the animals loose.*

Of course, he didn't let Clemmie in on his thoughts.

When they returned to the parlor, Rosie had resumed her seat and was twisting a few unruly curls into place in her bun.

She'd lost her sprig of jasmine and blue ribbon somewhere during her struggles earlier in the day. She didn't mind losing either of those, but somehow during her tumble down the hill she'd also lost her small corncob pipe which was always in her bosom. Her pipe was the one vice she allowed herself. No whiskey or wine. And none of Cooter's homebrew. But she did enjoy a puff on her pipe now and then.

Clementine set the tray on the oak table and served Rosie a slice of cake, along with another cup of tea.

"Thank you, Clementine. This will be just what I need to finish my story."

Clementine sat in her same place near the window. A few seconds later, Dean exited the library where he'd made a small detour. He joined them and placed one of his crutches on the floor next to Clementine.

Then he handed her a couple of items he had tucked under his arm. A small pillow and a crocheted throw blanket from the sofa in the library. Somehow, the interlude in the kitchen, the exchange of thoughts, had removed a barrier. A barrier that had existed only in his mind to begin with.

"Thank you," Clementine said, then placed the pillow behind her back and spread the throw across her lap. Then she picked up her writing pad. She noted that Dean, too, now had a notepad.

But Dean wouldn't write notes. He knew this story almost as well as Rosie. No writing for him. Instead, he began to make small sketches of Clementine's profile. He thought maybe later he'd do a full face one.

"Y'all ready?" asked Rosie.

"Clementine, I told you this was a long story and might not be something you would enjoy, but if you want me to, I'll go on. You understand, though, the telling ain't quite as good in English. When *Keke* told it, that Gullah language flowed from his lips like syrup on hotcakes. And it was like he was in touch with her. With Kadie. Like she was telling it herself."

"It's still our story, Gramma. You just tell it. It's our story in any language," Dean said. He sat back and closed his eyes. Yes, this was their story. And as surely as Rosie was telling it tonight, he knew he'd tell it one day.

Clementine chimed in, "I want to hear it all, Rosie. Kadie was pretty special. Not everybody could survive what she did. We didn't learn anything about a Middle Passage at school. Are you going to tell us more about that?"

"I'm gettin' to that part. Y'all be patient."

Once again, she stared into her teacup, then lay her head against the back of the chair, closed her eyes and appeared to be channeling Kadie as she entered the room again . . .

*By the time we got to the ship the kidnappers had anchored down on the coast, there were thirty-two of us. I know because I counted everyone as they led us on board.*

*The name Wanderer was printed on the side of that ship, which seemed enormous to me, and it appeared to have many compartments. I learned later the Wanderer was a ship that brought many slaves from Africa. We were just the latest passengers to board her.*

*Suddenly, I was being pushed forward, away from the group my mother was in. Mama cried, and I cried. She screamed as the kidnappers dragged me away.*

*"Don't take my daughter. Please! She's just a baby! Don't take her from me!"*

*But they didn't listen. Then me and Jenneh were put in a group of other young girls, and the ship was so large I could not see the compartment at the other end of the ship where they headed with my mother.*

*I slapped and kicked at the kidnappers so hard they cuffed my hands in iron chains. I wanted to put my hands over my ears to block out the crying children and the screaming mothers, but I couldn't. The iron handcuffs were so heavy I could hardly lift my hands.*

*After a few minutes, Jenneh didn't cry anymore. She didn't holler or scream either. She sat there, watching as our homeland began to look like a speck on the horizon as the ship moved away.*

*And she never spoke again.*

*Once we were out in the open sea, I kept praying my mother would keep calling for me and I would find her . . . somehow.*

*On that first day, one of the younger men called Mako planted one of his big fists into the face of one of the crewmen. Guess he was too young to know what trouble that would bring on. The next thing, there was yelling at the front of the boat and crewmen shoving us along.*

*"Git yourselves on up here. Watch this now. This is what happens if you act up," yelled one of the guards.*

*He brought Mako forward and tied him to a tall pole anchored into the deck. Even with us girls and women standing there, they stripped him of his clothing and chained his feet to hooks on the deck. Hooks that I learned were put there precisely for that purpose. Mako, again being a young man, spat at the crewman, who stood there holding his cat-o'-nine-tails, a dreaded whip that could bring a man to his knees with one lash.*

*Mako never uttered a sound until the sixth lash. The one that ripped his right ear off his head. I wanted to turn my eyes away, but they refused to obey my wishes. It was as if they wanted me to watch this horror. Only later did I understand that my body was helping me. Wanted me to learn from this. It was teaching me to survive.*

# 33

# *Fever Pitch*

Toby and Jesse climbed out of the truck. As they approached the door to the auditorium, however, they stopped. Jesse, never one to express much emotion, looked to Toby. His eyes opened wide.

"Good Lord, Toby! What in the world's goin' on in there?"

The racket was so loud they hesitated before moving closer. Women were rushing around the room, children were wailing, and Mrs. Watson appeared to have lost control of the rowdy group. A most unlikely event.

Toby went in first, his eyes searching for Theo or Marlee. Hopefully, they could shed some light on this chaos. A few seconds later, Marlee spotted Toby and hurried to him with Corina's two children in tow.

"Toby? Do you have any news?"

Toby understood what she was asking, and he shook his head slightly. "We're still looking. Something will show up. For sure."

Marlee got the message and nodded.

"But what the hell is happening here? From the look on Mrs. Watson's face, I'd say something is wrong."

"Yes, well, it seems one of the children, one of the white children, came in here with a fever. Now, it seems like half a dozen of 'em got one."

Toby looked down at the two small children standing by Marlee. "These two got it?"

"Not yet. Bennett's gone to fetch Nurse Gould, the school nurse. He should be here any minute now. Maybe she'll have a solution to this mess."

Toby and Jesse exited the auditorium and met Andrew and Larry as they pulled up. "You might not want to go in there, Mr. Mac. There's a lot of screaming women, and children with fever. I'm not sure it's a safe place to be."

Andrew and Larry smiled. Both had children and knew what that meant. Andrew then suggested, "I see. Then I think the four of us should figure out which direction we should go and not stop until we've found Corina. Skidder would do the same for any of us."

~ ~ ~

Bennett brought Nurse Gould in the rear door of the auditorium. Her mind still worked like quicksilver, and she moved as she always had. With purpose. And like Mrs. Watson, when she said jump, those close by fell over each other trying to do just that.

She was on the matronly side, with dark hair that was beginning to show a few streaks of silver, but she was still attractive in her own way. Her white uniform was starched so stiff it rustled when she moved, and she wore her snappy, white nursing cap tipped on the back of her head. To the community, that white cap was as important as the badge on Sheriff Burke's chest. It was a sign of authority and demanded respect. She had her medical kit in hand and moved forward, where she was immediately met by Mrs. Watson.

"Oh, Thelma. Am I ever glad to see you!" Mrs. Watson exclaimed.

"What's wrong here? Bennett said a child arrived with fever? Anything else I should know?"

"That's right. Ann Barber's child has had a fever for several days, according to Ann. But now there are at least six or seven more. You got any ideas?"

"Let me set up my nursing station by the door, away from the crowd as much as possible."

A couple of men hopped to and arranged a long table by the door, and Nurse Gould placed her medical equipment on a crisp, white tablecloth. Then she took a look around the room, where she counted some twenty plus children.

"I'll need someone to help me."

"Of course," Mrs. Watson answered. "Marlee knows all the black children. She'll be good. And Martha Jane. She knows the children from down in Blue Creek. And ask Gabra also. She knows most everyone."

Nurse Gould washed her hands, then examined three or four of the fevered children. That was enough for her to make a diagnosis of the problem.

She washed her hands again, made a few notes in her journal, and prepared to report her findings to Mrs. Watson. A report she didn't relish making. She took a moment, straightened her cap and laid her stethoscope on the table.

Mrs. Watson was waiting, if not patiently, and looked the nurse in the eye. "What do you think, Thelma. They all coming down with a summer cold?"

Nurse Gould shook her head. "I wish it were that simple, but it's not. These children all have measles. And we've got a problem on our hands."

"Measles? Then what must we do? Just tell me."

"Measles is a highly contagious disease that can have serious complications. It often leads to ear infections and diarrhea. Sometimes it brings on pneumonia and encephalitis."

"But, didn't these school-aged children get immunized at school? I know you were there once a week to make sure everyone was covered."

"Yes, they were immunized for some diseases. But we don't have a vaccine for measles. Many physicians, researchers, and the Center for Disease Control, are working on one. But as of today, there's not one available and many people die from it every year. It's a real problem for the entire country. "

"First the dam breaks, now this. What next?" asked Mrs. Watson.

"Well, if we don't confine these measles cases, we could have a whole community of sick folks on our hands. We need to take quick action."

# 34

# Dead Men Don't Talk

Andrew and Larry were to search the south side and Toby and Jesse were headed north. As Larry left the main highway and headed south, however, Andrew had a thought.

"Wait a sec. Let's go down to the Hollow again. There's a two-rut road behind the church. A back way that leads to Lirey. To an old settlement in those woods. Then we'll go on to the Kent place and check out the vacant buildings out there. That's pretty close to the Hollow, so Corina may have taken refuge in one of those. Might be a place to start."

When they passed the old church, Larry crept along, and wondered if the truck might completely stop on him. But the ol' girl kept on truckin' and they moved on. Like Larry had said, she seemed determined to prove he didn't need to replace her with some new, shiny Ford F-100 or something along those lines.

The road to Lirey was a dirt one with deep ruts made by the logging trucks that used it to get to their worksites deep in the forest. Andrew knew these woods. Had hauled timber from them for many years. He recalled there was an old log house back in those woods. Built long ago by Silas Kent.

“See that dilapidated place down the way? It was quite a fine dwelling originally, built by the old man himself with the help of his three sons. Lads I knew when I was a boy. The last I knew of the sons, they'd moved to the next county west of here and gone into the automobile repair business. And the old man passed on years ago.”

"Where does that other dirt road go? The one we passed a mile or so back?" asked Larry.

"I believe it’s the beginning of the old Blackshear Trail that eventually leads on to McRae and that area. Daddy's got some kin over that way. Distant cousins, I think. But I've never met them."

As the two neared the house, the truck lights showed the place to be rather run down and surrounded by tall dog fennel and gallberry shrubs, along with the remains of an old turpentine plant that told a story of long-ago times. They got out, taking their flashlights with them. It was totally dark now, and finding anyone would be difficult.

The roof of the house had caved in, but the interior was still pretty much intact. Andrew took a turn through the house, commenting as he did.

“You know, with a minimum of repair, the place could once again be a decent enough house. But I don’t even know who owns the property now. Probably the sons. But if so, they’ve certainly not taken an interest in the place.”

Larry nodded. "Andrew, I hate to say it, but I think we’re going to have to wait until morning. It's impossible to see out here. It's August, and I don't have to tell you how many rattlesnakes are crawling around in these gallberry bushes."

Andrew directed the flashlight onto his feet. Just checking.

"Yeah, you got a point there. And you can bet they see better in the dark than you and I do. Okay, let's go to my place, check it out, and find something to eat. Norah will have left enough food to feed Patton's army. And I've got a generator we can use if the electricity went out."

"I've got one at the Tea House, too. But you gotta go outside to the utility building to start it. Not sure Rosie would have known about that."

Andrew's "ridiculously logical" mind sent him a mental picture then of Clemmie sitting in the dark with this Rosie that Larry had so much faith in.

Clemmie would be afraid, certainly, but he also knew she'd deal with it. She was young, but he'd already seen she was made of stronger stuff than her brothers gave her credit for. She didn't only inherit Nana MacKinnon's size; she was blessed with her grit and determination as well. Or maybe cursed might be more correct.

They eased their way to the main road, headed to Andrew's place. A few minutes later they were moving along on Highway 12. Suddenly Larry slammed on the brakes and sent Andrew flying forward, whacking his head on the dashboard.

"Damn Larry! That's two times today you've pitched me to the dash. What the hell you doing?"

Andrew held his hand to his forehead, where a deep gash sent rivulets of blood down his face and where a goose egg now resided.

"Didn't you see that? That body in the road?"

"What? No. I was thinking about Clemmie. Wasn't looking I guess," he said as he pulled a handkerchief from his pocket and held it to his bloodied forehead. He chuckled inside remembering what Nana always said regarding one using curse words.

"That's language barbarians and the uneducated use, Andrew. Remember that when you toss one about." But he could remember hearing her say 'Oh shit!' when she dropped her frying pan on her toe.

Larry pulled off onto the shoulder of the road and the two hurried to the body to take a closer look, neither of them wanting to confirm what was going through their minds.

As Larry said, there, right in the middle of the traffic lane, lay a body. They shined their flashlights on it and both experienced a moment of relief. They didn't know this person. This man.

Larry quickly checked for a pulse but wasn't surprised when he found none. It was difficult to guess the man's age, as he was lying face down. His clothing led them to believe he might be a hobo, a vagrant passing through.

There were some shacks down south of town near the railroad tracks where hobos often camped for a day or so. Then they'd jump the freight train as it passed through and ride until it came to some other backwoods place. The townsfolk had never had any trouble with the hobos, so there was no reason to make them leave.

"This day just gets longer and longer. I reckon we better find Sheriff Burke. Let him take it from here," Andrew remarked.

"Yeah. You think we should move the body off the road? If we leave it there it might cause another accident."

"Uh-huh. Got no choice. Let's get it done."

They each took an arm and a leg and carefully lifted the body. As they placed him down on his back, Andrew got a better look at him, now face up. He was so shocked he hardly knew how to react.

"God Almighty, Larry! Look at him. Closer. His face!"

Larry bent down and shined his flashlight on the man's face. He expected to see road rash or bruising and scrapes. And those marks were there. But what grabbed his attention was the same thing that had gotten Andrew's. The man had a bullet hole in his forehead. Both men were experienced hunters and knew a bullet hole when they saw it.

Larry stood, "Holy Mother of God. I figured he'd probably misjudged the speed of a car and walked into the lane. Maybe it was too dark. And the rain didn't help. But, no. Andrew, this was not an accident. This man's been shot."

Once more the old truck was called on to go full bore, but now she had another issue. She was low on gas, and the service station was miles away.

"Hope we make it to the sheriff's office. We're awful low on gas," Larry grumbled, irritated to have something else to worry about.

When they arrived at the sheriff's office, there were several other vehicles parked in the pine straw lot and Sheriff Burke was on his radio when they went in. He motioned them to take a seat, and when he ended his conversation, turned to them.

"Andrew, what the hell happened to your head?" he asked as he leaned back in his chair.

"Ah, just a scratch. It's nothing."

"That goose egg doesn't look like nothing to me," Sheriff Burke said, but didn't question him any further as Andrew had a reputation for keeping his business to himself.

"I've been talking with Tri-County Electrical in Brunswick. They're sending several trucks and some linemen early in the morning. We should have some electricity by noontime. That'll be a godsend."

Andrew nodded. "That's good. Cleveland, I hate to be the bearer of bad news, but we're here to let you know about the latest problem."

The sheriff nodded. "You mean the outbreak of measles at the auditorium? I've been briefed on that already. Nurse Gould is manning that station. For the moment, anyhow."

"Uh, no. That's not what we came to tell you. We've just come from out on the McRae Highway. Some ten miles out from my place. We found a body on the road. A dead body."

The sheriff jumped out of his chair which was a feat, as he was quite a heavy man.

"What are you talking about? A dead body? Who is it?"

"Don't know. Appears to be a hobo, a drifter. But we're guessing."

"What'd he do? Wander into the roadway in the dark and get hit?"

"That's what we thought at first, but that's not what happened. He's been shot, Cleveland. Shot in the forehead."

Sheriff Burke sat down heavily in his chair, looking first at Andrew then at Larry as if trying to determine if they both had lost their minds. No one said anything for a second, then Larry started for the door.

"We moved the body to the shoulder of the road, hoping to prevent another accident."

The sheriff nodded. "Yeah. Yeah. Good idea." Like Andrew and Larry, he was exhausted. He'd been on duty for more than twenty-four hours, and he'd now been presented with one more issue for his already very full basket.

"I'll get on the radio and call the sheriff's office in McRae. I think that's actually in their county that far out. Even if it isn't, we don't have a man to spare. Huh. I guess that'll be a crime scene now."

He rubbed his chin and sighed. "All right then. You two go on home. We'll talk again in the morning."

He shook his head. "Jesus, a dead body on the highway. But at least it wasn't one of our folks. Go on now. See you men tomorrow."

# 35

# *We All Have a Story*

Rosie stopped for a moment, holding her empty cup in her lap, and Clementine took this opportunity to ask a question that had been bothering her throughout the entire telling of the story.

"Rosie, I know you said not to ask any questions until you were finished, but would you answer just one?"

"I don't know, but I suppose I can try. But you gotta remember, I only know what my *Keke* told me. If it's something else 'bout them bad times, I can't answer yo' question."

"Yes, ma'am. Well, I know that Kadie must have survived, or else you wouldn't be knowing the story. And you said Kadie was the same age I am now. But I can't imagine being kidnapped and becoming a slave.

"If you had asked me, I would tell you my biggest problem is that time goes so slow, and I want to hurry through this time of my life and get to be twenty years old. Or something like that. Then I'll do what I want and become a veterinarian.

"But Mama's always telling me to enjoy my time being young. To stop wishing my life away. That the time will all pass too quickly. Now I wonder if maybe she's right.

“Listening to Kadie’s story makes me sad. It seems like she never even had a childhood. Like she had to become an adult even if she didn't want to. She didn't have any choices."

"Uh-huh. So, what's yo’ question?" Rosie pushed up her spectacles, which refused to stay properly placed since her tumble down the hill.

Clemmie glanced across the room to where Sarah, a child without a mother, was still sleeping. Then she focused her gaze on Dean, a child who had a mother but had never known her. He was leaning against the wall, his eyes closed. Maybe he was taking a short nap. If he was listening, she hoped he didn't take offense, as they seemed to have buried the hatchet. For now, anyway.

Her eyes filled with tears which she quickly wiped away before Dean could see them. Then she turned her attention to Rosie.

"I was wondering . . . did she ever find her mother?"

"Oh, now. If Rosie tells you happenings out of their place in the story, it won't be right. Just keep listening. We're coming on to the end in a short while now, and then yo’ question will be answered. I bet yo’ own story has to be told in the right order, too."

"I don't have a story, Rosie," Clementine said quietly.

"What? 'Course you do. We all have a story. A story that tells where we come from, who our people are, why we become the people we are when we grow up.” She peered over her spectacles again and lifted her eyebrows.

"Do you have any oldsters still living? A grandma or grandpa?"

Clementine nodded. "Granddaddy MacKinnon is still alive, and his sister, Aunt Maori. And she's really old. Even older than Granddaddy."

"Uh-huh. Well, when you get home, you get yo’ granddaddy or auntie to tell you the story of yo’ people. It will be different than mine, but even more interesting to you, as it will be about people you be related to, yo' ancestors, yo' blood kin."

"Do you have other stories about your people?" asked Clementine.

"Oh, I have many more. But this one is the most important. Where my story started. With Kadie in Sierra Leone."

"But what about your sister, Tonja? Where is she? Is there a part where you tell about her, too?"

Rosie stared in the distance for a moment, then shook her head. "No. I don't have a story 'bout Tonja. As far as I know, she still lives up on St. Helena Island. She writes once or twice a year, but I ain't heard from her since Christmas, and she was complaining about breathin' problems. She could even be gone on to the Lawd for all I know. But, no, there's nothing about Tonja or me in the story.

"You know, I never thought of that. That our story didn't stop with these ancestors. Time keeps on moving along, and each generation brings more to the story. I suppose Dean could add some new parts, about me and Tonja. And *Keke* and Vanna. And himself. I just gotta get him to write it all down."

Rosie held her cup out again and Clementine hurried to refill it. If keeping Rosie in tea was all it took to complete the story, then that was easy enough.

Clementine was amazed at how Rosie was able to change the pitch of her voice to sound like another person from another time. And she was so anxious to know that one thing. Did Kadie ever find her mother?

Rosie sipped the tepid tea, rested her head on the chair and called on Kadie to make an entrance . . .

*When the flogging was done, three crew members dragged Mako to the side of the deck. They chained his hands and left him bleeding. Then they threw his bloodied ear overboard and left him lying there for hours. And we all had to parade past him. And, yes. This one example of how cruel they could be did leave an impression on all of us.*

*I thought being on that deck was the worst thing that could happen to me and Jenneh. And my mother, wherever she was. But I was wrong. In fact, it didn't take long for me to pray to be back on that bloodstained deck, where there was at least fresh air.*

*When the ship was far out in that never-ending ocean, and Mako had been taken away, they began separating us again. How I prayed that maybe this time I'd be placed in the group with my mother. But that didn't happen, and this wretched situation was shortly to become even more tragic.*

*When I was shoved harshly from behind, I grabbed on to Jenneh's hand, pulling her along with me. I found it odd that her hands were cold, even in the heat of the day. She stared at me, and I put my arms around her shoulders, trying to comfort her.*

*"We gotta stay together, Jenneh. You and me will be all right. And I'll keep looking for Mama. I'll find her."*

*Jenneh didn't appear to understand what I was saying, but she followed after me quietly as we stood in a long line.*

*When it was my turn to enter the small door in the deck, I breathed a sigh of relief. It appeared that we were going to be taken down inside the ship, away from the blazing sun. Maybe this was where we would be allowed to rest, and hopefully, be given some food and water.*

*I squeezed Jenneh's hand. "We're gonna get to rest now. And I know they'll give us some food. And water."*

*But when the door opened, the stench that came flooding out of that hold was so intolerably putrid that I fought nausea that welled up in my throat. Surely, something was dead down there. This couldn't be where they were taking us.*

*And I was right about that. There was something dead down in the hold. In fact, there were several dead things in that crypt—which is essentially what it was. And these dead things were all human beings or had been at one time. Now, they looked anything but.*

*My nostrils had never experienced such an assault as this. And then, to my horror, I became sick and emptied my stomach in the corner, where more vile refuse had been deposited. Human waste had been pushed into that corner, right next to the dead bodies. Some of which were adults. Some were children.*

*The hold was quite small, but Jenneh and I could stand, whereas the adult women had to bend over, as the hold was only maybe five feet tall from the ceiling to floor. It was so crowded I could hardly put one foot in front of the other. But still, I held onto Jenneh's hand.*

*Even in my worst nightmare, I couldn't imagine such a scene as what was before me. The word horror wasn't strong enough, but I had no other word. The shrieks of the women and the groans of the dying slithered into my ears and planted themselves in my brain.*

*They're still there today.*

# 36

# Sleepless Night

One look at Andrew's drooping shoulders and Larry's drawn face told their stories. The two weary men arrived at Andrew's place, parked the truck and entered by the front door, leaving their dirty boots on the porch. Both looked like they might drop to the floor at any moment.

Andrew made a suggestion that Larry found quite appealing. "Let's get a shower and find a bite to eat. Then we'll rest a few hours. Start again at daylight."

"Sounds good to me."

"All right. Bathroom's second door on the left. You'll find towels in the bottom of the vanity. Help yourself. I'll see what Norah left us to eat."

After the men showered, they were almost too tired to eat. But Norah's chicken casserole, even when served cold, was delicious. They topped that off with a dish of her peach cobbler and at the end of their meal, Andrew poured them both a small tumbler of Jack Daniel's. His chosen libation.

"Norah would say we need this. For medicinal purposes." He laughed as he took a swallow and felt the mellow, smokey liquid travel down his parched throat.

Andrew searched Larry's face for a moment.

"Larry, do you think . . . " he paused.

Larry understood Andrew's question without him asking it.

"They'll be all right, Andrew. Rosie won't let any harm come to them. They're safer at the Tea House than here in town with some maniac going around shooting people in the forehead."

Andrew didn't argue with him, but in the last few hours, his anxiety level had crept up several notches.

"Yeah. You're right. Okay, you can rest in the guest room. There are two bunk beds in there. Used to be James and Jeremy's, but James has his own place now, and Jeremy's away at the university. We'll grab coffee in the morning and get to searching for Corina."

Larry crawled under the fresh-smelling sheets and pulled the top one up to his chin. There was no air conditioning, but the windows were open and a breeze brought the heady scent of longleaf pine and the enticing aroma of jasmine from the front porch.

And somewhere, somewhere close, a bit of evergreen was growing. But Larry didn't stay awake long enough to enjoy those scents. He was asleep before his brain could take time to sort through such unimportant details.

Andrew, however, tossed and turned for a while before he finally gave in to his body's plea for rest. His mind kept returning to Clemmie, holing up at the Tea House with a black woman she didn't know. And with no electricity. He had no doubt she would be wanting her daddy to come get her. And she'd be scared. Yeah, she'd be scared.

And even though Larry was convinced this Rosie would take care of her, Andrew was more worried about Clemmie than he'd ever been in his life.

Sleep eventually overtook him, and he slept the sleep of the dead. Or near-dead at least. Some three hours later he was awakened. Not by a sound, but by a feeling. Something he couldn't quite put his finger on. An uneasy sensation in his gut. Made him recall what his mother had told him once when he was a small boy.

*Andrew, you must learn to tune in to your body's messages. It knows much more than you might imagine, but you have to pay attention when it's talking to you. Sometimes it might just be an inkling, a sensation you don't quite understand. Something that awakens you from a deep sleep. Something important.*

He sat on the side of the bed for a minute.

*Something that awakens you from a deep sleep.*

He pulled his pants on and walked down the long hallway. He heard the rhythmic sound of Larry snoring as he passed the guestroom door. He made no sound as he padded on, pausing to look into Norah's sewing room, then the closet at the end of the hallway. Nothing. No one. But he still had that nagging feeling. A sense of urgency. But about what?

The back door creaked as he slowly pushed it open. The moon had risen high in the sky, and he gazed across the pasture next to the barn. What did he hear? Nothing unusual. A couple of cows lowed, and Missy snorted in greeting as he passed by her stable. Nothing more.

*Maybe I'm just tired. Maybe it was a dream I can't recall.*

But the feeling didn't abate. If anything, it became even stronger as he went toward the end of the stable, down to the empty stalls where he stored hay for Missy. He walked as far as the tall dog fennel that grew in the far corner of the pasture. Still nothing. He shook his head as if to clear his mind.

That same uneasiness followed him back to his bedroom. He lay on his bed again for a while, then went to the front porch. It was still dark and the only sounds were the skittering of a small covey of quail searching for breakfast.

This was Andrew's favorite time. When darkness yields its hold and gives way to light. A new day is born. He often wondered if that was what happened when a person died. Did death give way to a new beginning? He'd never been given to dwelling much on such subjects until recently. But since his mother died, he found himself pondering such questions as this. At times, he felt her presence even more now that she was gone.

The first soft rays of pale-yellow light came peeping through the pine trees, their boughs still dripping with moisture from last night's rain.

When the yellow tones gave way to deeper shades of orange and finally brighter crimson, it brought to mind the dead man on the road, the one with blood caked on his face.

Was there a maniac on the loose in the community? And on the heels of that depressing thought was another, only slightly less morbid one. Where was Corina? And his mind raced on. Was she dead too?

He went to the kitchen and made a pot of strong coffee. Rummaging around in the pantry, he found Norah had left a tin of muffins. He placed several on a plate, grabbed a cup of the coffee and returned to the porch. He pulled his boots on, and it wasn't long before he heard Larry stirring. A few minutes later, his houseguest appeared with his coffee in hand and joined Andrew on the porch.

"Morning."

"And to you. You sleep all right?"

"That's the best bed I ever slept in. Tell James and Jeremy if it's missing from their bedroom when they come home, they'll know where to find it."

Andrew smiled.

"You? How's your head feeling this morning?" Even from where he sat, Larry could see there was a good size lump of Andrew's forehead, with a bit of bruising around the edges.

"Oh, my head's all right. At least on the outside. But somethin's niggling at the back of my mind. Can't explain it. Just a feeling. It'll sort itself somehow.

"But I was wondering about the body we discovered last night. The look on Cleveland's face was telling. He's got more work than one sheriff can do."

"Yeah, and we got a lot to do ourselves. I suppose we should down this coffee and get on about it."

"Yep. Here, have one of these," Andrew said as he pushed the plate of muffins toward Larry. "Norah left some of her blueberry muffins in the pantry. We'll woof down a couple of these and get on to the sawmill. See what's happened that we don't know about yet. You want to take my truck today? Give yours a rest?" Andrew asked.

Larry smiled. "Nah, might hurt the ol' girl's feelings. And she's shown herself to be dependable even in her old age." He grinned.

They both felt better this morning. A few hours of sleep helped. Andrew pushed that nagging feeling to some far corner of his mind. He'd dwell on that later. This morning he had enough to think about, and Clemmie and Corina were at the top of that list.

~ ~ ~

When they arrived at the sawmill, the menfolk had already begun assembling. And like these two, they were all raring to start doing their part to restore their community to working order. Rufus was relaying information, same as yesterday.

"All right then. Sheriff Burke informs me that several utility trucks and linemen will be coming from McRae. They ought to be here any minute now, so by the end of the day some of us will have electricity. And Stu at Tall Timbers sent Bud Black over again. Early this morning. Woke me up and started reporting before I even had my first cup of coffee. And I ain't in the best of moods when that occurs."

A few chuckles came from the group. Most of them knew how gruff Rufus could be. But they also knew how much he cared for this community.

"Bud said the barriers at the dam are still holding, and the water is flowing at its normal pace. The Corps will be there for as many days as it takes to get everything in order, but there shouldn't be any more floodwater coming down on us."

"Hallelujah. That's good to hear," said Wiley Duncan, one of the older men in the group. He'd had his own accident many years ago when a log fell from one of the logging trucks, pinning his leg beneath it. He had a noticeable limp, but his life had been spared, and he was never one to complain about the chronic pain that accompanied this limp.

"Bennett's got an announcement before we get on to our tasks. And we got enough, that's for sure."

Bennett walked to where Rufus stood with his foot propped on a stump from an oak tree that had been cut down years ago. Bennett needed to stand on the stump since he was quite short. Truth was he wasn't any bigger as a fully grown man than he was when he was fifteen.

"You look like a scrawny pup that never did get anything but the hind tit," his mother had said more than once.

He ran his fingers through his dark, unruly hair, tucked at his shirttail and cleared his throat.

"I just come from the auditorium. Mrs. Watson and Nurse Gould got their hands full. According to Nurse Gould, we got an outbreak of measles there. Right now, there's eleven children with the ailment, and she assures me there'll be more in the coming days."

He rocked to and fro on his heels and toes as he spoke, much like Pastor Evans when he delivered his scalding Sunday morning sermons at Corinth Baptist.

"Well, dealing with measles ain't so bad. Both Jennie's nieces, Margie Nell and Dorothy, had 'em a couple of years ago. They were sick enough all right, but it only lasted a week or so.

"Nurse Gould said it does seem to afflict children often, but she also told me to tell y'all that the whole community, even the grown-ups, are liable to come down with it.

"She believes the fact so many children have come down with the disease in only a couple of days, we might have an epidemic. She also said people die every year from measles, and it seems to be worse on the grown-ups than the children. Don't make sense to me, but that's what she said."

"Did she have any suggestions about how we might avoid getting it?" Thomas asked.

"No. She said we probably can't avoid it, what with so many folks all in the same place where the sickness is.

"And the auditorium was the first place it showed up. I spoke with Jennie this morning—she's helping at Corinth Baptist—and she said they got two cases there already. So, it seems we're doomed."

Rufus took the stage again, lifting his voice so all could hear him. "Well, let's not go so far as to say we're doomed, Bennett. That's that then. Measles or not, we're going to get on with our work. Removing debris from the roadways, checking homes to see if they need repair, and getting stray cows and horses in their proper places. Any other questions? Other announcements?"

Andrew raised his hand to be recognized.

"Andrew?"

Andrew came forward, but being rather tall, didn't need to stand on the stump to be heard.

"There is one more item we need to call to everyone's attention. Last night Larry and I were driving on the McRae Highway searching for strays and checking water levels in the ditches.

"We came across the body of a man lying in the roadway. We hurried to help him, but it was too late. He was already dead. But the thing you need to know, what we all need to think about is this. The man didn't die from being hit by an automobile. He was shot in the forehead."

Several gasps were heard, and mumbling from the group grew louder.

"You mean somebody murdered him?" asked Hoyt.

"Well, I don't know what Sheriff Burke will call it, but he's aware of it and said he'd be on the case. It seems to me that we all should be on our toes. We know everybody in this town pretty much. So, if someone sees a stranger, it might be a good idea to hightail it to the sheriff's office and let him know."

Rufus took a deep breath. "Well, then. That's a bit alarming. And gives us more reason to get moving on our tasks, the first of which is to redouble our efforts at finding Corina Sanderson. So, get on about your work. If you find Corina, come to the mill and give the whistle three quick pulls. Let's get to work."

# 37

# Don't Tell Me Anymore

Rosie shifted in her chair, but it was Kadie who was still holding court . . .

*There were so many of us confined in that place it was unbearable. And it wasn't long before I understood about the piles of human waste in the corner. And the dead bodies close by.*

*Some of the older ones, especially the women, simply couldn't survive the fevers and illnesses that ran rampant down in that hold. When someone died, it might be several days before a crewman would come down and remove the body.*

*Once the crew had gotten everyone sorted, the men and women were kept in separate holds. And the men were secured by leg irons. Most often two chained together. The women were tied or chained at the ankles, but not together.*

*The crew knew they had to keep us alive if they were to receive their payment, so occasionally some of us would be permitted to go on the deck for a while, to breathe the fresh air. Of course, when we weren't chained to the floor, our feet would be tied together with enough rope length to allow us to take small steps.*

*When we'd been down there maybe six days, me and Jenneh were in the group selected to go on deck. I could hardly wait to feel the breeze on my face and see the sun sparkling on the ocean. Once again, I grabbed Jenneh's hand and pulled her along. When we got topside, I found a place along the side rail of the ship and pulled Jenneh next to me as we watched the huge, white-capping waves splash over the deck. I knew that white capping meant there might be bad weather coming, but at the moment I closed my eyes and smiled when the wind lifted my hair. For a moment, I felt almost human again. It was only for a moment, however.*

*Then, one more thing happened before we were shoved down into the hold. As we lined up to go down inside, a group from another compartment was being brought from the opposite end of the ship. Another group of women.*

*From across the deck, I briefly saw a face among the crowd. I could only see her eyes . . . huge, brown eyes with long thick eyelashes. When I saw those eyes, I stared harder, trying to see the entire face. I knew those eyes. Those eyes that could smile even when her lips didn't. Those eyes that leaked water when she found a small bird that had fallen from its nest. Yes, I knew those eyes. My heart fluttered wildly and I felt like singing.*

*When the crowd thinned a bit, I saw the woman's entire face and head . . . a woman with Mama's eyes . . . a woman with tear-stained cheeks . . . a woman without hair . . . a bald woman. And my heart crumbled into small slivers of sadness. No. This woman couldn't be Mama.*

*Shaving a woman's head was one of the favorite punishments the crew would dish out for some behavior they didn't approve of. And this woman's head had been shaved. But Mama had beautiful, long dark hair she kept tied with her many colorful ribbons. A different one each day. No. That bald woman couldn't be Mama. Not Mama.*

*Then—too soon I thought—we were ushered down to the hold again. During that next week, I became weak from lack of food. They brought us beans, yams, and rice. But the bowls they served them in were never washed. Just used again and again each time they brought our food. No wonder there was so much illness on board.*

*I don't know how many days passed before we sailed into a port. When we did, I saw several other ships. Ships like the Wanderer. And I could see dark faces lined up along their rails. Despair and hopelessness stamped into each. It was then that I realized they were a mirror of us. The faces were the same no matter which ship you were on.*

*We picked up even more kidnapped persons at that port, and then we were out in the great water again. I had no idea there was so much water in the world. You couldn't see land in any direction. Then the days ran together, and I quit trying to count them. They were all the same anyway.*

# 38

# *Keep Your Distance*

Nurse Gould and Mrs. Watson—both highly competent women—were at wits' end. Mrs. Watson was accustomed to keeping order in her school and classrooms, and Nurse Gould ran her weekly clinic in an orderly fashion when she made her weekly excursions to the schools to give injections or administer medications.

But this morning both discovered that managing rowdy children was a whole lot easier than dealing with a group of worried, irate mothers.

Mrs. Watson stood tall, lifted her chin, then made another trek across the auditorium, her ever-present, stylish, high-heeled shoes clicking as she moved along. She would make yet another attempt to calm the waters between two women who appeared to be close to blows.

"Move your son's cot to the other side of the room. We don't want his fever on our side!" yelled Tiny.

"The nurse said to put it here, and that's where it's staying!" said Alex.

Mrs. Watson rubbed at her forehead, wrung her hands, and stepped between the two women.

"Alex, Tiny, you need to calm down. Nurse Gould is doing all she can to keep the children's fevers down. Arguing over where to place a cot doesn't help."

"My Robbie doesn't have a fever, Mrs. Watson. And if Alex will keep her son away, maybe he won't get it."

Mrs. Watson glanced around the room and spied Elsie Mae standing in the far corner. Just the person she needed. She called out, "Elsie Mae? Could you give me a hand here?"

Elsie had been her student some years ago, and Mrs. Watson was aware the young woman possessed such a calm nature that she could handle these two women if anyone could.

"Elsie Mae, I wonder if you could help me with Alex and Tiny? They're both a bit worried and need someone to soothe them.

Nurse Gould stopped for a quick moment. Her uniform was still as spotless as when she arrived, but her cap had become askew. She removed the bobby pins, made an adjustment, then, satisfied she was put together again, continued her tasks.

She knew it was too late to do much quarantining since so many folks had assembled in the auditorium, but she could attempt to keep any others from entering. She also had to make a few changes in the room that had become her clinic.

Children with measles were one thing. Adults were something else entirely. She was putting off checking temperatures of adults but would need to do so eventually.

The black folks had pretty much stayed on the right side of the auditorium, and the whites on the left. But with so many children with fevers, all the children would now need to be brought together in order for Nurse Gould to make rounds with her medications and check each child for any new problems. She thought for a moment, then approached Marlee, the attractive, young woman from Smokey Hollow.

"Good morning. Marlee, isn't it?"

"Yes. I'm Marlee Anderson. Theo's wife."

"I'm Thelma Gould, the school nurse. I wonder if I could ask for your help?"

"I'll be glad to help. Tell me what to do."

"Marlee, what I need is two large posters. One to put on the front door of the auditorium and another for the rear door. We must try to stop anyone else coming in here. We also need to make sure each child has his own paper cup to drink from. We don't need anyone sharing anything. If we can manage even a small bit of quarantine, it would be helpful. Would you take care of that for me?"

Marlee nodded and took herself off to find materials for her task. She was glad to have an assignment. Anything to keep her hands and mind busy as Corina's disappearance was constantly on her mind.

Marlee was still struggling with Corina's daughter who had not stopped whining all night. But Corina's son, Luke, appeared to be fine and was playing with one of the white boys in the corner. Skidder had often voiced his opinion that the problems between blacks and whites would ultimately be solved by the children. Watching these two boys today, sharing toys and laughing, she was inclined to believe that was true.

~ ~ ~

Toby and Jesse had stayed the night at Toby's place in the Hollow. They wanted to be there if the water did come flooding in. Wanted to know the extent of damages and be able to report it to the others.

Even though he'd never verbalize it, Toby was feeling a heavy weight on his shoulders. Responsibility for his people. They didn't have a city council like the whites, but it was understood that Skidder was the leader of Smokey Hollow.

Now, with Skidder no longer with them, and without it being said, Toby was aware his people were looking to him to step in. Somehow, he'd never thought of himself as a leader, but the situation at hand demanded that he be one.

As he and Jesse were readying to leave, Andrew and Larry drove up. "Morning, Toby. Jesse. How's it going?" asked Andrew as he climbed out of the truck.

"Mr. Mac." Toby nodded. "The water came over the bank but didn't get into any homes. But we'll have to bring in a big load of sand to build the creek bank to its original height, else next time the water rises, it'll come flooding in here again.

"And there's a huge puddle that covers a large area behind the marketplace. We'll have to fill that in, too. But neither of those are causing any problems at the moment."

"You think you can safely bring your people to their homes?"

"Yessir, I believe I can."

Andrew let out a sigh. "I'd say that's good news. Could use more of that this morning. Wish I had some to report but I'm afraid I don't. When Larry and I were checking downed lines last evening, we came across a dead body on the McRae Highway. The fellow had been shot in the forehead."

Toby's face registered his fear. "What? You mean somebody in this community shot this man?"

"We don't know who shot him, Toby. But we have to be on our toes. Maybe the sheriff will know something more today."

Toby hesitated before his next question. "Was he white or black?" He so hoped this wasn't another incident like the one that took Emmitt Till's life in Mississippi.

Andrew looked directly at Toby before he spoke. He understood what Toby was asking.

"He was white. Not anyone we knew. Don't think he's from this community."

Toby sighed, "Well, I hate to hear about a death. Makes me even more concerned about Corina."

“Yeah. I know what you mean. But that just means we all got to get busy and find her. Today.”

Jesse was quiet, but then he always was. Toby might be the leader, but Jesse would be in his back pocket, ready to step in when needed.

"You know we got a measles outbreak, right?" asked Andrew.

"Is that what's going on there at the auditorium? Marlee told me some of the white children had fever. Didn't know it was measles, though."

"Yeah, and according to Nurse Gould, there are many cases already and she expects there'll be more. So, don't go in the auditorium if you can avoid it. The disease is contagious."

"But I gotta go there at some point, Mr. Mac. Gotta bring my folks home."

"Of course. Find Bennett and ask him to bring the bus again. But right now, all hands are turning to search for Corina. Once we find her, then the two of us need to head to the Tea House, Larry's place, to see about our girls. He thinks they're in good hands with Rosie, his supervisor at the tobacco barn, but we're anxious to get there."

"Yessir. Me and Jesse'll look here one more time. Seems to me Corina would be hiding some place close. Maybe in the morning light she's come to her senses. The death of someone can bring some awful consequences. Corina's a fine lady, you know. Skidder worshiped that woman."

Andrew nodded, "Well, when you leave here, you and Jesse go north like we planned last night, and we’ll take the south route. With the whole town searching, we're bound to find her."

Toby pulled off and Andrew threw out several ideas to Larry about places Corina might have chosen to hide.

Larry listened before he responded. "Well, yeah, those places all sound like where you and I would hide out. Places where you'd be protected, places where you'd see someone coming before they saw you. But, Andrew, that's what logical folk would think, and obviously, Corina's not thinking logically or she wouldn't have left her children.

"When Ellen was alive, she didn't even like leaving Sarah to go to town to get groceries. Women are fearsome when it comes to their children.

"And another thing that baffles me about this woman missing is this. Toby seems to think she's not thinking well and has gone off somewhere. But what if she's not taken off on her own? What if somebody's holding her somewhere?

"I keep picturing that body last night. Who would have thought we'd have such a happening here in Harper's Mill? I don't know. Maybe whoever killed that drifter is holding Corina. There might be more to this than we're considering."

Andrew stared at Larry. "That's a hell of a thought, but you've got a point. Well, whatever the story is, we need to find her. And soon. Let's go."

They met Bennett coming along in the bus and flagged him down to tell him the news regarding the Hollow.

"Everyone's searching for Corina, but it would be helpful if you made it your job to get the black families to their homes. Toby says everything there is all right. But be sure they know they won't have electricity for some time. Maybe not even until tomorrow."

"Yessir. I'll get on to the auditorium. 'Course, Nurse Gould is in charge. And believe me, she's even more of a drill sergeant than Mrs. Watson. If she says I can move them, I'll do it. But the black folk all been in there with the sick children. Don't know what that means."

"Then do what you can. That's all any of us can anyway. See you later."

~ ~ ~

The south end of town was less populated than other areas. The woods were thick with stands of longleaf and loblolly pine, tyty bushes grew to be six feet or more, and walking through that brush, thick with catbrier vines, was difficult. Plus, beggar's lice would attach itself to every inch of clothing you were wearing. Andrew and Larry looked across the huge expanse of pines and a spreading patch of beautyberry shrubs.

"A person could hide anywhere in these shrubs, Andrew. Unless we walk every inch of these woods, we could miss her if she's hiding in here."

Andrew's mind was screaming at him this morning. And the message this morning was the same as last evening. Get to Clementine!

"Got any other ideas?" Andrew asked.

Larry answered by beginning to stride toward the tall loblolly pines up ahead. Andrew went in the opposite direction, covering a lot of ground with his long legs.

"Corina? Corina?" Larry yelled. He reasoned that maybe if she could hear them calling, she'd show herself. He called out again and listened carefully. The only sounds he heard were the calls of two crows, apparently communicating their displeasure at these men invading their space. After a couple of hours of stomping through the woods, the two men returned to the truck.

"Let's move on. I know we decided to cover the south end of town, but it's a bit far for her to have come. I believe Toby had it right. She's still somewhere close to the Hollow. Let's check it out one more time."

Larry nodded. He had no better thoughts himself, so they headed back.

# 39

# *Going Home*

The minute Bennett pulled the belching bus behind the auditorium, Nurse Gould hurried across the parking lot.

"Bennett, I need your assistance, please."

"Yes, ma'am. What can I do?"

"Could you go to Corinth Baptist and see how those people are faring?"

"No need, Nurse Gould. I just come from there. Went by to check on Jennie."

"What did she say? Did she say if anyone had a fever?"

"She said they got two cases of fever. 'Course they ain't got a nurse there, but they're using them thermometers you sent. Like you said."

"I see. Two cases. That makes it more important that we contain these cases here in the auditorium. Which means no one comes in or goes out. And that includes you, Bennett. By the way, have you been checked for fever?"

"No, ma'am. But I'd know if I had one, wouldn't I? I mean, I'm skinny as a rail all right, but I'm healthy as a tick on a hound's hide."

"Maybe so. But since you're here, let me check you over."

She scooted inside, grabbed a thermometer, her stethoscope, a blood pressure cuff and returned. After a quick assessment, she smiled.

"No fever. No rash anywhere. And nothing that appears to be a problem. One thing I would point out, however, is that you need to have that blood pressure checked again. You got a doctor in Brunswick? Or maybe in Savannah or Jacksonville?"

"What? No, ma'am. I ain't got no doctor. Never needed one."

"Well, I suggest you find one, and let him keep a check on your blood pressure. Nothing too concerning today, but still something to keep tabs on."

"I never . . ."

Nurse Gould was already striding toward the auditorium. Bennett called to her. "Wait a minute, Nurse Gould. I been sent to get the black folk. Toby says the Hollow wasn't flooded, so they can go home. I'll take as many as I can on the bus, and make two trips if I need to."

"Oh, what to do, what to do?" Nurse Gould asked herself. She gazed down at her white nursing shoes and reached down to brush a bit of grass from the toes.

"So far, I haven't found an adult with measles here in the auditorium. But it could be that it hasn't manifested itself yet. If I send them home, there's a possibility one of them might still come down with it. And if one, then more than likely others." She took a deep breath and sighed.

"Well, I can't keep them here forever. You stay outside here. I'll get them organized and send them out one by one after I've checked them over."

"Yes, ma'am. I'll wait right here." He went to the bus and sat down in the driver's seat. His thoughts spinning madly.

*What's she talkin' 'bout? I ain't never had nothing wrong with me. And if I tell Jennie what Nurse Gould said, she'll be dragging me to some fancy doctor somewhere. Knowing her, she'll think we gotta go all the way to Savannah or Jacksonville. Humph. Maybe I'll keep this to myself. No need to worry Jennie 'bout something that probably won't amount to a hill of beans anyway.*

Nurse Gould announced that the sick children, along with their mothers, would be staying at the auditorium until she felt they had a handle on this measles outbreak.

She made her rounds of the adults. Still no sign of measles, so she gave her okay and they began to form a line getting ready to go home.

The first to board the bus were the two ladies who were confined to their beds. Two young men lifted them from their cots and placed them into the seat on the first row. One of the women came along and helped get them settled.

Next were the older residents, and that included Rooster and Elvira. Rooster stepped out of the line and was making his way to the kitchen when Elvira spotted him. She watched a moment, then began walking in his direction. When she got within a few feet of him, she coughed. Loudly.

"Rooster? What you doing? Get yourself back in line. We going home."

"But I ain't ready to go. The ladies in the kitchen said we would be having lunch any minute now. I don't want to miss that. They gonna be serving blackberry cobbler. They told me that already."

Elvira crept closer. When she reached Rooster, she stomped her cane on the floor. "We going, Rooster. And we going now."

Rooster nodded as if that had been his plan all along. He'd learned long ago that no argument would ever be won with this woman, even if she was only five feet tall.

Elvira stomped her cane once again. "And I make my own blackberry cobbler, you feeble-minded old coot."

Bennett stood at the front of the bus and made a headcount. Didn't want to go losing anyone else. That woman named Corina still hadn't been found, and that had everybody concerned.

He'd been at the sawmill early this morning and, along with the other men, learned the story about the body Andrew and Larry found on the McRae Highway. Guess he'd better lock the doors tonight. That was disturbing to him. No one ever locked their doors in Harper's Mill. No need. No telling how many more changes would come as a result of this flood. And Bennett didn't welcome changes. They were kinda like doctors. Not much needed in his opinion.

As the bus pulled to the marketplace in the Hollow, Bennett smiled to himself. The place didn't appear to have suffered much from the water. He saw a large puddle behind the marketplace, but even as he watched, two men were already shoveling dirt to keep it from spreading.

Everyone waited patiently as the two young men once again lifted the two invalids from their seats and carried them to their beds in their homes.

Then the old folks began to disembark, with Elvira leading the way. Rooster followed along behind her, and as they stepped off the bus he pulled at Elvira's sleeve.

"So, when you serving my lunch? And I'd like some of that blackberry cobbler you said you make." He stepped forward and left Elvira grinning behind his back.

# 40

# *Are We Finished?*

Rosie stopped her monologue a moment and closed her eyes, her head still leaning against the chair. Clementine waited, hoping her question would be answered. When Rosie didn't begin again, she kept quiet. Maybe Dean would ask Rosie to continue. It sounded as if he liked to hear the story again and again.

Clementine had never heard of the Gullah/Geechee people. She knew about the Native Americans who were here before the Spanish and a little about the slavery years and how the black folk had been mistreated. But Gullah people were not ones she ever heard anyone speak of.

Apparently, Rosie needed a rest as a few seconds later her soft, even breathing told Clementine she was asleep. Looking over at Dean, lying on the floor, Clementine could tell he was sleeping as well. Sarah, still wrapped in her blanket, hadn't moved since Rosie placed her on her pallet.

Clementine stood, walked to the large, damask-covered sofa and borrowed a larger pillow. The one Dean had given her was quite small. She sat down, placed the pillow on the floor, then took the blanket Dean had brought her and snugged it around her legs.

With everyone sleeping and no one making noise, Clementine smiled when she heard the *diga-diga-diga* call of the pine woods tree frog. Then their cousin, the Southern cricket frog, joined in with their metallic *gick* notes, and somewhere in the distance she heard the nasal *quanks* of the green tree frogs. This amphibian chorus was comforting to Clementine. Sounds of her world. Sounds of home.

As she lay quietly on the floor of this grand mansion, her mind kept presenting her with images of Kadie and what her life must have been like.

*Could I have survived such an ordeal? No, I don't think so. Any time I have a problem Daddy or Granddaddy always make it go away. Is that a good thing? To have someone who always makes things right? Will I ever be able to figure things out on my own?*

*Were my ancestors as strong as Kadie? Did they suffer similar happenings in their lives and I just don't know about it? I know they came from Scotland, but that's all I know. Why hasn't anyone told me more? Is there something they don't want me to know? When I get home, I'll ask Granddaddy and Aunt Maori to tell me our story. The whole thing. Like Rosie's story. And maybe I'll memorize it like she did.*

Her last thought before succumbing to the suggestion coming from her heavy eyelids was that she fervently hoped this last passage Rosie had relayed wasn't the end of the story. So far, this story was a sad one. She might have called it a tale, but a tale was usually something someone made up, not a true happening. Sadly, this wasn't a tale.

It was a true story about a girl her age who had nothing to live for. She had been taken from her home, her land, and finally, from her mother. No. This couldn't be the end. No one would retell a story that ended like this. Then, as had Rosie, she rested her eyes for a moment, and these four survivors let their bodies have a short moment of peace.

# 41

# Pigeons and Bobcats

As soon as Bennett arrived at Smokey Hollow, he was helping get the oldsters inside their homes.

"Here, take my arm," he called to an old woman who appeared to be having difficulty climbing the steps to her house. She was wrapped in a colorful shawl and wore a red wool hat despite the heat.

She looked at him a moment before she nodded and reached out toward him. Bennett took her hand, so wrinkled and thin it made him wonder if she was sick. His own grandmother's hands had looked like that in her last days. Tissue-paper thin and small as a child's hands. He wouldn't think on that right now. And, no, he wouldn't think about Nurse Gould's comments about his blood pressure either. Not today.

"I assume Nurse Gould gave them a clean bill of health, else you wouldn't have brought them home," said Andrew as he approached Bennett.

"Yeah. She says none of the adults have fever at the moment, but she didn't know what tomorrow might bring. And she won't let anyone in or out of the auditorium. She's insistent the place be quarantined."

Larry breathed a sigh of relief. "Well, that's one good thing, Andrew. At least Clemmie and Sarah haven't been exposed to the disease."

"Yeah, but I gotta tell you, Larry. If we haven't found Corina by late afternoon, I think the two of us should take a jon boat and get ourselves to your Tea House. But before we head there, I need to go by Daddy's place. Check on him. It's not far past Lirey. I'm not worried, but still.

"And I know him. He'll be there, sittin' on his front porch readin' his latest Louis L'Amour western novel. But I'll feel better if I lay eyes on him."

"Then let's take the path behind the church where we searched yesterday. We'll go the back way to Lirey, to your daddy's place. You're right. It's not much farther. Let's make sure he's all right."

This time when Larry started the truck, it sputtered for a couple of seconds before it caught, and then the engine began to purr. Larry chuckled. "Don't go quitting on me now, gal. We're not done yet."

They rolled on past the old church, the one where Skidder's funeral had taken place, and Andrew could still hear that soul tingling, uplifting music ringing in his head.

On they drove, past the old settlement where the turpentine distilling plant had been years ago. They bumped along across the rough ground, some of it still covered with clumps of the sticky, amber resin commonly called turpentine gum.

Turpentine had been a booming industry in many places in the early 1900s, and these piney woods were the ideal place for a plant. Today the small, round pebbles of resin sparkled in the sun. Larry stopped the truck and they got out for a moment to take a look around. Andrew bent down and picked up one of the amber clumps.

"Clemmie's spent more time with Daddy and Nana than she has with me and Norah. The boys always liked staying with them, too. But not like Clemmie. She says they listen better than we do.

"She used to collect these pebbles. Called these bits of resin 'amber diamonds' and would string them on a piece of twine and wear them as a necklace. Guess she thinks she's too old for that now."

He pocketed a couple anyway. Maybe he'd take them to her at the Tea House. A reminder of one of her special places. They made several walkabouts through the fields and the old remains. Nothing.

"Think I'll take a quick turn around the old house again. Maybe the ceilin' won't crash on my head," Andrew said.

He stood for a moment at one of the doorways, the one going into what would have been the kitchen.

"Look here, Larry. Marks at various heights. A blue one, a red one, and a green one. That's probably one for each son. Norah and I made those same kinds of markings on our wall in the hallway."

Larry ran a finger across the markings. "Hmm. Hadn't thought to do that with Sarah. But not a bad idea. See how she's growing."

Andrew went on. "On her eleventh birthday, in January, we made a mark for Clemmie and I had to laugh. The boys were taller at age seven than she is at eleven. That's when Norah and I realized Clemmie apparently inherited many of her physical traits from my mother."

After convincing themselves Corina was nowhere in the area, Andrew and Larry moved on toward Lirey, another three miles farther into the forest. They jostled across a rickety bridge where dark water flowed silently beneath, bits of wiregrass floating along.

Crossing the bridge meant they were close to their destination. They ambled up the long, gravel driveway to Andrew's boyhood home. His mother had planted azaleas along both sides of the driveway, just as Norah had planted crape myrtles on theirs when they first bought their place.

Larry stopped the truck, sat a moment and took a long look at the house. "I always liked this dogtrot-style house."

"Well, it's not exactly the Tea House," Andrew said with a laugh, "but I like it too. When I was a boy I would streak down through that open hallway in the center, my dog, Buddy, trottin' alongside me. I'd be chasing my sister, her screaming as she tried to outrun me. Mother would be yelling, 'Stop runnin' in the house, you two. Andrew, you and that dog need to get in the yard if you're going to tromp around like a herd of wild horses. And you, Carrie, young ladies shouldn't scurry about like senseless chickens.'"

He grinned as he recalled how Carrie squealed with delight as he got closer on her heels. The older Andrew got, the more important he realized memories were. At some point, they were all one had of those who had gone on. He looked out the truck window and chuckled. Larry twisted his head toward him.

"Don't know what you're finding funny, but I'd sure like to hear it."

Then he took a closer look and laughed aloud as well. There, as Andrew had predicted, was his father, Dougie MacKinnon, puttering about his pigeon coop which was located on the west side of the house.

What had the two of them chuckling was obvious. The old man was wearing his usual attire of a light-blue chambray shirt and a threadbare pair of stained khaki pants. With his ever-present pipe hanging from his mouth. And a small Louis L'Amour paperback book sticking out of his back pocket.

"As I said, there he is, safe and sound. And that book in his back pocket will be dog-eared he'll have read it so many times. When Mother was alive, she made a point of getting the latest Louis L'Amour novel when she went to Jacksonville or Brunswick, but now he just rereads the old ones. Says he can't remember them anyway."

Larry nodded. He was glad to see the old man. He was tall and thin, and still had a head full of hair. Silver now. And Andrew looked so much like him it was uncanny.

Larry pulled the truck off the driveway and parked under a giant oak tree, its limbs draped with long strands of Spanish moss, and resurrection fern growing along the trunk. It was a good place to park in this heat.

They walked past a stack of firewood that was placed alongside the chimney and then to the large pigeon coop where pigeons squawked their disapproval at their presence.

Dougie smiled, "Son, you didn't need to come out here. I'm fine. I know you got more important things to be doing, what with that damn flood tearing through every stream and waterway within a hundred miles."

Neither of the two was given to expressing much emotion, but Andrew went closer and placed his hand on his father's shoulder.

"Figured you were all right, or I'd have come sooner. But glad to see you and the place are in one piece."

"Course I am. Takes more'n a flood to get rid of a MacKinnon," he muttered.

"The biggest problem I got today is that blasted bobcat that keeps prowlin' about my pigeon coop. I saw him in the early light this morning, so I'm gonna set a trap for him today. Those pigeons are good eating for him, but as far as I'm concerned, he's had his last supper. How's your place? Any damage? Norah and my girl all right?"

"No, Daddy, no damage. Everything's good. Norah's in Brunswick checking on her Aunt Alice. And Clemmie's fine."

The old man nodded then and greeted Larry.

"Larry, what are you doing down here in these parts? Surely, you're needed at the tobacco barn. I know the

Appahoochee lies between here and there, and all those creeks gotta be flooding out in the woods everywhere. Some of them are bound to be going through your fields."

"It's a long story, sir. I was down here when the dam broke, and Sheriff Burke and Stu at Tall Timbers Station said no one could get across the river yet. But this morning, Rufus said Stu passed on that the dam was holding. So soon as we're finished with our assigned task, we're headed to my place."

"I see. So, what task you two been assigned?"

Andrew took control of the conversation then. He didn't want Larry to let on that Clemmie was at the Tea House. Andrew had no doubt her granddaddy would swim across the Appahoochee if he thought she was in danger.

"The whole community is out searching for Skidder's wife, Corina. You remember Skidder? He worked for me for years."

"Of course. He came here to Lirey once and helped me when your mother wanted a couple of trees removed from the side yard. Fine fellow. But wasn't he the one who was killed recently? Or was that somebody else?"

"No, that's the one. His wife, Corina, has been missing since everyone from Smokey Hollow had to be moved to the auditorium at the elementary school. For fear the place may be overrun by the water. Everyone is accounted for except Corina. We're putting every man available on the case."

"Anything I can do? I'm still able to turn my hand to whatever you might need."

"Thanks. We got it covered. But there is one more thing I feel you need to be made aware of. Last night we came across a dead body on the McRae Highway. Think the fellow may have been one of the hobos that frequent the area. He'd been shot in the forehead, so that's kinda got everyone on edge.

“The sheriff's working on it, but I don't think he knows much yet. Anyway, he suggests we all keep our doors locked and our eyes and ears tuned in to anything unusual."

Dougie shook his head as if in disbelief.

"I've lived here my entire life, and I don't believe we've ever had a murder. Lord, but I'm glad your mother isn't alive to know about that. She'd have me sitting on the front porch pointing my .410 at anything that moves."

They all laughed at that, probably as a way to smother the fear they all felt but certainly wouldn't' give voice to. Maybe not even to themselves.

"Daddy, if you need anything you can come to the house, you know. You don't have to stay here in these woods all alone."

"I'm never alone here, Andrew. There's a family of raccoons hiding out in the barn, where a huge barn owl was already residing. And if you take a peek in that spreading oak every morning, you'll see a red-tailed hawk when he comes screaming in like a fighter pilot. And after a couple of minutes, his female mate will fly in and join him. And on that bottom limb of that small pear tree, a wren has set up housekeeping. Got three eggs in her nest. As I said, I'm never alone."

Andrew smiled. At least this part of his family was secure. Now, if only they could find this woman. But as he'd told Larry earlier, if they hadn't found her by afternoon, then he was going to find a way to get to the Tea House. He wasn't going to let another night pass without making sure Clemmie was safe and home with her family.

"All right then. It's back to the sawmill. See if there've been any new developments. I’m not sure if the folks at Corinth Baptist will be allowed to go home yet. Bennett said they have two cases of measles there. In any case, we’ll go by what Nurse Gould says.”

"Get going, then. Go on with you," smiled Dougie.

Larry glanced at Andrew and held his breath when he attempted to start the engine. It made a deep thump-thump and then died. He shook his head.

"She's trying to tell us something, Andrew."

But then he stomped on the starter again and after a few spats and splutters, she finally found her second wind and hummed along as if nothing had happened. Larry reached out and patted the dashboard as if the old truck were a dog who'd obeyed a command from her master. "Good girl, good girl."

When they arrived at the sawmill, there was a buzzing sound. But it wasn't coming from the usual saws that were always humming in the background. Instead, it was coming from the many men gathered about. There was a lot of chatter, but the men's faces told the same story. Corina was still missing, and there didn't seem to be anyplace else to look.

Rufus spoke up. "It's noon already, and I think we gotta' realize that finding Corina will take some time. I know you men need to get home to your families and attend to whatever issues you may have at your place. So, I say we gather here again in the morning, maybe at eight o'clock. That will give everyone a few hours to recover, and we'll know more about how the community has weathered this flood.

"Sheriff Burke will come by and give us an update on the tragedy on McRae Highway, which is one problem I wish we didn't have. Not that you need to be reminded, but he suggests you lock your doors tonight. Anybody got any questions or comments?"

Toby raised his hand.

"Yes, Toby. What's on your mind?"

"I understand what you saying, Mr. Rufus, but me and Jesse gonna keep looking for Corina. Skidder was my friend, and my conscience won't let me rest if I stop looking for her. So, that's what me and Jesse going to do. Keep on looking."

Then Dewey spoke up, "We all gonna keep looking, too, Rufus. Ain't much that can't wait at our places."

"All right then. Yeah. Skidder had many friends, and I agree with you. Y'all keep on searching, but you all gotta get some rest at some point. I still say Corina will show up, and she'll have a perfectly good reason that will explain where she's been." Toby nodded and walked over to stand with Andrew and Larry.

"Mr. Mac, I know you and Mr. Sutherland gotta' check on your girls, and that's the right thing to do. Y'all do what you gotta do and me and Jesse'll keep looking. Ain't no way in hell that woman hightailed it and left her children. No way.

"I didn't want to mention it in front of everybody, but I'm getting worried now that maybe whoever killed the man on the McRae Highway might be holding Corina somewhere."

Andrew nodded, "Sometimes our imaginations can run away with us, Toby. Mine's been clawing at me all day picturing Clemmie floating down the Appahoochee calling for me. I understand your thinking. So, yeah, you men go on. If we don't see you before, we'll catch you tomorrow."

# 42

# Mothers and Daughters

A couple of hours passed and Rosie awoke, feeling as if she'd slept for an entire night. She scanned the room without moving her head. The kerosene lamps were still glowing softly, and the large parlor had a warm, welcoming feeling.

Sarah was sleeping soundly and Dean turned over, carefully, as he'd learned to do since his bout with polio. Then she glanced at Clementine. The girl was sitting against the wall, frantically writing on her pad. Rosie cocked her head to one side. She stood, stretched her long, thin arms and motioned to Clementine to come with her.

"Where we going, Rosie?" whispered Clementine as she stood, the long shirt she wore falling below her knees. Mr. Sutherland would probably laugh if he could see her wearing it. But it covered her well and was cleaner than her dungarees and tee shirt.

She was barefoot as her tennis shoes were so caked with mud and grass that she'd had to throw them in the trash. But her braid was still intact, even though several strands of hair had escaped and wispy curls appeared all around her head, reminding her that some things just couldn't be tamed.

"Just making a bathroom call. Then Rosie'll make a fresh pot of tea. When it gets daylight, we'll use the Sterno stove and have some kind of breakfast if we can find some eggs and bread."

Clementine was thankful for the bathroom visit and hurried to the kitchen to help Rosie with the tea. Shortly afterward, she heard the clank of Dean's crutches as he answered his call to nature.

It was still dark out, and Clementine had no idea what time it was. Did it even matter? However, she did realize she felt refreshed after a few hours of sleep. And the more time passed, the sooner Daddy would come for her.

When Dean got to the kitchen, he took over the tea making, as he appeared to know how to perform that task. As soon as they got their tea, they all sat down in their accustomed places. Rosie in her chair. Dean and Clementine leaning against the wall.

Clemmie looked at Dean and took a chance on a bit of conversation. "You make really good tea, Dean. Is there something special you do that makes it so good?"

"No, silly, there's nothin'—" He was just before dishing out a smart-ass response, but then checked his razorblade tongue. He'd not forgotten Rosie's harsh words. For her to speak to him in such a manner meant he'd really tried her patience.

But this girl had surprised him. He could tell she was as interested in Rosie's story as he was. So, instead of blistering her with another spiteful remark, he continued, "Nah, just gotta know exactly how long to let it steep. Even a minute too long will change the flavor."

Clementine nodded and offered a small smile. She had so many questions she wanted to ask. How did he get polio? Would he ever walk without his crutches? Might he get it again?

She was sure her brothers would have said, "Too many questions, Clemmie." So, she thought it might be better to listen.

Once Rosie finished her tea and held the cup in her hand, Clementine knew they would continue. She simply had to know if Kadie ever found her mother.

Rosie looked at the two listeners. "It'll be daylight soon, and we comin' on to the last part of the story now. Some of this part is hard to tell. And even harder to hear. So, Clementine, if you need to close yo' ears, or leave the room, Rosie understands.

"I know the story by heart, and this part still hurts when I tell it. But the story is the story. And if you leave anything out, then you've not been true to yo' people and haven't been true to yoself, either."

She sat straight, leaned back in her chair, and sighed aloud. "Now, y'all. As I said, this part is truly going to be difficult. Just so you know."

Then, in a matter of seconds, her voice tone changed and Kadie took the stage again . . .

*We'd been on the ship for weeks. I can't remember how many, but I learned that if I stayed up close to the door of the hold when it was time for our compartment to go topside, Jenneh and I could be among the first ones on deck. And if we hurried, we could find a place along the rail. The breeze was always better there, and the hideous odors of the dead bodies and the waste in the hold below were gone . . . if for only a short while.*

*Then there was that morning when we marched along side by side. The guards had stopped tying our ankles together. Guess by now they saw we were too small and scared to cause many problems.*

*We passed another group moving on the other side, across from us. I looked and then I looked again. Hoping to see that woman, the one I had seen and thought might be my mother.*

*Two of the women looked like older versions of me and Jenneh. One was clinging to the other, and the shorter one pulled at her hair as if pulling it might ease some pain somewhere. She had bald spots all over her head, so I guessed she must have been doing this a while.*

*Then, out of the corner of my eye, I spied a thin woman wearing a purple dress wrapped around her body and tied at her waist with a bit of rope. It was that woman again. The woman with the shaved head. For a moment I wondered if she had pulled her hair out, too. But no. Her shiny head had to have been shaved with a straight razor. It all but sparkled in the sunlight. And once I made myself stare—longer than I knew I should—I began to cry.*

*I saw the amulet hanging around her neck, a beautiful piece made from the kapok tree . . . circular in shape . . . the one Mama always wore . . . to protect her from evil she'd said.*

*My first impulse was to scream out to her, but I'd already seen what a disaster that would cause. Flogging was the usual. But I couldn't stop the tears when they began to fall. I didn't know whether I was crying out of despair, or for joy.*

*Yes, this was Mama. My wonderful, loving, beautiful Mama. I continued to stare, and then I realized her eyes were sending me messages. The same messages mine were sending her: I see you, my precious one. I see you. We have to survive. We have to survive.*

*But my heartfelt joy was short-lived. When we began to be herded and lined up to enter the holds again, I glanced one last time at Mama. She and the shorter woman were being dragged along the deck, both of them screaming, begging to be released. Their feet were tied together, so they couldn't even kick out at their captors.*

*Once they reached the front of the ship, the crew threw them to the deck, and like Mako, their clothing was stripped from their bodies and several men held them down. Even at my young age, I knew what would happen next.*

*As I entered the hold, Mama's scream was the last thing I heard.*

# 43

# A Woman's Tears

When Andrew and Larry started to leave the sawmill, both held their breath as they climbed into the truck.

"You can do it, old gal. You can do it," coached Larry. He cast a glance to Andrew, who sat there with a quirky smile on his face.

"Keep your fingers crossed," Larry said.

The old girl had done her duty. He turned the key in the ignition, stomped the starter on the floor, and she cranked right away, rumbling deeply like she did in her early days. Then she settled in with a rhythmic, soft hum that meant all cylinders were firing and she was raring to go once again.

The two men grinned and headed to Andrew's home. He decided when they got to his place, they'd use his relatively new Chevy pickup and give Larry's old truck a rest.

Entering the front door, Andrew said, "Let's get a quick sandwich then move on."

"We need to find a boat somewhere, Andrew. The Appahoochee is pretty wide up there where the bridge is. Or was. I'm sure it was washed away. Should have been replaced years ago. Probably after the last flood, which my father told me happened when he was a young man."

"James and Jeremy have an old wooden jon boat in one of the empty stalls in the stables where they keep it covered under a tarp. Last I knew, they had a decent five-horsepower Evinrude motor on it. That's all we need to get across the river."

"Sounds good," said Larry. "Once we get across, we'll have to hike a couple of miles or so to reach the tobacco fields and my barn. Then the Tea House is another quarter mile or so and straight uphill. I expect it weathered everything just fine," he said, maybe to reassure himself as much as for Andrew's benefit.

Only now was he beginning to let his mind wonder. What had happened to his workers? Their families? Until now, he'd only thought about Sarah and Rosie. But what about Jeremiah? His place was on high ground, but Larry knew the old fella would have tried to get to the Tea House this morning come hell or high water . . . which was exactly what the case appeared to be.

Andrew nodded. "I hope so. You'll find some peanut butter and jelly in the pantry. Make us a couple of sandwiches, and I'll go hook the boat to my truck. Won't take a minute."

He scurried out the back door. Noting that he might need to install a proper lock on it, what with some idiot going around shooting folks.

Andrew was aware that with James and Jeremy gone the place wasn't kept quite as well as he liked. He had to step over a couple of old tires he should have taken to the clay pit long ago. And over by the stable, the grass was waist-high.

He stepped into Missy's stall and was greeted with a snort and a head nudging his hand, hoping for an apple or treat as Clemmie would have brought. He then realized he had not thought to feed her this morning. Clemmie usually took care of that chore.

Missy's stall was the only occupied one now, as the boys had outgrown riding and sold their ponies long ago. As soon as they became teenagers old enough to drive, they were more interested in trucks than ponies and horses.

He quickly tossed a few cups of oats in Missy's trough, checked her water, then moved toward the stall where the jon boat was kept. The boat needed a new coat of paint but appeared to be in fair condition.

When he yanked the starter cord, the Evinrude responded in a flash. He hitched the boat to his pickup, checking to make sure the turn signals on the trailer were working. James and Jeremy had gotten more than one ticket for not having proper lights on the trailer. After they'd had to cough up money for the fines, they made sure they were in working order.

He made one more pass by Missy's stall and stroked the white blaze streaking down the pony's face. He was about to leave when, just for a brief moment, he thought he heard a noise, a whimper. Probably another critter Clemmie found and brought to the barn to nurse back to health. Most likely a kitten or baby squirrel.

He listened closely, and at first there was complete silence. Then he heard the whimper again and followed the sound past the last stall to a tack room where he stored Clemmie's leather saddle, her bridles and other items that needed to be protected from the elements.

He halted for a moment before he jerked the door open. When he did, he jumped back so quickly he lost his footing and landed on his butt.

The whimper became a desperate cry.

"No! Don't hurt me! Please, no! Don't hurt me!"

Corina was curled up in the far corner, cowering down in a deep pile of hay, clutching a horse blanket. She inched her body even farther into the corner as if afraid Andrew might try to grab her or harm her in some way.

Andrew stared for a moment, then got to his knees. He'd seen frightened faces many times, but nothing like the fear on Corina's face. Her eyes, beautiful dark orbs in her small, delicate face, shifted back and forth from one side of the room to the other, then searched his face as if afraid of what his next move might be.

"Corina? It's me, Andrew MacKinnon. I'm not going to hurt you. You know that, Corina."

But he wasn't sure she could even hear him. Her wild-eyed look told him to keep still and make no attempt at getting closer.

Corina stared for a moment, then blinked several times. Andrew stayed still.

"It's all right, Corina. No one's going to hurt you. Let me help you."

Corina craned her head to one side as if to see if anyone else was behind him. Andrew waited, knowing if he reached for her she would only retreat farther into the corner of the room. And maybe farther back into her mind as well.

"Mr. Mac? Is that you?"

"Yes, Corina. It's me. Everything's all right. Come. Take my hand. Let me help you," he said as he reached out to her.

She didn't take his hand, but slowly crawled from the corner and stood. Bits of hay clung to her flower-print dress, which had been torn from her left shoulder and was barely hanging on. She again looked behind Andrew as if expecting to see someone or something there. Andrew waited patiently.

*God Almighty but I wish Nana was here.*

His mother had a way of seeing into folks' souls, a trait he wished she'd passed on to him. But she wasn't here, so he'd have to work through this on his own.

"Let's get to the house. Get you some food. And maybe some coffee."

Corina nodded. "He's not here, is he? Please tell me he's not here."

"Who, Corina? Who's not here?"

"That man. That white man, Mr. Mac."

"What white man, Corina? Someone you know?"

She shook her head. "No. Not someone I know. I've never seen him before, but I won't ever forget his face."

Andrew scanned her face closely, and when he did his heart skipped a beat. Dried blood was caked near her hairline and the right side of her face was swollen. Even with her dark skin, he saw a large area of bruising, and her upper lip had a cut that was seeping blood.

"You're hurt, Corina. Did this man do this to you?"

She nodded and tears began to stream of their own accord. Andrew decided he'd better get her inside before he questioned her any further. He'd thought things were already bad, but they had just gotten a whole lot worse.

"Come on. Let's go in. Get you some coffee."

"No, Mr. Mac. There's something I need to tell you first. But if I do, then you'll turn me in to the sheriff."

"Corina, I'm not going to do anything but get you inside and give you a strong cup of coffee. Come on. You can tell me whatever you need to inside."

He reached his hand out to her again. She looked into his eyes before taking it, then she grabbed Andrew's arm with both hands as if she needed something to anchor herself to.

"I'll help you, Corina. Come on now."

"I was afraid he'd followed me."

Andrew held her arm and observed that she limped as she walked along beside him. When they came into the house, Larry had his back to the door and called out, "Sandwiches ready. Let's down them and get going."

When he looked around, he saw Andrew standing in the doorway with a small, black woman. A young woman with a face that could have graced *Ebony* magazine. High cheekbones and narrow face. Almost childlike. So striking. She clung to Andrew's arm with both hands, as if afraid to let go.

"Larry Sutherland, this is Corina Sanderson. The woman we've been searching for."

Larry smiled. "Ma'am. Am I ever glad to see you."

Corina nodded but didn't speak. She knew of Mr. Sutherland but had never met him.

"Corina's been through an ordeal, Larry. We need to let her tell us the story. See what we can do to help her sort through it. Maybe some coffee would be a good idea."

Larry nodded, poured three coffees, and they sat around the kitchen table. Andrew sat next to Corina and put his hand over hers.

"Corina, whatever has happened is finished now. You're safe here with us."

He expected her to begin telling her tale, but instead, she immediately broke down into slobbering, heart-wrenching sobs. The two men looked at each other, each hoping the other may have some words of comfort to offer the distraught woman. They were both in over their heads.

"Mr. Mac, I don't know what has happened to my babies! When I left the cemetery, I could barely walk, but I made my way home. But everybody was gone. There was no one around anywhere. My house was empty, the church was empty. The marketplace was shut. I was alone. And it was dark.

"So I did what Skidder told me to do if I was ever in trouble and he wasn't around. I walked to your place. I came through the backwoods, which took a long time, and I hid in your barn. But I must have fallen asleep.

"When I knocked this morning, you must have already left. No one answered. I went into the kitchen, but no one was there. I waited a few minutes, then decided it was safer to go back to that tack room and hide again. I mean, that man may have watched me. Maybe followed me here. I don't know, Mr. Mac! I don't know!"

She sobbed loudly and Andrew pulled out a handkerchief and offered it to her, but she ignored it. Larry left the table and poured them all another cup. His mother would have given them tea, but coffee would work as well, and for a moment he was tempted to put a taste of Jack Daniel’s in there as well.

Andrew was continuing to try to soothe Corina. "First things first. Your children are fine. Marlee and Theo took them to the auditorium at the elementary school. And I'm sure they're still in Marlee’s care. Nurse Gould is ramrodding the show there, as we've had an outbreak of measles, and any child who has a fever is being cared for by her. So, fever or not, they're in good hands."

"Oh, thank the Lord. Marlee is a good friend." Her sobbing subsided a bit, which was a relief to both Andrew and Larry.

"Now, tell me about this man. What happened?"

Corina shifted in her chair, pulled at her torn dress, trying to keep it on her shoulder. Then once again she looked around, as if still afraid someone was going to grab her.

"Well, Mr. Mac, when they said we all had to leave I got everything in order. I put a change of clothes in a valise for the children and one for myself. And I put Gracie's rag doll in the valise, too. She needs that to go to sleep. Surely, I thought, we wouldn't be gone from our home for too long. But there was one more thing I needed to do.

“You see, Mr. Mac, I had to go to the cemetery. I had to tell Skidder what was going on and let him know why I wouldn't be there that evening to talk to him. I go every evening, just before dark, and tell him how my day went.

“That's what he always wanted to know when he came home from working with you in the woods. He'd clean up and then sit in the kitchen while I got our supper ready. He wanted every detail. What the children had done, and what I had done to keep myself busy. His childhood had been difficult and he wanted better for Luke and Gracie. He didn't want to miss anything in their young lives."

Andrew listened. Was Corina not thinking straight as some were saying? Or was she still in such agony over Skidder's death that she was coping as best she could?

Andrew couldn't find anything wrong with talking to those who had gone on. He, himself, had visited his mother's grave several times already. And when his sister had died when he was a young boy, he had often thought he saw her in a crowd or walking down the street. He had gone to her gravesite many times over the years.

No, he didn't think Corina was not thinking straight. He simply thought she needed time to deal with her loss. Still, he refrained from throwing too many questions at her and waited for her to continue. When Corina finally reached for his handkerchief, his fingers briefly touched hers and he felt the tremble pulsing through her body. At that point, he ventured to try to get more information.

"Now, if you can, tell us what happened to you. It might be important."

Andrew's mind was working a double shift. A flood, a measles epidemic, a dead man on the highway, and now a woman who had obviously been attacked. Good God, could it get any worse?

Corina pulled again at her torn dress, trying to arrange it on her bare shoulder. Andrew left the table for a moment and brought a soft, thin sweater from Norah's closet and draped it across Corina's shoulder. She smiled briefly, nodded, and began her tale.

"You were at Skidder's funeral, Mr. Mac. And he would appreciate that fact. And if you recall, his grave is way back on the far side of the cemetery. That's where his brother is buried, so I had him placed there, too."

Andrew nodded.

"I hurried down to that side of the cemetery and started telling Skidder about the flood and how we needed to leave for a couple of days, but that we'd be back and I'd come and tell him all the details. Then, after I'd been talking to him for a few minutes, I leaned down to place a bouquet of flowers on his grave. Petunias from my garden. And the next thing I knew I was flat on my stomach. On top of Skidder's grave!

"I couldn't move my head. I couldn't see what or who was holding me down. But I felt something metal poking me in the back of my head. It was a gun, Mr. Mac, a pistol!

"I kept still. I wanted to scream, but the breath was done gone out of me. I couldn't move a muscle. The man on top of me was so heavy. I was trapped.

"When he finally raised up slightly, enough for me to breathe, I scrambled to my knees, but he quickly flipped me on my back and began tearing at my dress. I kicked him in the stomach, but he just laughed and fell on top of me again.

"The next thing I knew, he laid that pistol aside and grabbed my wrists and held both of them above my head with one of his huge hands. He was pulling at my clothes with his other hand. And I guess the good Lord was looking out for me because I managed to free one of my hands and grab that pistol. And before I even thought about it, I pointed it at him and pulled the trigger. It jerked my hand so hard I dropped it. And the sound was so loud it hurt my ears. And that sound echoed for the longest time.

"Then he pushed up again like he was going to get off me, but then he collapsed on top of me again. And this time he felt even heavier. He was a really big man, Mr. Mac. Even bigger than my Skidder, and you know how big he was."

Andrew and Larry were spellbound. Neither thought it was a good idea to ask anything, but hoped she'd continue. Or perhaps they hoped she wouldn't. They knew the remainder of the story would be difficult to hear. Andrew, however, needed to know as much as possible.

“Did he . . ."

Corina understood the question even if he never completed it because she was sure the intention was just that. Rape.

"No, Mr. Mac. I stopped him with his own pistol. It took all I could do to wiggle my way from under that weight. But when I did, I felt something sticky on my dress. It was getting on to dark by then, but even in that twilight, I knew it was blood.

“Then I saw a dark stream flowing from beneath that man and spreading to Skidder's grave, weaving through my bouquet of petunias. I didn't look again; I just threw that pistol as far into the bushes as I could and took off running. And I ran until I couldn't breathe. Until I had to stop. It was then that I remembered what Skidder had told me once.

“He said, 'If you are ever in trouble, Corina, and you can’t find me, you get yourself to Mr. Mac's place. He'll know what to do.’

"But Mr. Mac? I don't know if that man's dead or alive. He was bleeding something awful when I last looked at him. I might have even killed him! I don’t know. But he was bleeding a lot. I don't know, but maybe he followed me? Or maybe he's dead? I don't know!"

Her sobbing was uncontrollable. Andrew held her hand in his and let her cry until she simply had no tears left.

Larry cleared away the cups and set them in the sink. Andrew helped Corina stand. "Why don't you get yourself cleaned up in the bathroom. I'll find something of Norah's for you to change into. She's small like you, so that should work." He led her to the bathroom and brought a pink-striped shirtwaist dress with a belt for her to change into.

Andrew now had a new situation to deal with. Should he report this to Sheriff Burke, or keep it to himself for a while at least? Corina was in no shape to undergo the questioning the sheriff would be obligated to put her through. He thought for a moment, then joined Larry where he was sitting on the porch, so deep in thought Andrew had to call his name twice before he heard him.

“Larry?” He waited a moment. “Larry?”

“What? Oh, sorry. Just daydreaming for a moment. I was wondering how one community can deal with so many issues at one time. And that woman in there, she's one heck of a lady. She might be sobbing, but she fought that man off and made her way here. She reminds me of my mother, able to deal with trying situations better than most. Always better than my father.

“Ellen had that quality, too. Even in her last days, she didn't let cancer change her attitude regarding life and how it should be lived. I think Corina has some backbone that will carry her through this ordeal."

"Yeah, but now we need to decide whether to take her to the sheriff's office or take her to see her children."

Larry shrugged. "Not a question as far as I'm concerned. She needs to see her children. Everything else can wait."

"But what if this man is still out there? Maybe preying on some other woman?" Andrew didn't like that thought.

"Well, certainly sounds like she wounded him. I doubt he's giving a lot of thought to chasing her or any other woman. Probably laying low or hoping to find a place to hide, maybe trying to get medical help somewhere. Either way, I don't think he's much of a problem at the moment."

"But if he's alive, he might have found that pistol Corina threw into the bushes. Which brings me to another question. Do you think maybe he's the same one who shot the man on the McRae Highway? I'm no weapons expert, but I would bet that hole in that man's forehead came from a pistol. Could be the same person maybe?"

"Christ! Hadn't considered that. No matter. I still say we take her to the auditorium and let her see her children."

"I agree. We'll take her there, and we'll get on about getting to our girls. Sheriff Burke won't be too happy with us, but that's his problem. We've got our own to deal with."

# 44

# Hold On

Rosie glanced out the front windows of the Tea House. The first golden tinge of light could be seen creeping along the horizon. Stretching upward, desperately struggling to make claim on a new day.

This night of tale-telling had been her way of coping with the disaster that would certainly have ramifications yet untold. She prayed this new day would bring sunshine and hope. Something they could all use.

She was continuing to tell her story, the story of her and Dean's people, to a young white girl who knew nothing of the tragedies of Rosie's people, but who was so eager to learn that Rosie felt compelled to finish it.

Would the story be re-told by this child? Would she even understand that it wasn't a story, but a true accounting of a grievous time that still brought tears to many in today's world?

Rosie thought about stopping the story at this point, but from the looks on Clementine's and Dean's faces, she knew she must complete the tale. And whether he knew it or not, she felt that each time Dean heard it he would commit another piece of it to memory. After all, he would soon be the only one who could pass it on. But to whom? Dean was unlikely to find a woman to marry, so who was she hoping he'd tell this story to?

Well, if for no other reason than she'd promised *Keke,* Rosie would never let the story die. It needed to be told, and she'd kept her promise. Now, as she glanced at that small white girl, so enthralled with the story that she barely even blinked, she had a thought she'd never considered before.

Rosie was sure similar stories had been written, but they would have been written by a historian. A researcher. And would simply state facts and figures.

But would a first-hand account of the Middle Passage give more insight than a historical document might? What if white folks could hear this story? What if Dean perhaps even put it down on paper? Would it then become a story that could be told again and again?

She was quite sure many of the barn workers had ancestors who'd suffered the same hideous tortures as hers. But they may not even know about them.

But why tell the story other than to keep it alive for herself and others whose ancestors had similar ones? To Rosie, that was an easy question. If the story were told enough times, maybe such inhumane treatment of anyone would never be allowed to happen again. And yet, she recalled *Keke* talking about how the Jewish people were killed and persecuted in the last war. Was that any different than what occurred in slavery times?

So, with that thought, she rested her head on the back of the chair and let Kadie continue spinning her tale . . .

*Even though I held my hands over my ears, Mama's screams still rang in my head. But just the fact I had seen her gave me reason to hope. For what I wasn't sure. But now that I knew she was alive, I could endure the daily hardships of existence.*

*I could hardly bear to go down into the hold again, but the alternative was that I would be beaten to a bloody pulp if I refused. And so far, my ankles were only rubbed raw and swollen, not like those of some of the women who had been on board longer. Their ankles had festering wounds often riddled with maggots eating away at their flesh.*

*Some slaves, so miserable they couldn't endure any longer, would try to starve themselves by refusing to eat. But if they did so, they'd be whipped or held down and force-fed by the crew.*

*As my brain tried to make sense of all this, it became quite simple. At least in my child's mind. Slaves had no choice but to endure horrific conditions. And now that I knew Mama was still alive, I would endure. I had to endure.*

*Once I'd made that decision—to endure no matter what—I no longer wished or hoped we'd have more than one meal a day. I no longer wished or hoped we'd be given water more than once a day. I no longer wished or hoped the dead bodies and human waste would be removed more often. None of that mattered. I would endure. I would survive.*

*It didn't take long for us to learn that if the ship ran low on drinking water, the crew would throw some of us overboard to make sure the rest of us survived. They needed live slaves when they arrived at their destination. They didn't get money for dead ones.*

*The ones who were truly past being able to make even another day figured a way out of their misery. A way to escape this unbearable captivity. They would simply walk to the ship's rail and step off.*

*In my weeks onboard the Wanderer, I'd observed that schools of sharks would follow the ship. I suppose they were as hungry as we were, and following a slave ship was an easy way to get a meal.*

*And, to tell the entire truth—which I am determined to do—even some of the crew were subjected to cruelty, too. If they became sick, which they often did, from the same conditions they inflicted on us, they would be thrown in the ocean just as quickly as we would have been.*

*The women, such as Mama, were allowed more freedom than men. I guess they were considered less of a threat, and often went on deck and helped with the cooking. But, as I had witnessed, they paid a price for this bit of freedom by being subjected to constant sexual harassment and rape, either at the hands of the crew or the captain himself. I suppose the fact that Jenneh and I were only eleven was why we escaped such treatment.*

*As the weeks dragged on, I only saw Mama a few more times, and always from a distance. But she still wore that amulet, and I decided it was doing what she always said. In some way, it was protecting her from evil. I was sure that if it hadn't been protecting her, she'd have disappeared long ago. I had to hold on to my hope that we'd be together again. I no longer even had to utter a prayer or say the words. They were simply the mantra that ran through my mind all day, every day: We will be together again, Mama.*

*And I was sure I heard the message being carried on the waves, the constant waves as the ship continued to plow through the churning water.*

*We will be together again, Mama.*

# 45

# *Mamas and Babies*

By the time Corina returned to the kitchen, wearing Norah's dress that fit perfectly, Andrew and Larry were in agreement about how to proceed. Corina had arranged her hair, and the dried blood in her hairline had been washed away. But the bruise on her cheek was quite large, and it would take some time for her split lip to heal.

Her wild-eyed look had abated and been replaced by an expression that spoke of one who had sustained an ordeal and was now resolved to move on to whatever life held next.

"I'm ready now, Mr. Mac. Could you please take me to my children?"

"That's where we're headed. But I do need to ask you one more question, if I may."

"Yessir. What do you need to know?"

"Would you recognize this man if you saw him again?"

"I'd know him anywhere. As I said, he's a giant of a man. And he's white. And unless he's found some different clothes to wear, he'll be easy to spot."

"Why's that?" Andrew asked.

"He was wearin' a uniform, Mr. Mac. A striped uniform. You know, the black and white striped uniform the chain gang wears when they're out working on the side of the road."

Andrew and Larry exchanged a meaningful look. Most states had passed laws forbidding outfitting prisoners in black and white striped uniforms, but there were a few places that were behind on implementing the new law. So, it was certainly possible Corina was correct.

"You mean he's a prisoner?"

"Yessir. And he'll have a hard time finding any clothes big enough for him to wear."

"Well, that changes things a bit. But we're still going to take you to see your children first. And Corina, I'll have to tell Sheriff Burke about this man. But don't you worry. If you did kill him, it was certainly in self-defense. And if you didn't, the sheriff and the Department of Corrections will be searching for him already. You leave this problem with me and Larry. We'll sort through it.

"But there's one thing we have to do before we take you to the auditorium. We gotta go by the sawmill and pull that whistle three times. That's the signal that means we've found you. Every man in the community has been searching for you, Corina, and they'll all be happy to know you're safe."

Corina reached up and placed her hands together in front of her face. "Oh, my Lord! I never thought of that. I'm sorry I caused so much trouble, Mr. Mac. I can't say anything else. I was confused. As I said, without Skidder I don't know what to do sometimes."

"Not to worry, Corina. Let's get to that sawmill. This will be one time I'm glad to let that whistle blast off."

"There's one more thing, Mr. Mac."

Andrew nodded. "What's that?"

"If I was you, I wouldn't leave dirty cups in the sink. Took me two years to teach Skidder to wash things up. And

I'm sure Mrs. Mac won't like coming into the kitchen with dirty dishes and utensils in her sink."

Andrew and Larry shared a quick smile, "You're right. She'd have a few choice words to say to me. Thanks, Corina."

Larry rinsed the cups and placed them face down on a tea towel. Andrew turned to Corina and grinned.

"No, thank you, Mr. Mac. Some days I don't think I can make it without Skidder. But I still have Gracie and Luke, and they're what keeps me going."

The three pulled up to the sawmill, jon boat in tow. Rufus and a half-dozen other men were sharing various bits of information about what conditions they had found in their areas of town.

"Rufus, give that whistle three loud pulls," Andrew called as he stepped up on the porch of the sawmill.

"You mean you've found Corina?" Rufus hurried to the steps where Andrew was standing.

"Yep. She's in the truck with Larry, and we're headed to the auditorium so she can see her children."

"Thanks be to God."

"I'll give you details later, but pull that whistle now and let the others know the good news."

The three screaming blasts could be heard throughout the community, and what a welcome sound it was.

When they arrived at the auditorium, Larry helped Corina from the truck, and she looked around. The only person she saw was Eddie, the janitor. Nurse Gould had him doing duty as a security guard, meaning he had to stop folk from coming or going into the auditorium.

Just then, another truck wheeled in next to Andrew's. Toby jumped out. When he saw Corina, he ran to her and pulled her close. "Corina, Corina, Corina. Where have you been, woman?"

Toby and Skidder had been friends since childhood, and Corina was ever so glad to be held close by such a caring friend.

He held her at arm's length and saw her bruised face and cut on her lip.

"What's happened to you? You need a doctor?"

"No, Toby. I'm fine. I'll tell you about it later, but right now I want to hold my children. Can you help me find them?"

Toby led the way, and Jesse stood by the truck. He didn't want to go in that place full of measles, and that Nurse Gould lady had a table full of sharp needles!

Andrew and Larry talked for a minute with Eddie, and he nodded to Corina as she entered the rear door of the auditorium. There were cots all around the room, and Nurse Gould was giving instructions to several women.

"Isabel? Can you take a final count of the children with fever? I need to know if we're making any progress here."

Isabel was a teacher in the elementary school. She'd volunteered to help Nurse Gould with the children as she'd already had measles so was not concerned about getting it again. Where there had been chaos yesterday, today the place was functioning as if a drill sergeant was in charge, as indeed she was.

Marlee spotted Corina at the doorway. She grinned and waved to her. "Over here, Corina. We're over here."

Corina didn't wait for Nurse Gould to give her the okay, she just fled to the cots where Gracie and Luke were lying. She tried to hold back her tears, but they flowed despite her efforts.

"Oh, my babies! My babies!"

Nurse Gould gave her a couple of minutes to embrace the two, then made her way to them. "Well, then. I believe seeing you is much better medicine than any I've given these two." She smiled and moved on to the next cot.

Marlee explained that both had come down with the measles yesterday, but were doing well, eating, drinking, and Nurse Gould believed the epidemic was coming to a halt.

"Then I can take them home?" asked Corina.

Marlee frowned, "I don't get to make that decision. Nurse Gould is in charge here. Let's see what she has to say."

Toby spoke with Andrew and Larry for a few minutes and assured them he'd stay close by Corina until he felt she was able to manage on her own.

"Skidder has come to my aid more times than I can count on all my fingers and toes. I owe him. Between me and Jesse, she'll be watched over."

Andrew and Larry left then, both anxious to get to their children. How close they could get to the tobacco farm depended on how wide the Appahoochee was at the bridge. The one they both knew was no longer there.

# 46

# Night Prowler

After Andrew and Larry left that morning, old Mr. Mac, Dougie, went searching for a trap for his nocturnal prowler.

Once he had trapped him, he'd call the Wildlife Refuge Center in McRae to come get him. If they couldn't take him, then the Four Paws Center in Brunswick might.

He rambled around in the smokehouse, which these days wasn't used to smoke anything, but was more of a catch-all for things Nana always said he didn't need but simply couldn't part with. Like most folks his age, he'd not forgotten the Depression days, and something within him wanted to hold on to most everything, even if he never used it again.

After turning the smokehouse upside down, he thought he had finally found what he was searching for. A couple of traps to capture his worrisome visitor. But upon closer inspection, he changed his mind.

*Nah. That cat is too large to fit into either of these cages. I gotta have something else.*

When he dug down inside an ancient wooden trunk—something he'd saved from his Army days—he came across the perfect item.

*All right, then. This paw-grip trap will do a number on you, my pesky little friend. It'll grab your paw, but it won't kill you. 'Course when I release that trap, you might want to lunge at me. But then I'm not planning on being the one to do that. I'll leave that bit of fun to the wildlife ranger. Today, I'm just taking care of my pigeons.*

The trap was a bit rusty, but Dougie thought it would catch its prey in one quick, grabbing motion if he put a little oil on it. Next, he dug a small hole at the rear of the pigeon coop, precisely at the place where he'd seen the cat's tracks yesterday.

*I'm certain you can't resist this can of sardines. Even if you don't try to get into my pigeon coop, the lure of sardines will be too inviting for you to ignore.*

He placed the fish in the hole and covered it with several inches of pine straw. After he fed the pigeons, gathered the eggs from his dozen or so chickens and shooed off a few potracking guineas, he poured himself a glass of sweet tea and mosied to the front porch.

Then he pulled his Louis L'Amour novel from his back pocket-an older one he particularly liked, *The Rustlers of West Fork*—and picked up where he'd left off yesterday.

# 47

# Morning has Broken

Rosie had talked so long her voice was beginning to crack and her throat felt scratchy. She stopped, cleared her throat, then turned her head toward the kitchen. Listening.

*Was that a voice? I know somebody was talking. I'm not so old I'm hearin' voices, so I know I heard someone. And they're outside that kitchen door.*

She held her finger to her lips, meaning for Clementine and Dean to keep quiet. Dean began to rise, but Rosie shook her head and whispered, "No, Dean. Y'all be quiet. Don't move."

Then she stood, grabbed one of Dean's crutches and headed to the kitchen door. She hadn't seen any lights coming up the lane, which meant whoever was outside had come on foot.

Rosie wasn't one to panic or worry about "what might be" situations, but she figured this flood may have caused many folks to be seeking shelter, someplace to be safe from the rising water. Or to do any number of other things she didn't particularly want to think about, like looting fine homes such as the Tea House.

After that thought registered, she continued toward the door that led off the kitchen. A quick moment of unbridled fear produced a rush of adrenaline as she reached the door. She raised the crutch above her head, fully prepared to bring it down on whomever was coming in.

When the door swung open it almost hit her in the face, but she still brought that heavy crutch down, barely missing her target. The crutch slammed to the floor with such a thud it made her arms tremble.

"Oh, what in the world?" she screamed as she backed away from the door.

Old Jeremiah stood there, neatly dressed in his black jacket and matching string tie holding his stiff, white collar together. This was the uniform old Mrs. Sutherland had thought appropriate for him. And, if truth be told, he enjoyed dressing in it. It spoke of his importance in the household.

He opened his eyes wide and stared at Rosie with an expression that matched hers. Frightened down to his toes.

"Rosie? What you doing? Tryin' to break my head? And what you doing here in the Tea House?"

Rosie put her hand to her throat.

"Dear me, Jeremiah. You pretty near scared me to death. I heard someone talking, but I didn't know what to make of that, it still being dark and who knows what's going on out there after this flood."

"I talk to myself all the time, Rosie. And I come here every morning just before sunrise. Like Mr. Sutherland wants me to. I open the doors, turn a couple of lights on, make a pot of coffee, fix him a small bite of breakfast, and as soon as it's light, I sweep the brick walkway. They's always something to do to keep this big place in order."

"Your place didn't get washed away then?"

"Nah. The roof leaks in a couple of places, but it's always been that way."

"Then that's a blessing. I'm afraid to see what my place looks like. Although, it's on stilts, so I expect I'll be all right. But there's gotta be some trash from all that water. And you won't ever hear me complaining 'bout climbing them steps anymore."

Jeremiah poked his head to the side, peering about the room. "Where's Mr. Sutherland? He not heah?"

Relaxing a bit now that the frightening situation had passed, Rosie explained to Jeremiah what had occurred. "No, he went down to Harper's Mill yesterday, so I 'spect he got stranded down there. And there is no way that bridge over the Appahoochee is still standing. So, I don't know when he might get here. But he will. I know he will."

Jeremiah closed the door behind him. "When I saw a light in the window, I thought maybe Mr. Sutherland was up early, maybe reading. He does that sometimes."

"The lights you see are from our kerosene lamps. We been having storytelling time. I guess you could call it that."

Jeremiah raised his eyebrows. "That so? Yesterday, that young white girl was having storytelling time with Miss Sarah. She reads real fast, too."

Rosie was not surprised to hear that. "I see. Well, tonight I was not reading but was telling the story of me and Dean's people. The Gullah folk."

"You don't say. Wish I'd heard that story. My gran come from South Carolina, and she said our people up that way is called Gullah."

"That right? *Keke* told me that some of our ancestors, who all come from the African slaves, still live in the Sea Islands. He said those in South Carolina are called Gullah. And those in Georgia, like me and Dean, and my sister, Tonja, and *Keke* and Vanna before they passed, they're called Geechee. I say Gullah/Geechee as that seems to cover everyone, 'cause I do know Kadie lived in South Carolina for a long while, you see?"

"Who's Kadie?"

"She's the ancestor my story tells about."

"Uh-huh," Jeremiah nodded. "I'm glad you came to the Tea House with Miss Sarah, but why you sitting in the dark, using them old kerosene lamps?"

Rosie smiled. "Well, it's not only me and Sarah. Dean's here, and so is Clementine, you know, the young white girl that showed up at the barn yesterday."

"What? She heah, too?"

"She missed the bus, so I brought her heah. And she's not what we might have thought. I figured she couldn't do much of anything, but that's far from the truth.

"She saved the horses and the mules, and Mr. Sutherland's hounds, too. She went tearing down to the stable and the dog pen in that pouring rain and let 'em all go free."

Jeremiah smiled, "Well, I'll be. You know it'll be light soon, but I can turn the lights on now. They do make it easier to see things."

"Don't think you can do that, Jeremiah. The 'lectricity is off everywhere, and I haven't seen any trucks coming to repair anything during the night."

"We don't need to wait for any repair, Rosie. All I gotta do is go to the shed and start the generator."

Rosie began to laugh. "I didn't know nothing 'bout a generator, but we spent the night occupying ourselves just the same."

Jeremiah stepped into the parlor and saw Dean and Clementine sitting side by side. Dean appeared to be showing her some of his drawings. "So, the young ones been drawing, I see. And Miss Sarah?"

Rosie pointed to the dining room, where the child still slept.

Jeremiah shook his head. "Looks like she's dead to the world. Sometimes when I get here early, she's already downstairs. And she talks to me while I'm making Mr. Sutherland's coffee. She misses her mama something awful."

Clementine and Dean glanced up as Jeremiah greeted them. "Well, how 'bout I make my usual coffee, find us some leftover biscuits and blueberry jelly, and we have ourselves some breakfast. Since Miz Ellen passed, I make something for Mr. Sutherland every morning. But he don't want much. Usually only his coffee and maybe a biscuit."

"Jeremiah, you have just become my favorite man," Rosie said, and the old man shook his head and started toward the kitchen.

Rosie came back to the parlor and was relieved to see Dean and Clementine conversing and him showing her his drawings. Perhaps sharing her story had made it possible for these two, opposites in more ways than skin color, to find neutral grounds to meet on.

It wasn't long before the aroma of Jeremiah's coffee filled the room. This coffee was a blend Jeremiah himself had created: a few spoons of Maxwell House, a few spoons of the brand called Eight O'clock, and the most important ingredient—to Jeremiah at least—a few dashes of Luzianne Premium Blend Coffee, because it contained that special taste he loved. Chicory. And Mr. Sutherland always raved about Jeremiah's coffee.

Rosie looked again out the windows, gazing at the eastern sky which had now become amber and rose.

*What will this day bring? Ain't no doubt in my mind that the bridge will be gone and water will be flowing out into the woods. How many people are homeless? And what about the tobacco fields? My life and the other workers' lives depend on that tobacco. Will we all still have jobs? And what about the old ones who can't care for themselves?*

She closed her eyes and uttered a prayer; the same one she prayed every morning: *I can do all things through Him who strengthens me.* She could no longer remember the particular place in the Good Book where the passage was found but thought it was somewhere in Isaiah. Or maybe Philippians. But it didn't matter. She would continue to repeat it as she had her entire life. It was her mantra.

A small voice from the dining room broke her reverie. "Rosie? Is Daddy here? I think I heard his truck."

Sarah slowly edged into the parlor, dragging her Madame Alexander doll behind her. She rubbed her eyes and looked around. Then a smile lit her small face.

"Jeremiah's here! I smell his coffee!"

She hurried to the kitchen, and Jeremiah greeted her with a big smile and his usual question.

"And how is Miss Sarah this fine morning?"

The old man was fond of the child, and his heart ached when she would ask him to tell her stories about her mother. It was as if she couldn't remember everything herself, but liked to hear him tell about her. He'd put her on his knee and begin a tale, a true one, but he may have embellished the tale just a tad.

“Oh my,” he would say. “Yo’ mama would dress you in one of them lacy, fine dresses, tie a pretty little bonnet on yo’ head, and push that fancy baby carriage down the brick walkway. And later, after the sun went down, she would sit in her favorite rocking chair and sing the sweetest lullaby you ever heard.”

Jeremiah’s job didn't require much in the way of physical labor, but these days he had an even more important position. He was the keeper of memories for this child.

"Jeremiah, is Daddy lost?" Sarah asked as she came closer.

"What you talking 'bout, Miss Sarah? Yo’ daddy knows every inch of these woods. He couldn't get lost if he tried. You don't need to worry 'bout him. It’s daylight now, and he'll be coming this way. Ain't no broke bridge gonna keep him from coming home to you.

“Come on in heah, now. We gonna have our breakfast in the parlor. 'Course yo’ grandma wouldn't normally have approved of that, I ‘spect, but I think she'd be understanding in this circumstance."

"Are we having biscuits?"

"For sure. Along with blueberry jelly.”

He brought a large tray with everything arranged in perfect order. He was in his element now. Doing his job. Being needed.

Clementine was not accustomed to coffee but didn't make a fuss when Jeremiah handed her a cup.

Dean, who had been standing for a few minutes in order to get the blood circulating in his legs, sat back down and took two biscuits along with his coffee.

Rosie wasn't much of one for breakfast, but she took the coffee and munched on a biscuit.

"I can't make yo’ plans for the day, Rosie, but I think Mr. Sutherland would want us all to stay here 'til he comes,” Jeremiah said.

“When I was walking from my house this morning, I saw a couple of wild hogs rushing through the woods. I 'spect there are other wild things moving around, too. Normally, they wouldn't bother folk, but they be looking for food and might not be too choosy 'bout what they eat just now."

Rosie nodded. "We'll do that. Stay here until Mr. Sutherland comes."

Clementine hadn't spoken, but the question she had was burning a hole in her tongue. Finally, she could stand it no longer.

"Jeremiah, your coffee and biscuits are good. Like Nana's.”

Then she turned to Rosie. “I was just wondering something. Rosie, are you going to finish Kadie’s story?"

Rosie sighed and looked at Jeremiah. "I'd like to finish my story, Jeremiah, but it might not be something you'll enjoy listening to. It's 'bout the Gullah/Geechee people we were discussing earlier."

"Well, Rosie, if my gran was Gullah, then I gotta have some of that blood in me, too. She told me some things about the slave days, about their music and dancin', but not a lot.

"Course, she had trouble remembering things, 'specially when she got older. I want to hear your story, too. Let me pull up a chair from the dining room. I can't sit on that floor like these young'uns can."

Rosie nodded, "We're coming to the end, but maybe one day I'll tell it again and you can hear the whole thing. And if you don't mind, Jeremiah, let's leave the kerosene lamps burning. I think Kadie likes those lamps with their soft light when she's talking to us."

The coffee had hit the spot, and Rosie was energized once again. She looked at Clementine, who had her pad and pencil in hand. The young girl would remember this night and tell her own story to someone. Someday.

Rosie clamped her lips together, took a deep breath, and with the lamps casting wavering, soft shadows on the walls and in dimly lit corners, she summoned Kadie once more . . .

*I lost count of the weeks because every day was the same as the day before. The floggings, the starvation, the raping of the women, the rotting, revolting, reeking bodies in the hold. This was our daily existence. And I now began to wonder if it would ever end.*

*Then came the day of the storm. The wind was so violent it had the ship all but laying on its side, and enormous, foam-filled waves crashed over the railings.*

*But earlier that same morning, the sun was shining, and even the great water appeared to be taking a rest. No whitecaps were seen anywhere. A perfect day.*

*Me and Jenneh had been among the first groups to be taken on deck, and we lived for those moments. We'd throw our heads back and let our faces bask in the warmth of the sun, and for a while we'd pretend we were home, lying on our backs in the lagoon in our village, letting the water lap over our bodies and telling each other our deepest secrets.*

*It was only a couple of hours later when the chief crewman, the one who manned the tall sail where he could see for miles, called out, "Get 'em below. Bad weather's coming. Get on with it now. I see lightning in them clouds ahead."*

*Even though we were not chained together, Jenneh stuck by my side like a young child clings to her mother's skirts. And since she had quit speaking on the first day, she only communicated by gesture. But I didn't mind. There wasn't much we needed to say anyway. Perhaps by keeping our worrisome thoughts to ourselves, one didn't add to the misery of the other.*

*We managed to stay far at the end of the long line, hoping to stay out as long as we possibly could. One of the guards came up behind us and grabbed Jenneh by her hair, pulling her close to his large, sweaty body. But she still held my hand. Then he leaned down close to her face and slowly ran his grubby fingers down her cheek.*

*"Next time you two pretty things come on deck, maybe we'll have a bit of fun with you. Look at you. You both just about ripe."*

*He pushed us along then, laughing behind our backs. Suddenly, the wind changed directions, jerking the ship about, and there was such force behind the wind that several women fell to their knees on the deck. The crew immediately lashed them with their leather whips and yelled at them to keep moving.*

*A scorching bolt of lightning seared across the sky, and the deafening rumble of thunder that followed had everyone scurrying along. Within minutes, Jenneh and I were drenched, our clothing dripping, and we smelled even worse than usual. Jenneh stood still for a moment. As if she couldn't move.*

*"Hurry, Jenneh," I said, tugging at her hand, trying to get her to move along.*

*"We could be struck by lightning, and if we don't move on, they'll flog us for sure."*

*Jenneh turned to me, and for the first time since we boarded the ship, she let go of my hand. Then she took my face in both her hands and caressed my cheeks. I wondered what she was trying to tell me, but I knew it was pointless to ask. She never responded to any questions or statements.*

*Then she quietly walked to the railing, and before I could even call her name, she climbed over. I screamed, then ran to the rail and watched as the greedy ocean swallowed her in one quick swirl of murky water. And I prayed that it snuffed out her life before the sharks could get a whiff of her sweet body.*

# 48

# Daddy's Coming

After Toby stepped in to take care of Corina, Andrew and Larry headed to the Tea House. As they left the edge of town and passed the "*Jesus is Coming*" billboard, Andrew snickered.

"Well, Jesus, this might be a good day for you to make an appearance!"

Larry grinned, but Andrew had no doubt he understood this was indeed a prayer, not merely some comment to lighten their mood.

Somehow, finding Corina had freed the minds of both Andrew and Larry, which might not have been a good thing because now they were both imagining all the horrendous events that could have happened to their girls.

Andrew tried to keep his imagination in check, but he was well aware of Clemmie's penchant for charging ahead before checking things out. If anything harmful was about to happen to an animal, she'd jump in with both feet trying to save it from injury.

And it was obvious that Larry simply refused to entertain any ideas of something disastrous happening to Sarah.

"Larry, have you considered that if Rosie's grandson was in trouble, then she might have left our girls and gone to help him?"

"No. She'd have figured out some way to help all of them. Trust me, Andrew. She's an exceptional woman."

Andrew nodded, but he figured Rosie must be getting on in years now, and surely that was something to be concerned about.

They continued driving. Slowly now as water was collecting in places you'd never expect to see it. Andrew knew exactly where the Appahoochee bridge was located. Six miles north of the now-defunct, drive-in movie theater.

The drive-in had been a success for many years, but was finally closed down because the owner got too old to keep the speakers in working order, and it seemed every teenager in the area delighted in tearing them from their posts.

About two miles beyond the drive-in, Andrew slowed down. Water was standing on both sides of the highway, and he watched as a long, smokey-gray snake swished through the ditch. Like Clemmie, he wasn't too fond of snakes himself.

"Larry, there's no telling what kind of wildlife we might encounter."

"Yep, I was just thinking that myself. I keep a rifle in the rack in my truck, but that's at your place."

"Yeah, and I gave up hunting some time ago. Clemmie goes crazy if I even talk about hunting anymore. No matter. Never was a very good shot anyway." He smiled.

They traveled another mile and water now covered the road, reaching far out into the forest. Andrew stomped on the brakes and brought the truck to a screeching halt.

"Good God! This is where the Appahoochee Bridge ought to be," he yelled as he saw nothing but acres of water.

"Yeah. But it's long gone now," answered Larry.

The only portion of the bridge that was visible today was a small section of that rusted, dilapidated truss Clemmie had seen on her bus trip yesterday morning. Today it was laying on its side, trapped in tree branches with water swirling about it.

"Well, I guess this is where we launch the boat. Hope we don't get the truck stuck in the mud," Andrew said.

He turned the truck off and Larry got out, released the winch, and the small boat floated off the trailer easily. Andrew then pulled the truck to higher ground, and they waded into the water and climbed aboard.

"It's not far now. Maybe two-three miles. We'll get as close to the barn as possible, but no telling what we'll find once we get there."

Until now Larry had not given much thought to his tobacco fields, the barn, his animals, or even his employees. He was somewhat chagrined when he realized he'd only been thinking of Sarah, the only family he had left. And Rosie, of course.

What about his workers? Most of the younger ones had children, and some others were getting on in age. What if their homes had been flooded? And the tobacco crop? This was how he survived, and his workers only survived if he did.

He shook his head. "My mother used to say, 'Son, don't borrow tomorrow's troubles. Just take care of what you can today.' Guess that was pretty good advice. But not so easy to follow."

Andrew opened the throttle, but with only a five-horsepower outboard, they moved at a slower than desired pace.

"At least we'll get there before dark. Then maybe this nightmare can come to a close," Andrew commented. The old Evinrude puttered along, and in a few minutes, they could see the tobacco fields in the distance.

"Thanks be to God for small favors," Larry murmured as they motored closer. Water was standing everywhere, but the barn was still erect and appeared to have survived the onslaught of water that would have come through it.

"Could be a lot worse, Andrew. I'll know more once I walk the fields. Most of the crop's already been brought in, but this last bit will be a loss for sure. I'll need to have the soil tested and see if anything can be salvaged." His mind was running rampant thinking about things he'd need to do to get his tobacco fields in order.

"Later we'll see if any of the mules and horses survived. Right now, though, let's get on to the Tea House."

Andrew had been to the tobacco barn numerous times but had never been inside the Tea House. His mother had toured it one Christmas when it was one of the homes the Garden Club ladies were showcasing. She'd said it was quite impressive. Of course, that was when Larry's grandmother, old Mrs. Sutherland, was still living. Somehow, Andrew couldn't see Larry opening the place for a Christmas gathering.

Andrew was already guiding the boat down to a small creek that would bring them closer to their destination. Larry nodded as they made the next corner. But shortly they were in a predicament. The water had become so dammed up with debris there was no room for the jon boat to get through.

"All right. I think we'll have to stop here. We're going to get wet up to our asses anyway we do this, so might as well start walking."

Andrew tied the boat to a cypress stump and they climbed out. Larry was right. They were now waist-deep in water and Andrew struggled to keep his thoughts of moccasins from rushing through his mind. When he lifted his head and saw the stately, two-story home at the top of the hill, his heart beat faster. Clemmie would be here. He'd bring her home now.

With the rays of the sun glinting off the sparkling windows, Andrew thought the place might just look like the

"*Mansion Over the Hilltop*" that the church choir sang about every Sunday morning. Or at least the mornings when he occasionally attended services.

# 49

# Gunslinger Territory

Dougie closed his book. No matter how many times he read this particular novel, it was still his favorite. Louis L'Amour had a way of ending all his books that left a reader satisfied and wanting to read another one. Catriona (Cat) often chided him about reading his books more than once.

She'd stand in front of him, hands on her tiny waist and stare up at him. "Dougie MacKinnon, I do believe you would have liked living in the Old West days. As for me, I prefer the present time, when we women are allowed to vote, and we have modern conveniences such as a Frigidaire and a washing machine. But I still don't want a dryer. I prefer to hang my clothes on a clothesline. There's no fresher smell than clothes that have been dried in the sunshine."

"Yeah? Well, Cat, my darlin', it's probably a good thing you didn't live back in the Old West days because they'd have hanged you early on and you'd be fertilizing tumbleweed up on Boot Hill. They didn't care much for highly opinionated women in those days."

Then he'd laugh, and she'd give him a smile that made his heart sing. She was gone now, but he had enough memories that he could recall a fresh one every day and never run out of them.

He'd thought he might ride into town and see if Clemmie needed anything. Andrew would be busy for who knew how long. But as he started to the carport, a stand-alone building situated next to the smokehouse, he heard a guttural scream that had the hair on his neck standing up like a porcupine in heat. Then a voice yelled loudly.

"Somebody help me! My foot! Oh, God!"

Dougie hurried, following the sound coming from the rear of the pigeon coop. He stood for a moment, taking in the sight before him. There, writhing in agony on the ground, was one of the biggest men he'd ever seen.

The fellow was screaming and pulling at the paw-grip trap, trying to remove it from his foot, which was bleeding and undoubtedly paining him something awful.

As Dougie had suspected, the quick release mechanism wasn't working, even though he'd oiled the contraption. Presently, he was glad it hadn't worked. If it had, the man would have gotten out of the trap with little effort.

Dougie's first inclination was to help the screaming man. That was until he took note of the man's clothing. Those black and white striped pajamas were a sure giveaway as to what kind of "cat" he'd caught in his trap. Still, he knew the man had to be in a lot of pain.

*He's obviously a convict, so if I release him he may come for me. Good God Almighty, what am I going to do? Guess this old dog finally caught the hubcap.*

He ran his fingers through his thick, silver hair, then looked more closely. He noticed that in addition to the man's bleeding foot, there was a considerable amount of blood on his pants as well.

*That foot couldn't have caused that. That blood's comin' from some other wound.*

The man continued to cry out when Dougie approached him. "Hey! Can't you see I'm hurting? I need your help!"

Dougie nodded, "I'm sure you're in pain, but those black-and-white-striped pajamas you're wearing tell me you've probably caused pain for some other folk somewhere along the way."

"You can't leave me in this trap. For God's sake have some mercy!"

Dougie stared down at his feet. The man's face was as white as Clemmie's hair. No way of knowing how much blood he'd lost, but Dougie couldn't just let the man go.

However, his conscience wouldn't allow him to leave him in such pain forever. It only took a moment for him to come to a decision, and he stalked off with the man still begging.

"No, please don't leave me here!"

Dougie went to the smokehouse, dug through his Army trunk again, and found what he needed.

"These will do the trick," he mumbled as he picked up a pair of handcuffs. He'd bought them years ago in a pawn shop in Texas, along with a few other Old West paraphernalia items, such as a lariat, a Stetson hat, and a pair of calfskin boots.

He'd worn the boots for years, but the hat was still covered in a cloth bag and was as good as the day he bought it.

His prize item was an old Colt .45, and he also had a .38 Chiefs Special, a .22 rifle, and a .410 shotgun. These he kept in his gun cabinet under lock and key.

Cat had teased him when he bought all that Old West stuff. "I do believe I'm married to a gunslinger!"

If the phone had been working, he'd have called Sheriff Burke, but this morning he'd tried and it was as dead as a Thanksgiving turkey in December.

He grabbed the handcuffs, retrieved his .38 from his gun cabinet, and started toward the pigeon coop. His visitor was still twitching and turning in pain, but Dougie was no fool. Even in his condition, this man could still deliver a jaw-breaking wallop with his huge hands.

Dougie held his .38 in his right hand and tossed the cuffs to the convict.

"Here. Put these on."

“What? What you doing?" the big man yelled. "You can't do this! You ain't the law!"

"We're not going anywhere 'til you put those cuffs on."

The man slapped one on his right wrist. "These things are too tight."

Dougie stared at him. "As I said, we're not going anywhere until you put the cuffs on."

Once the cuffs were in place, Dougie tucked his pistol in his waistband, then, using his lariat, hog-tied the man's ankles together.

Finally, he took his hammer and pounded the quick-release mechanism on the trap. When it opened, pulling the jagged edges away from the man's foot, the fellow cried out louder than ever. One look at the foot told Dougie it was most likely broken. So be it. He was satisfied the man wouldn't be walking far.

The wounded man continued to beg. "I need a doctor. You gotta get me to a doctor. Can't you see I'm hurt? I've been shot in my leg, and now you’ve broke my foot."

Dougie saw blood seeping from the man's leg wound. "How'd you get that bullet in your leg?"

"Huh? An accident. It was an accident. I was cleaning a gun and it went off."

"And since when did cons have access to weapons?"

At that juncture, Dougie threw a half bale of hay into the bed of his truck and pulled it close to the coop. He helped the man stand, which was quite a feat because when he stood, he was exceedingly tall. Dougie, himself, was about six-foot-two, and this man towered over him. Still, he managed to hold the man erect long enough for him to sit on the tailgate of the truck.

"Get yourself on in there. That hay will be a good enough bed for the time being. I'll take you to Sheriff Burke. Let him decide what to do with you."

The fellow yelled as he inched his body onto the bed. With his hands cuffed, his feet tied, bleeding from his leg and now sporting a broken foot, he was glad to lay down on that bed of hay. Even the state penitentiary, where he usually resided, was sounding like a better place to be than where he was at the moment.

Dougie stepped on the accelerator and the truck jerked forward, bouncing along on the rough, gravel lane, scraping the gallberry bushes as he made sharp turns. He wanted to get to the sheriff's office as soon as possible. He didn't know what crimes this man had committed, but something told him it was more than petty theft.

When he parked at the front of the jail, a deputy came out, headed to his vehicle. He recognized Dougie and approached him.

"Mr. MacKinnon? What brings you to this side of town? Getting lonely out there at Lirey?"

Dougie motioned with his chin. "I've made a citizen's arrest. Take a gander in the back of my truck."

The deputy let out a string of swear words that Cat would have smacked him for.

"Well now, you've earned yourself a deputy's badge for sure. Who is he?"

"Don't know. Don't even want to know. I just want you to take him off my hands and get him to a doctor. He's got a bullet in his leg, and I believe his foot may be broken."

The deputy took a closer look, blinked several times, and his mouth opened like a cottonmouth moccasin.

"Bless my gramma's bloomers! I think that's Big Jack Simmons. He's an escapee from the state prison in Reidsville. In Tattnall County. He overpowered the guard, cracked his head open with a shovel, then stole his pistol and took off through the backwoods of Big Hammock swamp. Been missing more'n a week now. He's got a record as long as a Sunday sermon, and if that guard dies, he's gonna fry. Wait here. I gotta get Sheriff Burke. He ain't gonna believe this!"

A minute later the sheriff came to the truck and looked at the man. Cuffed, tied at the ankles, and bleeding from the leg and foot.

"Dougie, I've seen cattle and hogs tied like that, but never tried it on a prisoner. You've made quite a catch here."

Dougie nodded, "And the sooner you get him out of my truck, the better I'll feel. But I think he's in pretty bad shape, Cleveland. And I am sorry about the broken foot. I was tryin' to trap a bobcat that's been prowlin' around my pigeon coop. Never expected to trap an escaped convict."

The sheriff looked again at the fellow, who had yet to utter anything other than a groan with every breath.

"You know, I wonder if this is the man that attacked that woman from Smokey Hollow?"

He called out loudly, "Howard, Dexter," and two deputies came dashing across the parking lot.

"Boys, take the prisoner. Dash him up to the clinic in McRae. That would be faster than the ambulance coming down here to get him. I agree with you, Dougie, he's not looking too good."

The deputies loaded the felon into the prisoner transport vehicle and headed for McRae, leaving Dougie and Sheriff Burke standing in the parking lot.

"Officials in three counties have been searching for him for more than a week."

"What's that about a woman in the Hollow being attacked?" Dougie asked.

"Yeah. Skidder Sanderson's wife. Corina's her name."

"Skidder's wife? She all right?"

"Seems to be. She told me she shot the man that attacked her but didn't know how wounded he was as she ran away as fast as she could."

Dougie nodded. "Well, if she was the one who shot this big fella, she did a good job. She put a hole in his left leg, and it's still spilling blood."

Sheriff Burke nodded. "We've got him now, thanks to you. And he'll be residing in the pen shortly. If he makes it through this ordeal."

"Good riddance. Glad I set that trap. Else he might have come on to the house before I even knew he was there."

It was getting late, so Dougie headed to Lirey. Would be better to wait until tomorrow to check on Clemmie.

On the way home, he grinned to himself. This unlikely adventure was something that could have happened in a Louis L'Amour novel. He wished Cat had been here to share in his moment of glory. Capturing a convict! Maybe she was right. He might be a gunslinger after all.

# 50

# Can't Touch Your Soul

"But . . . no . . . that couldn't have happened. The sharks would have gotten her!"

The emotion-filled exclamation had erupted from Clementine's mouth as if her tongue had a mind of its own, blurting out words even she didn't know were forming in her young brain.

"But . . . but . . . then Jenneh died! If she had stayed with Kadie . . . just held on to her hand a little while longer, then she would have survived too. I didn't want Jenneh to die. She was the same age as me, and she had so many years to live still. It's . . . I . . . That's too sad."

Her lips quivered and she took a deep breath, then darted her eyes to see if Dean had seen the tears that were making tracks down her face. He was busy drawing, and if he saw her tears, he gave no indication.

Rosie nodded, "Yes, Clementine. Jenneh was much too young to die. But that's one of the reasons why we must continue to tell this story. To remind us, we folks in this room today, that we have a lot to live for. To thank the Good Lawd for.

“And we must never forget what strong folk we come from. Folk like Kadie and her mama.” She looked at Dean.

"And, young man, you need to remember that this same blood is flowing in yo’ veins, too."

Rosie drank the last swig of her tea and put her cup down, then turned to Clementine. “If you don't want to hear the final bit, I'll stop. Dean already knows how the story ends."

Clementine shook her head. "Oh, no, Rosie. I want to hear it. I'm sorry I spoke out of turn. That's another one of my irritating habits according to James. But I'm working on that problem. I guess I need to work harder."

Jeremiah, so engrossed in the story he could hardly wait for Rosie to tell the next part, decided to speak.

"And I want to hear it myself, Rosie. This is the first time I ever learned anything about my Gullah people."

With a small lift of her chin, Rosie leaned back. By now, simply a change in the tenor of Rosie's voice set the stage, and Kadie made her entrance . . .

*I stood at the railing staring down into the churning ocean until a crewman shoved me from behind, causing me to fall to my knees. Before I could regain my footing, the dreaded lash tore into my back and I screamed, praying I could get to my feet before another one ripped the flesh from my bones.*

*When I stood, my dress barely hung on my shoulders, as the lash had shredded it, and it was nothing more than strands of fabric billowing in the wind.*

*When I crawled down into the hold, I didn’t even notice the revolting, nauseating, odors and moaning. I felt as if I had turned to stone. I couldn't even cry.*

*And my hand, the hand Jenneh had held for so long, felt so empty. I stared at it for the longest time, and until that very moment, I never realized that a hand was so connected to the heart.*

*Several hours later, in the wee hours of the morning after the storm finally spent itself, I was one of the lucky ones to be taken up on deck. Mostly because the guards needed to remove several bodies that were so putrefied the eggs laid by the blowflies a few days ago had now become scores of maggots feeding like a flock of vultures on a dead animal.*

*Now that I no longer had Jenneh attached to me, I moved about quickly and kept myself hidden behind various boxes stored on deck. The moon cast shadows, and I darted in and out of them. The wind had died down, and there was a stillness I'd not experienced before. At least not on this voyage. The ship plowed so easily through the water that you could barely hear the waves as they sloshed off the prow.*

*From my hiding place, I lay on my back and looked up. The sky was a deep velvet black, and a thousand glittering stars winked at me. I wondered how something so beautiful as this night sky could exist in the same world as the misery that existed on this ship. Had Mama been lying next to me, she'd have had some words of wisdom to answer my questions and soothe my mind.*

*It was in this brief period of perfect peace—and I hesitate to say peace—that a sound . . . a sound so soft as to almost be imperceptible . . . came drifting across the deck of the ship and lingered in the air. I thought maybe I was hearing the soft voice of an angel and wondered if perhaps I'd gone off in my head the same way I'd witnessed others doing during this nightmare voyage.*

*The hush about the ship became even greater. When I dared to raise my head and look about, it was apparent I wasn't the only one hearing this angelic voice. All those on deck were listening to the soft, sweet melody floating through the air.*

*For another few moments, I still thought my ears were deceiving me. They wanted me to believe I recognized this voice. But that couldn't' be. I only knew two people on this ship, and one of them had died today.*

*Then, when I finally allowed my heart to open its ears, it confirmed what the two shell-like organs on the sides of my head had been trying to tell me.*

*'You know this voice . . . you know this song . . . and it needs a response. . .a response that can only come from you, mi gyal pikin (daughter).'*

*Yes, I did know that voice. I did know that song. It had been sung to me long before I even knew what a word was.*

*Before my brain could remind me of the danger of "acting out," I opened my mouth and responded to the angelic voice . . . and the words came from somewhere deep inside . . . probably from that same place where I'd discovered the hand is connected to the heart.*

*We sang our duet for several minutes, the angel sending her lyrics across the deck and me responding to them. Her voice was just as I remembered from my childhood. Warm. Soothing. A low-pitched voice for a woman. And mine—the voice of a child still—was much higher-pitched and filled with such wanting that the angel must have felt I was tugging at her skirt as I answered her plea. The last refrains of our song drifted away then, and all was silent once again.*

*My first thought was that I would hurry to the other end of the ship to try and find Mama. But that thought was dismissed as quickly as it formed when a crewman jerked me by the hair, opened the hold and tossed me down into the pit.*

*But those few moments of hearing her voice, knowing she was still alive, were more powerful than any food or medicine might have been. Mama was still here. And I was still here. And yes, we would be together again. Somehow, someway, I'd find her. I'd find Mama. I made that promise to myself. And I never break promises.*

*The next morning, even with my head aching and my shoulder screaming with pain from the broken collarbone I'd received from the headfirst entry down into the hold, I was able to smile when I heard the crewman on the crow's nest call out "land ho!" At last, we had sight of the port we were headed to.*

*As soon as the announcement was made, there was so much action on deck and below in the holds that it was quite confusing. One crewman was yelling for all the men to follow him to the front of the ship. Another was calling for the women and children to follow him to the opposite end.*

*"Hurry now, you foul-smelling, disgusting pigs. Get in line. We gotta clean you up before we get there, else they'll refuse to buy you, and we'll be stuck with you lot," one of the guards called.*

*We'd not had a bath for weeks, but now they had us stand in a line and one by one, strip off our clothing, and wash from head to toe. You'd think that by now I wouldn't detest the guards staring at my naked body, but I did. I did.*

*The men were shaved, the guards doing it themselves as they didn't trust the men to not take that razor and slit the throats of their captors. One guard would shave and another would hold his pistol on the slave.*

*After the men had been shaved and we'd all washed, the guards rubbed us with palm oil to disguise sores and wounds caused by our irons or by their whips.*

*Again, with Jenneh no longer attached to me, I had no one to share my worries and wishes with. But listening to the other women down in the hold, I learned that even though some families had managed to stay together on the slave ship, they might be separated once they got to the port. Or so they'd been told.*

*But I refused to think about that possibility. That Mama and I might be separated. That was not a thought I was willing to let flit through my mind more than a second.*

*So now, with a strong wind pulling at our sails, the ship moved into port. Some of us—the younger, healthier ones—were allowed to be on deck. It was said that the captains usually sold their captives directly to rice planters. If not, then they were bought at auction. Again, this was loose talk I'd heard down in the hold. However, I saw quickly that the story was true.*

*Within minutes after the ship was secured at port, several white men came on board. I learned these were the planters who grew rice and cotton. And lived on huge plantations. They would come aboard and select the most desirable slaves, preferably tall, healthy males, fourteen to eighteen years of age, and as dark-skinned as possible, for they believed these dark-skinned men were the best workers. Of course, they choose the most attractive women, who in addition to working the fields would be used for "entertainment" purposes as well.*

*When the women and we girls were all cleaned and oiled, we were crowded onto the stern of the ship, still naked. And the "gentlemen" paraded by us, lifting our arms, checking for diseases or wounds.*

*When one of them came close and lifted my budding breast, I flinched and cried out. He laughed and moved on, and it was then that I felt a hand on my back, warm and soft, and then came a whisper in my ear.*

*"Kadie, he can touch your body, gyal pikin,* **,** *but not your soul."*

*I didn't need to look. The feel of the warmth flowing from the soft hand was so comforting it could only have come from Mama. But, of course, I did look. She shook her head, meaning no, don't let them see we are together. Let us just get through this day.*

*Many of those on board, those who had diseases and sores, were hauled off to a small island off the coast of this new land. A place called Sullivan's Island where the sick ones would be quarantined before being sold in the slave markets.*

*Mama and I were among the healthier females, so we were allowed to leave the ship and go ashore that same afternoon. I didn't know what was to happen to us, but once again, I gave credit to Mama's amulet that was still resting on her breast.*

*Then we were taken into town. Charles Town, they called it. We were still naked and had no way to cover ourselves. The townsfolk were decent–at least most of them—and turned their eyes away from our nakedness. We were taken to a large, enclosed area behind a stone wall, where we huddled together wondering what was to happen next.*

*Shortly, a group of white men came into the walled-off area and stood watching us as we were made to walk about in large circles, giving the planters a chance to view us from all angles. They wanted to be sure they were getting their money's worth, I suppose.*

*I tired of the walking, but it was so good to be off the ship, and I kept shoving my nose up into the air, reveling in the many wonderful scents that drifted there.*

*I caught whiff of a small, white flower growing on a vine that covered the walkway where we entered the area. It was so like the moonflower vine that grows in our village.*

*After the parading came to a halt, we were then inspected even more closely. Each of us had to stand on a stone block about four feet by four feet, and they twisted us in every direction, made us bend over, raise our hands above our heads, and lift our legs, one at the time.*

*They forced our mouths open and looked at our teeth, and some of us were made to jump or dance to show our physical capabilities.*

*When Mama's turn came, I wanted to go to her, to push those men away. She'd already been abused and subjected to many hideous attacks on the ship, and I could hardly bear watching this degrading scene. Mama opened her mouth when directed, stood on one foot, then the other, then danced a jig when told to do so.*

*One of the buyers was a well-dressed man decked out in a top hat, a striped morning coat, dark jodhpurs and tall black boots that came to his knees. He carried a cane and used it to poke at us as he strolled about, deciding which of us he would buy.*

*When he came to Mama, he halted and checked her out from the top of her head down to her bare feet. He moved on, and a few minutes passed as he surveyed several other women.*

*Then he made a final round and returned to stand in front of Mama again. He removed one of his gloves and rubbed his hand across her shiny head. Then he smiled.*

*"I'll take her. Her bald head tells me she's been a bad little gal. She's got some spunk. With the right training, that can be a good thing in a slave. And she's good-looking and healthy enough to help the missus in the house."*

*Once someone had bought you, you were removed from the others and made to stand aside. Then chains were placed on your ankles, which was silly, as an armed guard was standing there already. No one was stupid enough to try to escape in the first place. I mean, where would we go?*

*At that point, you were given a shroud to cover yourself, as your new owner had already seen everything you might have to offer.*

*It was most of two hours later before it was my turn to stand on the block. One of the guards lifted me as I could not step that high.*

*While I stood on that block, I held my head high, as I'd seen Mama do. My heart skipped a beat when the same planter that had bought Mama came to stand in front of me.*

*He poked me with his cane a few times, and when I had to raise my hands above my head, my broken collarbone injury brought tears to my eyes. But I didn't make a sound, and I remembered what Mama had said earlier.*

*"He can touch your body, mi gyal pikin, but not your soul."*

*I looked straight ahead, never acknowledging that I found being poked such an offensive act.*

*He nodded. "Hmm. Young, but well built."*

*He looked closer then, staring into my eyes.*

*"I see intelligence in this face. I'll take her. Young enough to look after my children. When she's older, perhaps she'll look after me." He laughed and moved on to the next woman.*

*I looked across the way where Mama was standing. She never even smiled, but I could feel her thoughts as surely as if she'd spoken them:*

*'Someone is looking out for us, gyal pikin. Never forget that.'*

*Then she caressed her amulet, and the corners of her mouth lifted briefly. I bit my lip to keep from letting my smile spread across my face, as my heart wanted to shout out the happiness it felt within.*

## 51

# Did You Hear That?

Trudging through the swamp water was more challenging than Andrew and Larry might have wished. There were cypress stumps hidden just beneath the water causing both of them to stumble more than once.

Andrew fell to his knees when he caught his foot in a submerged fish basket, one of those traps made of chicken-coop wire where the fish get caught inside and can't make their way out.

"Guess I'm gonna be wet from head to toe by the time I get to your place," he said as he grabbed hold of a stump and pulled himself up.

"Maybe Clementine and Sarah won't even notice," Larry laughed and kept looking ahead. They moved on. Then Larry stopped, turning his head first one way, then the other.

"Something wrong?" asked Andrew.

"I don't know. Listen. What do you hear?"

Andrew stood still, turning his head in all directions. "I don't hear anything."

"Yeah. Exactly. We should be hearing horses snorting, mules braying, and most of all, my hound dogs would have heard us coming and should be howling like a pack of wolves."

He looked ahead, “Look, Andrew. You can see the roof of the Tea House from here. Not much farther.”

He looked across the tobacco fields in the distance.

“Looks like the barn is still intact. There’s water standing everywhere, and from here it looks like the tool shed was toppled. That’s too bad. There were a lot of tools in there the workers use every day. But maybe we can sift through the rubble and find some of them.

“I see several bales of hay strewn about the yard. Other than that, everything appears to have survived. Don’t see anything that makes me think something terribly destructive has occurred.”

Moving on, the men reached a lone pine sapling Larry knew marked where the old well was located. But the water was still high and they struggled to walk through it.

"Be careful, Andrew. There's an old well with a sweep right here somewhere. It's never used . . .”

He gasped as Andrew disappeared beneath the rising water. He didn’t have to guess what had happened. When Andrew’s head surfaced moments later, he spat and spluttered for a few moments.

“Larry, I think I found the well sweep.”

As he reached down to free himself, he felt something wrap around his wrist. Something slick. Something slimy.

Larry saw the expression on Andrew’s face.

“What? What is it? Are you stuck?”

Andrew grabbed his wrist with his other hand and uncoiled the long, thick, hideous snake that had latched on to him.

“Damn you!” he yelled as he flung the unwelcome hitchhiker into the scrubby trees close by.

“It was only a water snake, Andrew. Not poisonous.” Larry said. He wanted to laugh but thought better of it.

Andrew composed himself and they kept trudging forward and upward with each step. The next sight to greet them had both men halting their steps in midair. The water was now about waist deep, and right in the path where they were walking, the bodies of two sandhill cranes came floating by with their large wings outspread.

Larry sighed, "They must have been trapped or injured somehow. Sandhills thrive in the Okefenokee Swamp, but I see them around here fairly often. And usually in pairs, like these."

"Glad Clemmie wasn't here to see that. She'd have had us tryin' to resuscitate the poor birds," said Andrew.

Larry smiled. "Your Clemmie sounds like a special young lady."

"Yeah, well, she is. But she can be a handful. Has a mind of her own, and sometimes leaps before she looks, if you know what I mean. How about your Sarah? How's she comin' along?"

Andrew had refrained from asking, but then Larry had made the initial overture, had offered his thoughts, so perhaps it would be all right.

"Oh, it's hard to tell. Some days she still cries for her mother. Other days she seems content enough, I suppose. But I try to take each day as it comes. And the one thing I always have, that I can depend on, is Rosie.

"I've noticed when Mrs. Jefferson leaves in the early afternoon, Sarah hightails herself down to the barn and follows Rosie like a chick following a hen. Rosie has a special caring quality that comes through whether she's dealing with adults or children. I'm grateful to have her."

"She got family here?"

"Just that grandson I told you about. She had a younger sister who left years ago. Rosie never mentions her, so I figure she must have passed on. I don't know of any other kin. I knew her daddy, of course, but he's been gone for some time.

And her daughter died in a car crash years ago, leaving a newborn baby boy that Rosie took to raise."

"He the one with polio?"

"Yeah. Dean. He's about fourteen or fifteen by now."

"Huh. Don't envy Rosie being stuck with a teenager. Thought Norah and I would lose our minds when the twins were Dean's age."

"Rosie keeps any problems she might have to herself. I've never known her to complain about much, and the barn workers have the utmost respect for her. She keeps them in line, and they all listen when she talks. But, you're right. She's probably got her hands full with that grandson about now."

He stopped for a moment, giving them both a moment of rest. "Never thought this was such a high hill, but after wading through the water with these waterlogged boots, it feels like it's about three miles high. Again, be careful.

"You see that saw palmetto bush on the left? There's a footbridge somewhere near it. Never thought I'd see the day that footbridge was underwater.

"The tale I was told is that "Lady Sutherland," my great-grandmother had it built in her day so she could get across the stream when she wanted to come down to the barn. My father always said she was more the tobacco farmer than my great-grandfather.

"She'd bring food to the workers, and loved being in that barn smelling that sweet tobacco."

He smiled, "Funny how you don't realize how important your folks were until they're gone."

Andrew lifted his chin in agreement but said nothing. He still couldn't talk about his most recent losses yet. Maybe one day.

Larry gently stomped around a bit and his foot scraped across the edge of the footbridge. "Ah. Good. We'll be at the house in a few minutes now. We'll see the girls and Rosie, and then figure out what to do from there. Don't know that I particularly want to wade through this swamp again, so maybe we can check out that old logging path behind the house.

"Telogia Creek goes through there, and at one time there was an old bridge made of railroad ties somewhere in those woods. The CCC folk built it in the thirties, so it might have made it through the flood. If that bridge held, then we can get you and Clemmie home."

"Yeah, I know those woods. Daddy cleared property back there in his day. But we've got one problem, Larry."

"What? What problem?"

"We don't have a vehicle. We came by boat."

Larry laughed. "Hadn't thought of that. But as I said, I take one problem at a time, so we'll deal with that issue when it gets here." He began to move on, then stopped. Listening again.

"What? You hear your horses or hounds?" Andrew asked.

"No. I thought I heard music. Do you hear anything?"

Andrew shook his head. "No, but Norah says I can't hear well anyway. Actually, she says I don't listen."

Larry smiled. Seeing his home had lifted his spirits immensely, and they picked up the pace.

# 52

# Together Again

This time it wasn't Clemmie who interrupted Rosie's story. This time, Jeremiah was the culprit. He raised his hand as a child would in a classroom.

Rosie stopped and looked over her spectacles. "What is it, Jeremiah?"

"Rosie, you say this story is true?"

"I have no reason to believe it ain't, Jeremiah. Why in the world would anyone make up a story as sad as this one? And *Keke* read and read them history books from the library in McRae. He even went to Savannah and found more information in the library there.

“He also borrowed some books from right heah in the Tea House. From Mr. Sutherland's library. There's a lot of books here, and *Keke* read everything he could about those slavery days. And he memorized Kadie’s story word for word. So, yes, I say the story is true."

Jeremiah stared at her for a moment, straightening his string tie and sitting straighter.

"So then, you saying my own people suffered this same kind of treatment?"

"Uh-huh. They all did. And, Jeremiah, it wasn't just the black folks. Many white folks were also sold as slaves during some of those historical times."

"But this Kadie. Telling her story. Somehow it gives more meaning. Her being yo' kin."

Rosie smiled, "And you being Gullah, she some kinda kin with you, too."

Jeremiah nodded, "My gran didn't tell me much about the slavery times. But before she lost her memory, she did tell me about how, in her time, the Gullah folk would celebrate just about anything. There'd be food, music, folks clappin' hands, and they'd do a dance that come from our people in Africa way back when.

"The girls would dress in white and wear red kerchiefs, and the boys would move heel-to-toe and wave colored scarves. And, according to my gran, sometimes whole communities would come together to dance in celebration of some special day.

"Well, anyhow, she taught her children that dance, and when me and my sisters and brothers came along, she taught us that same dance."

Rosie shook her head side to side, "I know Kadie's story well enough, but as for dancing, *Keke* wasn't much on that. Like Dean, he could draw just about anything, but don't believe dancing was something he learned. What else you need to know?"

"Nothing. Go on. Continue, Rosie." He was ready to listen again.

Rosie cleared her throat. "And now I'm gonna come to the end of this tale. And Clementine, once I'm done, you can ask yo' questions. I'll answer what I can, but Rosie don't know everything."

Then Jeremiah witnessed what Clementine and Dean already knew. Rosie could bring Kadie into the room with just a sigh and a voice tone. And so she did . . .

*When the buying of slaves, the auction, was done, we were herded into waiting wagons. Wagons that would transport us to our new homes. To our new owners.*

*Our new owner, the one with the fancy clothes and boots, was a man named William Aiken. Later I learned he had been a special man in a country called England, where he was treated special by the Queen, and after that, he had to be called Sir William.*

*But maybe he was called Sir William because if you didn't use that term then you'd be accused of being disrespectful. And we all knew the consequences of that.*

*As the wagons pulled away from the auction block, I was sitting next to my dear, sweet Mama, and whatever thoughts we had, we kept them in our hearts.*

*We had no idea what would happen to us in the future, but there was nothing that could touch us now. At this very moment. We were together. Her arm was wrapped about my waist, and I leaned my head on her shoulder. She stroked her amulet and once again she began to sing the lullaby. My lullaby from so long ago. And I responded.*

*Mama and I continued our duet, and the lullaby was carried on the winds blowing through the giant magnolia trees, resplendent with their glorious, white, sweet-scented blossoms. These sounds and scents would become embedded in my soul. The same soul that can only be touched by those I invite within.*

*Some eight months later Mama would be singing that same lullaby to my little sister. When I asked her why she didn't rid her body of the baby—for certainly it had been the result of one of her many attacks on the ship—she simply replied, "This child is an innocent soul. It should not suffer for the actions of evil men on that ship. Our people, the Sierra Leone people, treasure our children. And I will treasure this one, as I do you."*

*And this sister, who we called Jenneh, held my hand for many years. As her namesake had.*

# 53

# Foot Stompin' Time

As they got closer, Andrew took in the splendor of the Tea House. It was spectacular. He wanted to run the last hundred yards. Wanted to get to Clemmie. But this wasn't his place. This was Larry's home. He had to lead the way. And Larry did, moving rapidly across the wide yard that was usually meticulously manicured, but not today.

He stopped at the edge of the brick walkway that led to the steps of the porch and looked to Andrew, whose expression told how surprised and confused he was. Same as Larry.

"Do you hear that?"

Andrew nodded. “Uh-huh.”

Delightful, foot-stomping music was blaring out from the open windows. They could hear a guitar, a fiddle, a banjo, and some kind of rhythmic drum beating in the background. There was loud clapping and people laughing. A high-pitched, young voice squealed with delight, and one deep voice calling out was heard above all the others.

"And now, four steps back, then four steps forward. Turn ‘round, stomp the floor two times, and clap yo’ hands over yo’ head."

Larry slowly stepped along the walkway which was strewn with small, downed tree limbs and covered with wet leaves and remnants of faded blossoms from flowering trees on the property.

*Limbs, leaves, and faded blossoms on the walkway?*

For a moment he wondered if something had happened to Jeremiah. He never failed to sweep the walkway. Even after a storm. That question was answered the minute he opened the door.

Jeremiah stood in the middle of the parlor. He had removed his jacket, loosened his string tie and was clapping his hands, keeping time, and stepping to the music as he, Rosie, Clemmie, and Sarah danced around in a circle.

"Now, take two steps to the right, then two to the left, then make another circle about yo' neighbor."

The fiery fiddle and clanky banjo were urging them on and Jeremiah clapped even louder, never missing a beat as he called the next moves.

For a few seconds that motley crew was so caught up in their joyful dance and uplifting music they weren't aware that Larry and Andrew had entered the room.

The two men stared at this unlikely gang. There was Rosie, outfitted in a pair of Ellen's slacks, and Larry knew those boots she was wearing were a gift he'd given Ellen last Christmas.

And Dean, sitting in the corner clapping his hands, was sporting one of Larry's hunting club shirts with a quail embroidered above the pocket.

Andrew did a double-take when he realized the small, barefoot waif dressed in a long, blue, man's shirt that went past her knees was his own sweet Clemmie.

With the music still blasting and feet still stomping, the first reveler to become aware of the interrupters was Dean, who had thought it better to sit out this dance lesson. Even so, he was clapping his hands and memorizing the steps. Just as he had memorized Kadie's story. This dance was from Africa, from Sierra Leone, and it had now become one more entry in his lexicon of Gullah/Geechee history.

"Gramma! Gramma!" Dean yelled.

Rosie turned to him and her eyes followed to where he was pointing. She stopped abruptly and brought both her hands to her cheeks.

"Oh, my goodness! Mr. Sutherland! You be home!"

Jeremiah stopped calling steps and stood still in the middle of the group, not sure what he should be saying. If anything.

And then Sarah, the reveler with the high-pitched squeal, rushed to Larry and grabbed him about the knees.

"Daddy! What took you so long? Rosie told us the story of Kadie. But it's way too long for me to tell you about. And I slept through some of it anyway."

Larry lifted the girl and squeezed her.

"I got here as quickly as I could. But I wasn't worried. You were with Rosie."

Jeremiah quietly moved to the Victrola and turned the music off. He quickly shrugged into his black jacket and tightened his string tie. Assumed his professional persona.

"Mr. Sutherland, I'll have everything in order in just a few minutes."

Larry put Sarah down and slowly strolled to Jeremiah, who stood as straight as a rail with his hands behind his back. Larry put his arm about the old man's shoulder.

"Jeremiah, I've never seen the place look better. I had no idea you were such a talented dancer. Now I know what we'll be doing in the evenings. Beats the hell out of reading the *Farmers' Almanac* by a long shot!"

Jeremiah nodded. "Yessuh. Now, I'll go make us all a fresh pot of coffee."

"Good idea. And you might add a little extra chicory this time, Jeremiah. Andrew and I are a bit tuckered out."

Jeremiah walked away; his head held high.

Larry stepped over to Rosie who had kept quiet. She'd been with him so long she knew all his moods and expressions. And the expression on his face now . . . this was one she hadn't seen in a while. He looked at her the way she'd seen him looking at Miz Ellen, a look that said so much without the need for words.

Larry went closer, stood before Rosie, and took her hands in his. "Rosie, I'm a simple man. A tobacco farmer. I don't have the words to express what I feel. If Ellen were here, she'd know what to say. But you know how much I respect you. You are part of this family, as was your *Keke* and Vanna. If you need anything, anything that I can . . ." He couldn't continue.

"Mr. Sutherland, I spent the last twenty-four hours saying more words than anyone needs to say. I learned a long time ago that words don't always mean a lot, but what you do and how you treat folks, that's what means something. Your family cared for mine before I even came along. And I try to care for yours when I can."

He nodded, afraid to try to speak. Rosie was right. Actions always speak louder than words. And speak the truth more often as well.

Andrew was down on his knees and Clemmie fled into his arms, oblivious to his soaking clothes and swampy smell.

"Clemmie, Clemmie. Are you all right, then?" he asked as he held her back and took a good look.

Clementine was happy to see her daddy, but she knew she might well be in for some serious punishment. After all, she'd known he probably hadn't truly given his permission for her to go to the tobacco barn. But, at this moment, she was so glad to be held by him.

"Oh, Daddy. I've got so much to tell you. And Daddy? I don't want to rush through my life any longer. I want to live every day of it. I don't want to miss anything. I always wanted to get older quickly so I can be like James and Jeremy. But not now. Now I want to be my age. I just want to be eleven." Her face was so animated it made Andrew want to squeeze her harder.

"Rosie told us a story. It was so interesting. But it was sad and heartbreaking, too. I'll tell it to you when we get home. Rosie is a wonderful storyteller."

"I bet she is. I've heard a lot about Rosie."

"Oh, and Daddy? I need something. Something important."

"Anything. Today, I will give you anything you ask for." He pulled her close again and sniffed at her hair, which for some reason smelled about as swampy as his. No matter. He ran his hand over her wispy, snowy curls and smiled at her.

"What do you need, Clemmie?"

"I need Granddaddy or Aunt Maori to tell me our story."

"What story is that?"

"The story of where we come from, who our people are. You know, why we have become the people we are today."

"Well, now. I've heard some of that story. It's quite a tale, and you'll have to get Granddaddy and Auntie Maori to tell it. But I can tell you that between those two you'll know more than you might wish for. It's a rather long story. And sometimes it's depressing. The Scots have a history that isn't all happy. They suffered a lot under the rule of a number of kings. And they fought for their freedoms. As I said, it's a long history."

Clementine stared at him, a whole list of questions just lying in wait on her tongue. But after a moment's thought, she decided she'd tuck them away and save them for another time.

"Oh, and we need to make a trip."

"A trip?"

"Yeah. I'll tell you all about that too, but now I need to tell Mr. Sutherland something. And I hope he won't be too mad."

"I doubt anything you could tell him will upset him today, Clemmie. We're both relieved to find you and Sarah safe here with Rosie. She appears to be quite a special lady."

"Oh, she is Daddy. And the story she told us is a true story. And she saved me from getting stuck in the stream. And Dean, her grandson, he helped us find the footbridge so we could climb up the hill . . . he used his crutch . . . he's actually pretty strong and then we . . ."

Andrew stood then. "Whoa. Slow down, Clemmie. We'll get the whole story soon enough. Now go tell Larry whatever it is you gotta tell him."

Clementine slowly walked toward Larry, who was still talking with Rosie. He smiled down at her, and that gave her the slightest hope he wouldn't be too harsh with her.

"Clemmie, Rosie tells me you took fine care of Sarah. And even though the tobacco barn will need some work before its operating again, I still need help with Sarah. I hope you'll come for a couple more weeks, 'til school starts, and help me with her."

"Oh, yessir. If I can find a way to get here."

Larry laughed. "We'll work out the details."

"But, Mr. Sutherland, I need to tell you something."

"What's that, Clemmie?"

"I let the horses and mules out. And then I let your hound dogs out, too. I was afraid the water might come rushing through the stable and the dog pen and they'd all be drowned."

Larry nodded, "Clemmie, that's precisely what I would have done had I been here. That was good thinking on your part. And don't worry, they'll all come back this way when the water drains off. They know where their dinner comes from."

Andrew joined Larry, Clemmie, and Rosie. Then he smiled at the woman who had kept Clemmie safe in his absence.

"Rosie, I'm not very good with words either, but I want you to know I can never thank you enough for taking care of Clemmie. Larry kept telling me how you'd keep the girls safe. About how resourceful you are. And I see he wasn't stretching the truth. I'm in your debt. If there is ever anything you need, anything I can do for you, I hope you'll call on me."

Rosie looked in his eyes, something her *Keke* would have told her to be careful about as sometimes you might see something you wish you hadn't. What she saw in Andrew's face was nothing more than gratitude and relief.

"We all worked together, Mr. Mac. And yo' chile is pretty special herself. She took care of the animals and didn't let that water stop her from doing what needed to be done. She's got a good head on her shoulders. She's a fine daughter, sir. A very fine one."

Andrew nodded and smiled. Rosie walked away then and began to help Jeremiah get the parlor situated, putting the chairs in place in the dining room which had been a dance hall for a short while. Then the two headed to the kitchen to make the coffee.

Andrew looked down at Clementine and had to stop himself from squeezing her again. "So now, tell me about this trip we gotta make. You itchin' to go to Brunswick, or maybe Jacksonville?"

"No, Daddy. We need to go to South Carolina."

"South Carolina? I don't know anyone in South Carolina. Why do we need to go there?"

"Well, I heard both you and Mr. Sutherland tell Rosie if she needed anything, she could ask you."

"That's right. And we both meant that, Clemmie. She kept you and Sarah safe when we couldn't come to you."

"Well, I know something she needs. She needs to go to South Carolina. To a place called St. Helena Island."

"St. Helena Island. Heard of it, but never been there. So, why does Rosie need to go there?"

"That's where her sister, Tonja, lives. And she's getting older. And Rosie hasn't seen her in a long time, so we gotta go right away . . . and she might be sick. . . and . . . "

"Hold on. All right then. That's the least I can do for Rosie. She's taken good care of you. Seems only right that I return the favor."

Andrew's thoughts immediately ran to his mother. He could all but hear her now:

"That's what you call synchronicity, Andrew. Simultaneous occurrence of events that happen by accident but seem to have some connection. A moment in time when we suddenly become consciously aware that we have made a deeper connection with the universe. We just have to be open to receive these moments. They don't come often, but when they do, they have meaning."

Andrew stared at his wet boots as his thoughts continued to whirl in his head. *Nana was right. This event is special. The fact that I was in Harper's Mill helping a black woman, while a black woman in the Tea House was helping Clemmie. All happening at a time when blacks and whites are struggling to find a way to exist in harmony. Is there some meaning here that I should be grasping?*

He was old enough to know that not all happenings can ever be explained. They just had to be accepted. But he would think further on this synchronistic event in the coming days.

Larry came over then and Andrew brought him up to date with his latest news. "Your Rosie is all you said, and more," Andrew remarked. "And it looks like I'm goin' to South Carolina. And soon I believe."

"Yeah? Got family there?"

"No, I don't, but Rosie does. A sister, according to Clemmie."

"Huh? Since Rosie stopped mentioning her, I assumed she was long gone. But that's like Rosie. She never tells anyone about her troubles or problems. I wonder what else she might need?"

Clemmie chimed in. "I know something else she needs, Mr. Sutherland."

"You do? What?"

"Well, not her. But Dean. He needs a prosthesis. I think that's the right word. He says the doctors in Savannah told him if he had a prosthesis he could walk without crutches. But he and Rosie never talk about it. He says there are just some things you can't do anything about."

"I see. Well, that is one thing I can do something about," said Larry. He was embarrassed to realize he hadn't given much thought to Rosie's and Dean's needs. But then, Dean's polio and Ellen's cancer had occurred around the same time, so he did have some modicum of an excuse for his thoughtlessness.

# 54

# Working Together

It took most of two weeks for Harper's Mill to right itself following the flood. A few homes in the low-lying areas had suffered damage, but nothing a few days' work by the men of the community couldn't deal with.

Earlier this morning Andrew had a few words with James. About his black eye and bruised face. "James, if we hope to have any peace in our lives, we have to learn to deal with problems. And using a fist isn't one of the better ways to do that."

James sighed with frustration, "Daddy, you had to be there. They were calling me Jim Crow and a few other names I never even heard of. They were looking for trouble."

"That may be. But I expect you to follow the teachings you mother and I have tried to instill in all of you. If you just react without thinking, then you aren't going to solve anything."

"Yeah. Well. Not all black men and white men get along like you and Skidder did. And I want to see how you react when one of them stands in your face and calls you honky and asks you where's your KKK robe!" At that juncture he walked out, slamming the screen door behind him.

Andrew had no doubt that James and the young black workers would get into more disagreements in the coming days. Just a feeling. But one he knew was probably accurate.

Meanwhile, he took several of his men and two dump truck loads of sand to the Hollow to help shore up the creek bank.

Toby, Jesse, and several other men were gathering their shovels and materials as Andrew and his men drove up. Andrew got out of his truck and approached Toby.

"Morning, Toby."

"Mr. Mac."

"Toby, some of the fellas from town have volunteered to help you men put that bank to rights. And whatever other repairs you need."

"We don't need help, Mr. Mac. We can do our own work."

Andrew hadn't forgotten his last conversation with Skidder regarding the racial issues in the country, but had hoped this community might be spared some of that tension after the blacks and whites had come together to survive the flood.

"Never doubted you could. Toby, these men, these white men, are the same ones who searched for Corina. Not one of them quit searching until she was found. And I don't recall the color of her skin being important to any of them.

"Skidder told me some of you are wanting to march and help bring racial reform to the forefront, and that's your right. We all have certain issues we feel are worth taking a stand for. Sacrificing for. And I'm sure we got some troubling times coming. For black folk and white ones as well.

"And I repeat what I said before, I can't right the wrongs of the world, but I can do my part to make the future better. That's all I'm asking of you."

Then Gabriel, who was spearheading the group that wanted to march, sidled up next to Toby. “Tell him we don’t need help from his white bunch.”

Gabriel’s mother had given him this name as she thought he had an angelic face when he was born. But angelic was hardly a word that was used when referring to him these days. He had a temper that flared as quickly as a lighted match on gasoline. But to his credit, he was equally blessed with intelligence. Not that he always used it.

Toby took a deep breath, rubbed the back of his neck, kicked the sand at his feet, then stared Andrew in the face. He’d known this moment would come, and he still hadn’t decided how to handle the situation. Well, here it was and now was the time.

He hesitated a moment, looked at Gabriel, then glanced at the men gathered behind him. Then back to Andrew.

“You know, Skidder once said that if we all work together, we can get a lot more done. Believe he might have been right about that.”

Gabriel snorted, “You just as stupid as Skidder was.” Then he stalked off.

Andrew, appearing to ignore Gabriel’s comment, smiled, “Yep. I believe Skidder did mention working together was better than going it alone. At least once or twice.

“And Toby? Don’t be too quick to judge Gabriel. That passion he’s so full of can be used for good purposes as well as for expressing anger. He just needs someone to help him bridle his emotions and direct his intelligence in a positive way. He could be a big help to your people. Eventually.

“And whether you like it or not, it seems your community is looking to you to pick up where Skidder left off.”

Toby nodded. “Maybe. Maybe. But those are some mighty big shoes to fill.”

"Uh-huh. But try them on for size. I'm willing to bet they'll fit pretty well."

With that conversation finished, Toby motioned for Andrew's men to follow him. Gabriel scowled but didn't say anything. Both crews nodded to each other and Andrew's men began to back their dump trucks to the edge of the creek.

Andrew headed to Corina's house where she greeted him with a timid smile. The bruise on the side of her face was still obvious, but overall, she appeared to be in good spirits.

"Mr. Mac. What a surprise. Come in. I'm about to take a blackberry cobbler out of the oven. Would go well with a cup of coffee and a bit of conversation."

"I'll take you up on that offer, Corina."

The two drank coffee, ate warm cobbler and discussed Corina's ordeal. She appeared to be coping, and Andrew felt Toby may have played a part in that transition. Skidder would like that.

~ ~ ~

At the Tea House, Jeremiah came in the back door as he did every morning. A few minutes later Larry came down the stairs and Jeremiah poured him a cup of coffee. Coffee laced with his famous chicory concoction.

"Morning, Jeremiah. You doing all right?"

"Yessuh. I am fine. But I was thinking about something on my walk here this morning."

"What's got you thinking so early?" Larry asked as he sipped Jeremiah's tasty brew.

"Mr. Sutherland, do you wonder sometimes if good might can come from bad? Like that flood. Now, if that hadn't happened, then I'd never have heard Rosie's story of her ancestors, which she says is the story of my ancestors too.

"And you would never know Rosie's sister is still alive. And after hearing Rosie's story, that lil' white girl knows she got a story, too. And now she's gonna learn about it from her old folks. And pass it on so those that follow her can know their history. So, yeah. I believe we can find something good from that bad event."

"Jeremiah, I believe you got something there. I never thought a flood would bring anything good, but you've just pointed out that I'm wrong. I believe if I give the subject more thought, I can think of several other good things that happened that day. And who knows? Maybe more good things will happen tomorrow.

# 55

# *No Words Needed*

As far as Rosie could see there was marsh. Where it's impossible to tell where water stops and sky begins. Where long-legged birds step gracefully in an endless sea of tall grasses and reeds. Where the air smells of salt and soggy vegetation. And where the eerie quiet wraps itself about you like a shroud. Where, if she listens closely, she can hear the far-off, mournful cry of an osprey seeking his mate.

She smiled when a large water bird with soft, pink feathers and a flat bill lifted its head. The birds in the marsh were quite different from those found in the piney woods surrounding the tobacco barn.

As they passed a brightly painted wooden cottage nestled at the edge of the marsh, Rosie saw a woman sitting in a rocking chair on the porch. She had a lap full of dried sweetgrass that had been bundled together and wrapped in coils; and her hands moved deftly as she wove baskets like the one Rosie had. The one passed on from Vanna.

Rosie wondered if she'd find that Tonja was like the birds in the marsh. Different. It had been such a long time since they'd been together, and Rosie knew time has a way of changing many things.

Shortly after they passed the cottage, Andrew turned down a narrow lane created from crushed seashells. He eased slowly onward, following along the edge of the marsh. Soon he came to another small cottage sitting some distance back from the lane . . . a cottage awash with flowering plants all about the yard. He brought the car to a stop.

"I believe this is the place, Rosie. We're here."

He came around to the passenger side, opened the car door, and extended his hand to help Rosie out. She stood tall, smoothed her thin cotton dress, then briefly patted her hair, neatly braided with a soft, blue ribbon woven within her bun.

She looked at Clementine, who sat in the rear seat, smiling as she chewed on the end of her braid. Dean sat next to her, his sketch pad resting in his lap.

Rosie motioned to Dean to follow her. “Come along, Dean. We heah now.”

Dean got out and stood next to the car, his new prosthesis holding him upright. He walked with a slight limp, but the crutches were long gone.

Dean shook his head. “No. You go on Gramma. I'll come along in a few minutes."

Rosie stood still for a long moment. She looked again at Andrew. He smiled and nodded.

“She’s waiting for you, Rosie. Go on now.”

Sierra Rose Aiken, *Keke's* little Geechee Rose, knocked at the door of the small cottage on St. Helena Island. The door was flung open and for a couple of minutes, the air shimmered through her tears.

As she'd told Mr. Sutherland, sometimes no words are necessary. Tonja's expression told her all she needed to know.

The two sisters embraced, and when they did finally speak, the sweet, lilting, Gullah language flowed from their lips as if they had never used any other.

Not surprising, though. The language of the heart always finds its way home.

# *About the Author*

Florence Love Karsner, author of The Highland Healer Series, is a Registered Nurse and Clinical Research Professional who creates hand-built pottery and enjoys golf and gardening. She is a fifth generation Floridian of Scottish heritage who lives with her husband in Ponte Vedra, Florida.

Several trips to Scotland inspired her Highland Healer Series, an adventure series set in $18^{th}$ century Highlands of Scotland. Her 2019 work includes The Molly McCormick Mystery Series which is set on an island off the coast of Florida during the Cuban Missile Crisis of 1962. Her latest project is Tobacco Rose, launched in 2021.